DARK ICE

DAN RENO BOOK 4

By

DAVE STANTON

www.bloodhoundbooks.com

Print ISBN 978-1-912604-17-3

For Adele Salle and Marvin Kohn

1

The cornice stretched three feet over the sheer face below. There was about fifteen feet of vertical drop before the snow-covered slope angled out at forty-five degrees. I inched my skis farther forward, the tips hanging over the void. I was wrong—it was more like twenty feet of mandatory air. And that was the shallowest entry the ledge offered.

I blew out my breath and ignored the sickly sensation of my testicles trying to climb into my stomach. Turning back now would mean a long uphill hike, while the reward for leaping off the cornice was five hundred feet of untracked powder. A slight dip to the left marked the most forgiving launch point. I pushed myself back and sidestepped higher up the ridge. A couple deep breaths, then I released my edges and glided toward the dip.

In a second, I launched over the precipice, my hands thrust forward, my knees tucked toward my chest. As I dropped, I could see the distant desert floor of Nevada fall behind the stands of pine and fir at the bottom of the bowl. I extended my legs in the instant before I touched down and absorbed the shock, blinded for a second by a blast of snow. Then, I cranked my skis on edge, bounced out of the fluff, and made a second turn through the deep powder. It had snowed about a foot last night, but here, the fresh coverage was at least two feet, maybe more. Bottomless under my boots.

Twenty turns to the glade below, my heart pounding, my body disappearing in blasts of powder, the white coating me from head to toe. When I reached the tree line, I skidded to a stop and caught my breath. Then, I looked up and admired the S-turns I'd left on the otherwise unblemished slope. *Not bad*, I thought, smiling at the understatement. Most of the winter storms that had blown through the Lake Tahoe region came out of the warm Pacific and dumped wet, heavy snow, creating the notorious Sierra cement. But last night's blizzard had swept in from Alaska, bringing colder and lighter snow. As a result, I was in the right place at the right time.

I skated along the terminus of the bowl and turned into the trees when they became sparse enough to allow passage. This was the Nevada backcountry, unpatrolled, accessible by ducking the boundary ropes at the highest elevation of South Lake Tahoe's ski resort, right at the California-Nevada border. Before me lay 4000 feet of descent to the high desert floor where I'd parked my truck, near Route 207 outside of Gardnerville.

It was slower going now, the terrain interrupted by tangles of deadfall and icy patches where the wind had scoured the surface. I picked my way through it, my skis alternately between sinking in powder then chattering and scraping across slick bands of ice. Finally, I spotted a clearing—a wide, sweeping snow bank that fell toward a collection of pines hundreds of feet below. I rode the section like a surfer on a wave, turning down off the lip then riding back up, staying high and avoiding a flat area that would likely necessitate a hike.

When I reached the trees below, I entered a broad glade, the trunks spaced at wide intervals, the snow as soft and uniform as a white pillow. The morning sun had just appeared from behind a swath of swift moving clouds, and the snow glittered with pinpricks of light. I took a long moment to take in the scenery, then I picked a line and pushed off into the mild grade. The pristine snow held no surprises, the powder light and consistent, making it easy to find a rhythm. Floating through the trees and leaving a wake of rounded tracks, I became immersed in the splendor of the moment, as if the setting had been created solely for my indulgence.

My grandiose thoughts came to a crashing halt when I came around a tree, and my skis rammed into something solid beneath the snow. My binding released with a loud click, and I flew forward and face-planted in a poof of powder.

"Son of a bitch," I said, wiping the snow from my goggles. I took a quick inventory of my body and found no injuries. Then, I crawled back ten feet to where my ski lay. When I pulled it from the snow, the edge caught, probably on a hidden stump, I thought. Then, the powder fell aside, and I saw a flesh-colored streak. I froze for a second, certain my eyes were playing tricks on me. Blinking, I used the ski to push away more snow.

"No way," I whispered, my heart in my throat. A bare shoulder revealed itself, then a snarl of blonde hair strung with ice. I reached down with my gloved hand and carefully pushed aside the hair. The face was half-buried, one eye visible, lashes thick with mascara, a blue iris staring blankly. Using both hands like a shovel, I pushed away the bulk of the snow covering the upper body. A sour lump formed in my gut. The body was naked, the skin that of a young woman, perhaps a teenager.

I stepped back and blew puffs of steam into the frigid air. After a moment, I took my phone from my coat pocket and dialed 911. There was no reception. I removed my pack, found a red bandana, and tied it to a branch overhead. Then, I turned in a circle, taking note of the surrounding features in relation to the sun over the granite ridgeline looming to my right.

The morning was beginning to warm up. It was close to zero at 8:30 when I had come up the chairlift, and now, it was probably ten degrees warmer. I looked again at the blonde-headed girl curled at the base of the tree. She'd not been there long, maybe only hours. Soon, the creatures of the forest would find her. Field mice, badgers, and mountain lions would make short work of the body, the big cats spreading the bones over miles.

I checked the surroundings again. The mountainside was unfamiliar to me, but I knew from a variety of accounts that as long as I headed downhill on a due east course, I'd not run into any cliffs, gorges, or otherwise impassable terrain. I clicked back into my binding and skied out of the glade, my turns lackluster and disjointed, the exuberance I felt a few minutes ago replaced by a creeping sense of dread.

***

Thirty minutes later, I sat on the hood of my truck and waited for the police to arrive. I'd missed the run-out leading to where I'd parked and had to trudge half a mile up the highway. Dark clouds lolled down from the sky, blotting the sun and shrouding the valley in a dense winter haze. An eighteen-wheeler down-shifted and rumbled out of the fog, chains rattling, a plume of gritty smoke billowing from the pipes above the cab. Streaks of mist lingered in the truck's wake, floating over the rutted road and hanging in the trees like a cast of ghostly spectators.

A Gardnerville sheriff's cruiser came along shortly and parked on the icy dirt next to my truck. Two deputies I'd never met climbed out, young cops, one pudgy and baby-faced, the other a studious looking fellow with glasses and mittens on his hands.

"I can't believe this," Baby Face said, his cheeks reddened. "The day before Christmas, and we catch a body."

They began interviewing me while we waited for snowmobiles to arrive. There wasn't much to talk about. A young, naked female deep in the backcountry, covered by the night's snowfall. Another foot or so of coverage would have hidden her scent, and she'd have been buried until spring.

The spectacled cop asked for my driver's license and began taking down the information. Then, he looked up at me. "You're the PI from South Lake Tahoe?"

"That's right."

An SUV towing a trio of snowmobiles labored up the road and crunched to a stop on the shoulder. Police Captain Nick Galanis from Douglas County PD stepped from the vehicle, while two more of his deputies released the straps securing the snowmobiles to a trailer behind the SUV.

"Hey, Dan Reno, right?" Galanis said, flashing his trademark smile, his face tan and handsome. He wore no hat, despite the temperature. His curly locks of black hair were unmoving in the wind.

"It's *Reno,* as in no pro*blemo.*"

"That's right, I remember. No problemo, huh? Sounds like we got a problem up there." He cut his eyes toward the mountainside.

"I'd say so, Captain."

"So, what happened?"

"I was skiing and ran into a body buried in the snow."

"Beyond the ski resort boundary?"

"Yeah. No law against it. It's national forest land."

He nodded, his expression one of casual agreement, a hint of smile still on his smooth face. Behind his back, local cops called Galanis 'The Snake,' a reference to both his habit of seducing college-aged women and his ability to instantly change his frame of reference to serve his personal agendas. I'd also learned in a case some months back that he was corrupt as the day was long, taking kickbacks for building permits, soliciting payoffs from a high-end escort service, and even selling confiscated drugs.

"You know how to ride a snowmobile?" he asked.

"Sure."

"I'll ride with you, then." He walked over to where the snowmobiles were staged, one with a body sled in tow.

"Actually, I'm a little rusty, Captain. I'd hate to see you get hurt on my account. Maybe you should ride with one of your deputies."

Galanis looked back at me, and for an instant, his eyes narrowed. Then, his smile returned. "Okay, we'll follow you."

We set out into the woods, and I was able to easily follow my tracks back a mile or so to the scenic glade where the girl lay half buried. I stood aside and watched while Galanis coordinated the crime scene. He made sure his deputies took plenty of pictures before they pulled the stiffened corpse from the snow. Once they lifted her free, I saw her face, her hair falling back behind her ears, an expression of shock and pain frozen on her features. She looked like a macabre Barbie doll, her red lips parted as if her hopes and dreams had died with a final gasp, her eyes wide with the realization that all she'd experienced in her short life had, in no way, prepared her for her final moments.

Galanis also seemed to be studying her face. He knelt and stared at her, his expression incredulous for a moment. I saw his head shake slightly, as if he was denying something. But he recovered quickly, and stood and motioned to the deputies.

"Get the snow off her before you put her in the body bag," Galanis said. "We don't want her in a pool of water."

The deputies began brushing the snow from her flat stomach and large breasts and thighs and scant pubic hair and buttocks and calves. They exchanged embarrassed glances and made quick work of it. I saw she had a couple tattoos, one on her upper thigh and a tramp stamp at the base of her spine.

With considerable strain, they unfolded her stiffened legs. Then, grunting with exertion and blowing steam, they placed her in the bag and arranged the dark folds of plastic until only a thin line of flesh showed. The cops hesitated for a long moment, as if reluctant to finish their grim task, then zipped the bag shut, enclosing her forever in darkness. In a detached part of my mind, I wondered whether she'd been a stripper. A cynical conclusion probably, but even in death, her body made me think of the lyrics to a song, something about shaking your moneymaker.

"Someone must have killed her somewhere else and dumped her here," one deputy said.

"We would have seen snowmobile tracks."

"No, last night's snowfall would have covered them," I said.

"Assuming she was dumped before the storm," the other deputy said. "Hell, she could have been dropped from an airplane."

"It's all mental masturbation until the coroner looks at her," Galanis said. "Put her on the gurney and let's go. It's freezing out here."

"Hope it's not me that has to notify next of kin," said a deputy, under his breath.

"Yeah," said the other. "Merry freaking Christmas."

2

A week went by, and I wondered what conclusions the Douglas County homicide detectives had reached, if any. The two calls I'd placed to Nick Galanis had not been returned. No surprise there; I was a private citizen, and he had no obligation to share information on the case with me. So, I tried to forget about the girl in the snow, but when I lay down to sleep, the death stare of her face was always waiting. But that would fade in time. It always did.

Christmas was a quiet event for me. Candi, my recent live-in girlfriend, decided not to visit her family in Texas, and my plan to drive us to my mother's home in San Jose was thwarted by another cold storm that closed Highway 50. So, we spent the down time between Christmas and New Year's around the house, staying busy with home improvement projects she'd instigated after moving in three months ago. A brightly lit tree besides the fireplace dominated our living room, and she had redone a sunroom I'd never used for anything but storage. The room was now full of easels and canvases and drop cloths.

In the years since my ex-wife divorced me, I'd defaulted to a sparse living style, my furniture utilitarian, my appliances old but functional. That changed when Candi moved in. In short order, she transformed my modest, three-bedroom house into something that still made me blink when I walked through the front door. My sagging couch was gone, replaced with a tan, leather sectional. Where my old tube TV had collected dust was a new flat screen, and the scarred table in my kitchen was chopped to kindling in favor of a fancy walnut unit. None of my artwork needed to be trashed, because I only owned a few pictures. My framed photo of Clint Eastwood as Dirty Harry now resided in the bathroom. Candi had hung my other favorite—a great picture of the Eiger north face towering above a Swiss hamlet—in the bedroom. The family room walls were now covered with a tasteful assortment of her paintings and modern art pieces.

At first, I'd protested, but I soon realized Candi had an impeccable eye, and I found myself enjoying what she was doing with the place. I'd bought the home mostly for the large lot and because it butted up against hundreds of acres of federally protected meadowland. A mile past my backyard stood the Sierra Nevada range, 5000 vertical feet of evergreen topped by sheer granite cliffs. A mile in the other direction was Lake Tahoe, claimed by many to be the most beautiful alpine lake in the Americas.

"Hey, doll, I'm gonna go to Zeke's, help out behind the bar for lunch hour," I said.

"See you in the afternoon, then?" she called out. She was in the sunroom, working on one of her paintings.

"You bet."

"Don't be long." A soft, suggestive edge to her voice.

My tires slipped on the unplowed residential streets as I drove out to Highway 50, the main drag of South Lake Tahoe. I turned away from the state line, where the casinos were filling with New Year's revelers. A minute later, I pulled into the parking lot at Zeke's Pit. I'd invested twenty grand in the joint last fall, dirty money I needed to hide from the IRS. I viewed the investment as a community service. The funky, old western-style barbeque pit and saloon had been an off-the-beaten-path favorite for locals and tourists alike, until it was shuttered for a month after owner Zeke Pappas died and left the place to his son, Zak, who promptly went on a cocaine binge and nearly fried his circuits for good before landing in rehab.

When Zak got sober, he was flat broke and gladly accepted not only my money but also my condition that Zeke's was to reopen and remain as before. No changes to the menu (which included the best goddamned barbeque chicken and beef brisket in California, I regularly professed to anyone who would listen). No changes to the interior, either—not to the saloon's wooden plank floor, or forty-foot oak bar, or the chandeliers above the cocktail tables, or the wood stove in the corner, or even to the off-color stickers plastered on the cooler doors behind the bar. Over the years, I'd seen plenty of my favorite joints replaced by strip malls or simply redecorated and voided of ambiance, so it was with no small satisfaction that I viewed my stake in Zeke's and the guarantee it would not fall victim to modernization.

But Zeke's had always done good business, so there was no need to reinvent the place. Hungry patrons stopped by for plates piled with smoked meats, beans, coleslaw, corn on the cob, potatoes au gratin, garlic bread, and green salads. Or they came in just to have a few drinks, to listen to the jukebox, and enjoy a setting that harkened a simpler time, a time when men earned a living with their backs, a time uncluttered with technology, electronic gadgets, and instant gratification.

I tied a white apron around my waist and began washing glasses in the metal sinks behind the bar. I didn't know much about the restaurant business, but I knew enough to fire the previous bar manager after discovering he was tapping the tills for $200 a week. Aside from my investment, that was my sole contribution to the resurrection of Zeke's. That, and filling in behind the bar once a week.

A few of the tables in the saloon were taken, couples having an early lunch. A family of tourists came in from the cold and chose the saloon rather than the dining room. Liz, her brown hair straight, jeans tight, breasts braless and pointy, grabbed a handful of menus and left the bar to wait on them. I poured Irish coffees for a man and his wife, and said hello to Bill, a young, mustachioed alcoholic on his stool near the stove. A strict one-pitcher limit for Soggy Bill.

The loud, unmistakable rumble of Harleys made me look out the plate glass window behind the small stage in front of the room. I caught a passing glimpse of a helmeted man parking his motorcycle in the icy lot out front. I shook my head and smiled, wondering what type of nut would ride a street bike in this weather.

My smile faded when the three bikers came through the front doors. They were dressed for the cold, bulky with layers beneath their black jackets, gloves studded with chrome points, chaps stiff and crackling with ice. They stood for a moment, glaring silently into the interior as all eyes turned toward them. Then, they walked across the saloon, their boots thudding against the creaking floorboards. A palpable musk of exhaust, grease, unwashed hair, never-washed leather, and stale sweat assaulted my nostrils. The odor thick enough that no amount of road wind would remedy it. They took a table at the far side of the bar where the stove flickered with heat.

Liz took their drink order while they peeled off their coats and rolled their sleeves to show the swastikas, hooded faces, and Celtic crosses inked on their forearms. One of the men had hollowed cheeks, deep eye sockets, and straggly hair down to his shoulders. When he looked at Liz, his mouth fell open in a hideous leer, half his teeth gone, the remainder brown and rotted. The man next to him surveyed the bar with eyes hard and still, his bush-like beard growing over a rash of tattoos rising up his neck. He acknowledged Liz's perky nipples with a brief nod, his face emotionless.

The third biker was a moose of a man, his chest and shoulders massive, a thin black goatee outlining his mouth. When he sat, the thick girth of his stomach sunk to rest on his crotch. He may have been carrying an extra fifty pounds, but that didn't mean the other 300 were any less menacing. He would be the muscle, his physical presence both a warning and a threat. Anyone wanted to mess with these dudes, they'd have to go through him.

"What are they drinking?" I said to Liz.

"Six shots, well whiskey."

I set the glasses in a row and filled them in one motion. Liz moved the shots to a tray and went back to their table. All three of them now seemed to be making a game of following her chest with their eyes, their faces split in smarmy smiles. The gaunt man pulled a pack of Chesterfields from his pocket and lit a cigarette.

"Sorry," Liz said. "No smoking. California law."

"That's right, boys," I said. The man with the lit cigarette shot a glare in my direction, but the other two ignored me.

"Come on, sweet tits," the man with the beard said. "That law's a crock of shit, and everyone knows it." He thumbed open a box of Marlboros and stuck one in his mouth.

"Goddammit," I muttered. I was at the far side of the bar, where it met the wall. I started walking toward the end that opened to the floor.

"Hey, man," Soggy Bill said, "It's the law." The bikers halted in midsentence and stared. Bill was a slight man, malnourished from taking the majority of his calories in beer. He often arrived here half-drunk at noon. Most days, operating his zipper and fumbling his pecker out before pissing himself was a significant physical challenge.

"I'm just gonna pretend you never said a word," Moose Man said.

"Is that right?" Bill slurred. He slid off his stool and took a step forward. Bill had a thing for Liz, and apparently, his boozy logic told him this was an opportunity to defend her. "Put out those smokes now!" he said, summoning a hazy rage that might have been funny if it wasn't so pathetic.

Just as I came around the bar, the big biker stood and pulled Bill forward by his shirt front and gave him a light slap across the head. "Dumbass trash, you're an insult to your race," he said, then fit his hand around the back of Bill's neck and pushed his head to the floor. Bill squirmed weakly, his face jammed into the floorboards under the biker's boot.

I moved toward them, but the beard stood and blocked me from where Bill lay writhing. "Get back there and pour us another round, barkeep," he said.

At that moment, a family of four walked through the doors. They froze, staring at the scene in the saloon. They looked like they stepped from a Norman Rockwell painting, the father wearing an overcoat over a suit, the mom with her hair pinned above her jacket's fur collar, the children dressed in their Sunday best. I paused for a second, watching their expressions turn from shock to disgust, before they turned and hurried out.

"The sheriff's on the way," I said to the bikers. "You all get your asses out of here." I jerked my thumb toward the door.

"You called the pigs?" the beard said, his eyes blazing. "You dumb, sorry motherfucker." He turned at the hip, his fist cocked.

Men who looked rough and talk tough liked to scare people, but that didn't mean they knew how to fist fight. A couple guys backing you up, you didn't need to be Mike Tyson. That's what being in a biker gang was all about; intimidation was easy when numbers were on your side. As individuals, though, most hardcore bikers were incompetent, frustrated losers, forever making excuses for their shortcomings and hiding behind the ridiculous claim that they were the one-percenters, an elite species that made their own rules and lived outside the law. Their ethos was so deeply ingrained that, even when imprisoned for life, they continued to claim they'd beaten the system.

As for the bearded biker, he jumped forward and threw a wild roundhouse at my head.

Spend a little time around people who liked to throw punches, and you learned a trained boxer was far more dangerous than most wild-eyed street brawlers. I once saw a featherweight boxer knock out a man a hundred pounds heavier. The featherweight was so short, he had to jump to land the punch, but the bigger man went down like a sack of rocks. In this case, though, I wasn't giving away height or weight to the biker who tried to take my head off. He was probably six-foot and two bills, and I had him by an inch or two and at least ten pounds.

I ducked his haymaker and snapped a left into his face, breaking his nose. Want to see how tough someone was? See if they came after you after their nose got busted. On the pain scale, if getting kicked in the nuts is a ten, a broken nose was a fifteen.

He fell to his knees, his hands clutching his face, blood spreading from between the fingers. He wouldn't be getting up—at least not for a minute or two. I turned to my right, knowing what was coming. Or so I thought.

The moose turned full toward me, his fists balling, smiling as if relishing the moment. I had a quick second to consider that this one fell outside my theory—what turned him on was causing pain, and he didn't need backup. But before he could take a step, Liz came from behind, swinging the heavy glass pitcher Soggy Bill had been drinking from. The thick bottom slammed into the big biker's temple. It was a hell of a shot, and I have high standards for that sort of thing.

His eyes rolling, the man pirouetted and fell on his back so hard the chandeliers swayed and ancient dust rose up through the floorboards. By this time, the saloon had cleared out, and patrons from the dining room were peering around the corner, their eyes wide with curiosity and fear.

"Remind me not to piss you off," I said to Liz. Her face looked like a snapshot of someone who'd just survived a near-death experience, eyes round, her lips a slash of red. In her white knuckled fist, she still clenched the pitcher, and I told her to set it down. She ignored me and looked poised to swing again, if necessary.

The skull-faced biker with the bad teeth had risen from his chair and backed off, apparently wanting no part in the altercation. I had discounted him as a non-threat, but suddenly, a small automatic was in his hand, pointed at my chest.

"You think you can disrespect the War Dogs and get away with it?" His voice was hoarse, his eyes smoldering like coals in his skeletal face.

"This is a family place, man," I said. "You want to raise hell, go to the Ho-down on 89."

He laughed unevenly, and I noticed his gun hand was shaking. Not out of fear, I suspected, but more likely because his heart was banging away on crystal meth.

"You…you think you can tell us where to go?" His cackle rose in pitch, and his face glowed with a manic sheen. I stood watching him, my hands half raised.

"Liz, why don't you pour our friend a drink?" I nodded at her, and she set down the pitcher and began walking behind the bar.

"Freeze, bitch," he said.

"Come on, man, let's have a drink. We can work this out," I said. Their shots had been spilled when the big man went down, the glasses scattered, whiskey dripping from the table where they'd sat.

"The only thing to work out here is your funeral."

"Liz, pour a couple shots of Wild Turkey for us, would you?"

"Make it three, you son of a whore," said the beard from his knees.

Ah, the voice of reason.

"Fine," I said, edging toward where Liz stood near the end of the bar. "No problem."

Skull-Face's eyes darted right and left, his gun roaming the room. I nudged Liz, and once we were behind the bar, I pointed to the rubber mats, then hooked a finger in her belt loop and pushed down. She squatted and disappeared from the biker's line of sight.

"Three whiskeys," I said, moving to my right. I grabbed a bottle and poured three shots, my free hand easing to a slot aside the ice bin.

"Tell the skank to stand up!" The gun was again trained at my chest. I didn't think Skull-Face would shoot me in cold blood, but his quivering lips and bugging eyes were a concern. How long since he'd slept? Two, three days? A man in the throes of a methamphetamine binge was an unpredictable thing.

"I believe she's fainted," I said. My fingers touched the smooth wooden pistol grip of my sawed-off shotgun.

A silent moment passed, then a burst of red and blue light flashed through the front window. From where I stood, I watched Sheriff Marcus Grier and a deputy park and climb out of their cruiser. Grier smiled at something his partner said, obviously unaware an armed man was inside. As soon as Skull-Face turned to look out the window, I brought the shotgun to my chest. At the same moment, the beard grabbed the bar rail and rose to his feet, his nose a bloody mess, swollen and bent across his face. Our eyes locked for a second, then he ducked and yelled, "He's got a gun!"

Skull-Face whirled and let off a wild shot in my direction, the round shattering a bottle of good tequila on the shelf above me. I leveled the shotgun and jerked the trigger, the blast deafening compared to the sharp rapport of the small caliber pistol. Skull-Face flew back against the wall and crumpled in a heap. I leaned over the bar and saw the bearded biker crouched down. I swung the shotgun's thick steel barrel and cracked him behind the ear. The blow knocked him out cold.

Outside, I spotted Sheriff Grier pressed to the edge of the window, his revolver in his hand. I hadn't called the police; a patron must have. I set down the shotgun and waved for him to come in.

"What in the hell?" he said a moment later, banging through the doors and covering the room with his pistol, his deputy following behind. They surveyed the three prone bodies strewn about the saloon.

"They came in and copped an attitude. When I eighty-sixed them, that one swung on me, and the one over there pulled a gun."

"You shot him?"

"A nonlethal round. Rubber bullet."

Skull-Face was curled in the fetal position, moaning softly. Grier found the small automatic on the floor and told his deputy to bag it. Then, they cuffed the three bikers and called for paramedics.

***

Half an hour later, the ambulances eased out of the parking lot, followed by a trio of police cruisers. The rubbernecking patrons and passersby finally dispersed, leaving me alone with Marcus Grier, who, after some pointed questioning, begrudgingly agreed

I acted without negligence or criminal intent in handling the situation. That resolved, we stood watching the flow of traffic on the highway.

"Looks like the crazies are flocking in," I said.

"Yeah, it's gonna be nuts at the state line tonight."

"You got to work New Year's Eve?"

He glanced at me, his eyes white against the dark shine of his skin. "Every cop in the region is on duty. You ever been at the casinos for New Year's?"

I shrugged. "Once, about fifteen years ago. Just a bunch of drunk college kids back then. Come to think of it, I might have been one of them."

"Times have changed. Last year was nearly a riot. Knifings, fistfights, drug overdoses. We even considered bringing in the National Guard this year."

"Yeah, I heard. The politicians still decided to let the party happen, huh?"

"The Chamber of Commerce pushed like hell. The street barricades go up at nine P.M."

A flatbed truck pulled up, and two men began wheeling the three parked motorcycles up an aluminum ramp.

"What are you charging the bikers with?" I said.

"Attempted murder for the gunman. Assault and battery for the other two. Possession and parole violation for all three."

"Slap them with a smoking violation too."

"Darn, I almost forgot," Grier said, and I think he tried to smile.

***

I drove home slowly after that. I was not looking forward to sharing the events of the afternoon with Candi. My first wife had left me as a result of a shooting, and though no one had died this time, I still didn't take it lightly. Even though I'd done nothing to invite the trouble with the bikers, I felt on the defensive, as if I was guilty until proven innocent.

Regardless, I marched right to the sunroom, where Candi was painting. At thirty years old, she was art director at South Lake Tahoe's community college. She came from rough cowboy stock, her father a sheriff, her uncles and cousins rodeo riders, oilmen, and one a cop in Austin. I thought, or hoped, she'd be less concerned than a typical woman over what had happened at Zeke's. You'd never guess it from her curvy body, but Candi was no-nonsense and not intimidated by conflict. But before I could say anything, my cell rang.

"Dirty Double-Crossin' Dan." It was Cody Gibbons, my good buddy from San Jose.

"What's happening, Cody?"

"Terr-bear and me are driving to Tahoe for New Year's."

"Who?"

"Terry, my gal. I told you about her."

"No, you didn't."

"Hey, not while I'm driving! Would you stop that? Jesus!" A pause and some laughter, then, "You'll love her, Dirt."

"I'm sure."

"What are you doing for dinner tonight? I made reservations for four at the fancy joint on the top floor of Pistol Pete's. You can make it, right?"

"Candi and I are going to Kalani's."

"What? Isn't that a sushi joint?" Cody knew I didn't like sushi.

"They serve other things too."

"Time for a change of plans, kemosabe," he guffawed.

"Let me call you back."

"I'll see you in a couple hours." More laughter, mostly female, then the line went dead.

"Who was that?" Candi said.

"Cody Gibbons."

"What's that wild man up to?"

"The usual, it sounds like."

"And?"

"He wants us to join him for dinner tonight."

"Do you want to?"

My phone rang again. I thought it was probably Cody calling back, but it was a number I didn't recognize.

"Investigations, Dan Reno."

"This is General Raymond Horvachek."

The voice was so gruff and authoritative that I almost replied, "And I'm Captain Kangaroo." I thought that would have been funny, but I resisted. "What can I do for you, General?"

"My understanding is you were the one who found my daughter."

"Ah," I said, my wise-ass temptations gone. I waved at Candi and walked to the spare bedroom I used as an office.

"Am I correct?" he said.

"I was skiing last week and found a body in the woods. I was never informed of her name."

"My daughter's name was Valerie Horvachek."

"I see."

"The police in Douglas County and Gardnerville are hitting dead ends. I want to hire a private investigator." He cleared his throat. "Are you available?" More like an order than a question.

"I am. When can we meet?" I said. Some private detectives were picky about their cases. Not me. My phone didn't ring all that often, and I had bills to pay, just like anyone else.

"I live in Sacramento. I'm available tomorrow morning at oh-eight-hundred."

"How about the afternoon?" I said. Sacramento was a two-hour drive.

"I start my days early, Mr. Reno. Force of habit."

"Noon, then."

"If that's the earliest you can make it," he said, the irritation plain in his voice.

He gave me his address and hung up. I sat at my desk and stared into space for a minute while images of the dead girl floated in my head. Then, I ran an Internet search on General Raymond Horvachek and quickly found a bio on him. He was a retired three-star general in the US Army, a West Point graduate, who insisted on working his way up from drill sergeant. Decorated for service in Iran and Afghanistan. Multiple decorations, including a purple heart.

I printed the info and began a file, then Googled Valerie Horvachek. Finding nothing, I logged onto a subscription site that provided access to a compilation of public records. Real estate transactions, addresses, phone numbers, rental history, and also criminal records. Not complete information, but enough to be valuable.

Valerie Diane Horvachek, twenty-two years old, address in Sacramento. An arrest for cocaine and marijuana possession, and a DUI. I wondered what the General thought of that. I guess I'd find out.

"That was an unexpected call," I said to Candi.

"Who was it?"

Candi continued to paint as I told her of the general's interest in hiring me, but she set down her brush when I changed the subject to the trouble with the bikers.

"Do you expect you'll hear from them again?" she said.

"Who knows? They're all looking at jail time."

"You're not worried, then?"

"I've dealt with their kind before."

She stood and curled a finger in the waist of my jeans. "I know how to use a gun, you know."

"You do?"

"My father taught me when I was barely a teenager. You're tense, aren't you?"

"Not really."

"I think you need a back massage." She reached her hand under my shirt, her palm warm on my skin. Then, she raised her lips to mine, put my hand on her breast, and led me to the bedroom.

***

Afterward, she said, "So, what's the plan for tonight?"

"I thought we'd bring in the New Year with a bang, but you jumped the gun."

"Oh, shush. Midnight is hours away."

"Cody wants us to join him and his date for dinner at the restaurant at the top of Pistol Pete's."

"At the Gold Lantern? He has reservations?"

"Said he did."

"Wow. I better go figure out what to wear."

"You sure you want to go? I mean, we've never met this girl—"

"Dan, are you kidding? It's one of the top-rated restaurants in the state."

She swung the blankets away and walked naked to the wall length closet. Standing on her tiptoes, she took a pair of heels from the top shelf. I sat up, enjoying the sight of her hourglass figure.

"There could be celebrities there." She pulled out my only sports coat and held it up for inspection. It was in good shape; I didn't wear it often.

"This should do," she said. She began going through her dresses, then spotted my black cowboy boots. They were the closest I had to dress shoes. "These need a shine, buckaroo. I'll iron a shirt for you."

"I'll let Cody know we're in."

She turned back to me, her nipples pink on her firm breasts. "Who's his girlfriend, again?"

"I don't know," I said.

***

We left a little after six and headed down Highway 50. The Nevada state line was only a mile from my house, but as soon as we turned onto the highway, I knew it would take twenty minutes or more to get to there. The road was jammed with cars, most on their way to the casinos that loomed at the border. As we crept along, the hotels grew more frequent, and all displayed neon *no vacancy* signs. Every room in town would be booked tonight.

When we finally crossed into Nevada, police on foot and horseback were patrolling the boulevard. Beneath the WELCOME TO NEVADA sign, heavy wooden barricades waited, ready to be moved into place. At 9:00 P.M., traffic would be stopped, and the half-mile stretch of 50 at the state line would become a pedestrian-only party zone.

The wide sidewalks that lined the street were teeming with people. I watched a group of young women come out of Harvey's Casino, carrying drinks, their jeans tight on their hips, coats unzipped, shirts revealing cleavage and midriff. A group of boisterous fellows followed behind, hoping sheer proximity might help them get lucky.

I rolled down my window and felt the air. "I'm sure the Chamber of Commerce is thrilled with the weather," I said. It was barely freezing outside, and it hadn't snowed in three days.

Candi shifted in her seat, her wrists glittering with bracelets. "You look spectacular," I said.

"Look out!" she yelled. I snapped my eyes back to the road to see a man stagger into my path. I hit the horn and slammed my brakes, missing him by a foot. He raised his eyes, an idiot's grin on his face.

"Happy New Year, dimwit," Candi said, staring hard at the fellow as he stumbled back up the curb.

"Amateur night," I muttered.

"Huh?"

"That's what hard core boozers call New Year's Eve. A perfect night to stay home while all the amateur drinkers go out and cause assorted mayhem."

"Well, I'm not worried, with a big stud like you to protect me."

"That's right, babe."

We parked, went into Pistol Pete's casino, and waded through the noisy sea of humanity to the elevators. Once the doors closed, I checked my duds in the mirrored elevator wall. Boots shined, jeans clean and pressed, shirt crisp. Not bad. Nothing compared to Candi's glamorous getup, but for me, not bad.

When we got off on the thirtieth floor, the dimly lit corridor was quiet, save for some barely discernable jazz. We found the entrance to the restaurant and went in. A middle-aged woman in an evening dress met us at the hostess stand.

"Your name?" she said.

"Cody Gibbons party."

"Ah, yes. They're waiting for you in the lounge." We turned and saw Cody and his lady come around the corner.

Cody was all smiles, his beard neatly trimmed, the blond mop on his head combed, to the extent it could be. He sported black slacks and a purple button-down shirt that somehow managed to fit his massive torso like a glove.

"Hello, Dan. Candi, you look lovely, just lovely." Cody grasped my hand in his huge paw. "And this is Terry," he said, gesturing to the woman at his side.

I tried not to eyeball her up and down, but her outfit demanded it. Her skin-tight white jeans were stuffed into the tops of gold knee-high boots on six-inch heels. Obviously enhanced breasts sat like overinflated balloons in a lacy white blouse split down the center to reveal a strip of tanned skin and a flower tattoo around her belly button. A pair of long silver and jade earrings hung within a mass of frizzy blonde hair cascading over her shoulders.

"Hey, shit, how y'all doin'?" she said. Her eyes were shiny, and there was lipstick on her teeth.

The hostess seated us at a table in the center of the dining room. Waiters and waitresses in white shirts and black bow ties hovered in the shadows.

"Are you from San Jose, Terry?" I said, once we'd settled in.

"Oh, hell no. I'm a SoCal girl, and I can't wait to get back to Hollywood."

"Terry, Candi is a painter," Cody said. "She teaches at the local college."

Terry took a long pull off her margarita, the ice cubes rattling against her lips. "Really?" Terry said. "Have you ever done nudes?

I used to pose. Man, was that boring." She raised her glass and looked around for the wait staff.

"I've never done nudes," Candi said. "It's—

"Photography was a lot more fun," Terry interrupted, her voice shrill and loud. "Paid better too."

"Cody, how's business?" I asked.

"Busy as a one-legged man in an ass kicking contest. Been nice to take a week off."

"I've been keeping him plenty busy," Terry said, elbowing Cody and casting a goggle-eyed smirk his way. The smile on Cody's face became pained.

A waitress came by and took drink orders and tried to tell us about the specials, but Terry seemed oblivious, talking over her, something about a magazine feature.

"Quiet, Terr," Cody said.

"What? Don't shush me."

"The waitress is talking."

"Come back later, sweetie," Terry said.

"Excuse me," Candi said, "I—"

"Oh my god, look," Terry said, pointing across the restaurant. "It's Sammy!"

I looked over and saw a red-haired man I recognized as a popular rock and roll performer. He was sitting with a younger man—likely his son. They both looked up when Terry stood and waved.

"Hi, Sammy!"

Every head in the place turned in our direction. Candi crossed her arms and sunk in her chair. I could sense the waitress in my peripheral vision, trying to gauge the right moment to return.

"I had a little fling with Sammy once," Terry said, winking. "But that was years ago."

A cocktail waitress brought a round of drinks. Sucking on a pair of straws, Terry drained half of hers. "Rock and roll, Sammy!" Terry yelled, pumping her fist. Our approaching waitress froze.

"Terr, kitten, you got to keep your voice down. This is a nice place." Cody's face had turned red.

"Whatever," Terry said. "I wish we could smoke in here."

"We'll go out to the hall in a few minutes."

The table became quiet, and the waitress quickly told us of the specials and asked if we needed more time.

"Candi?" I said.

"Yes, I'll have the Chilean sea bass, and could I get rice pilaf instead of the mash potatoes?"

"Oh, Cindy, you should just get the potatoes. I'm sure the chef knows what he's doing."

"Thanks for the advice, Tracy. I'll stick with the rice." Candi rolled her eyes, and I could feel a wave of negative energy radiate from her body.

"And for you, madam?" the waitress said to Terry.

"Madam?" Terry giggled. "What do you think I do, run a whorehouse?"

"How about a salad, Terr?" Cody said. "That's what you always get, right? They got a salad with poached prawns."

"Sure, why not?" Terry hit off her margarita, but it was empty. "What's with these miniature drinks? Could I get an adult-sized drink, please?"

The patrons at the nearby tables were trying to ignore us, but I kept seeing annoyed faces. The exception was an older couple. They were making no pretense of their irritation, staring at Terry and commenting to each other under their breath.

"Hey, gramps," Terry said, "don't get cranky, I know it's getting close to your bed time."

The redness was gone from Cody's face. His skin was now the hue of granite, gray and coarse and deathlike. His green eyes were fixed on the table.

After a moment, the waitress said to me, "Would you like to order, sir?"

"All right. A T-bone, medium rare, baked potato, and salad, with Italian."

"And for you, sir?"

"Are you going to behave?" Cody said very quietly to Terry.

She took her napkin from her lap and dropped it on the table. "I'm really not hungry. What I'd really like to do is get drunk and do a few lines and see if I can get laid."

Cody stood abruptly. "Cancel her salad," he told the waitress. "Put their dinner on my card."

"You don't have to," I said to Cody.

"Yeah, I do."

***

We didn't say much for a few minutes after they left. I apologized to the waitress and slowly felt my embarrassment recede as the tension around us dissipated. People went back to their conversations and their enjoyment of a holiday evening.

"What the hell was that about?" Candi said.

"For all the good things about Cody, he sure makes some bad choices when it comes to women."

"All the good things? Like what?"

"He saved my life twice."

Candi swallowed. "You never told me that."

"He's the bravest, most loyal friend a man could have. His personal life, though, tends to be a little rough around the edges."

"Why?"

I sipped my drink, thinking how to answer what sounded like a simple question, but in truth was not. "He's the product of an alcoholic father and a weak mother. He was married once to a stable type of gal, but it didn't work out."

"Why not?"

"I always thought he got married to try to create the normalcy of a family life he never had."

She thought about that for a moment. "Looks like he's given up on that concept, huh?"

I smiled. "At this stage, Cody's definition of normal is probably different from yours. Ours, I mean."

"You'll get no argument from me there."

My drink was empty, and the conversation was making me thirsty. I looked around for our waitress and saw a man in a dark suit escorting a young woman to a table along the floor-to-ceiling windows. I pegged the woman at twenty-one. The man was double that age. I knew that for a fact, because it was Nick Galanis.

"What are you looking at?" Candi said.

"The local police captain just came in. Same guy that was there when I found the dead girl."

"The ladies' man?"

"That's the one."

Candi turned and snuck a glance, and like I knew he would, Galanis looked up and spotted me. I nodded, and he smiled in return.

"He looks like he should be in the movies," Candi said.

"That's the popular consensus."

"And she looks like she could be his daughter."

"She's not."

We finished dinner, Candi only eating half her entrée, as was her habit. She had an incurable sweet tooth, and whenever we went out to dinner, we always stopped somewhere else for desert.

"How about The Rosewood? They have great apple cobbler," she said.

"Okay, doll." I would have just as soon gone home. The longer we stayed out, the more tempted I'd be to drink, and I was committed to not allow booze to sabotage my relationship with Candi. *Just one more drink*, I told myself. It would be a relatively sober New Year's Eve, a good way to start a new year.

3

The next morning, I woke early. While Candi slept in, I had breakfast, drank a pot of coffee, then went to my garage and pumped out a dozen sets of heavy weights, alternating between bench press, curls, and upright rows. When I came back inside, Candi was up, and I said a brief good morning before taking a shower. I needed to get on the road to be on time for my meeting with General Raymond Horvachek. I don't like being late.

I drove south and began climbing Echo Pass. Rock walls draped in snow lined the road as it corkscrewed toward the summit at 7800 feet. The skies were mostly clear, allowing the low sun to cast a bit of warmth through my windshield. There was no cellular reception at this point, but my phone rang as soon the signal reconvened, half an hour later in the little town of Kyburz.

"Cody," I said.

"Hey, man. You at home?"

"No, I'm driving to Sacramento."

"Really? Shit. I wanted to come by and apologize."

"Don't sweat it."

"Look, I came into town thinking I'd impress you and your old lady, and now, I feel like a complete asshole."

"It wasn't your fault. We had a good time, anyway."

"Well, I'm glad someone did."

"What did you do after you left?"

"We went to our room, and Terry pulled out a bindle of blow and packed a couple fat lines up her beak. I thought it might mellow her out, you know, the way Ritalin calms a hyperactive kid."

"Did it?"

"Uh, no. When I said her behavior at the restaurant was a joke, she started bitching me out, then she split."

"What did she have to say this morning?"

"Beats me. She never came back to our room last night. She won't take my calls, and I have no idea where she is."

I didn't say anything for a moment. This type of situation was not atypical for Cody. Since his divorce, his girlfriends consisted of strippers, small time porn actresses, closing time bimbos, and gold-diggers. They usually came laden with drug, alcohol, and money problems. All the relationships were unstable and temporary, and to my knowledge, none had ever ended amicably.

"What's so funny?" Cody said.

"Nothing, man," I said.

"What, you think I deserve this?"

"No, no, of course not."

"Bullshit. I do deserve it. Can I help it if the women I'm attracted to are freaking psychos?"

"I think maybe you should see a sex therapist," I said, breaking into laughter.

"Great, thank you, Doctor Ruth. Appreciate the advice. When you going to be back in town?"

"Four, maybe later. You going to hang out?"

"I don't see what choice I have. I don't want to strand her here." Cody lived where I used to, in San Jose, a four-hour drive from Lake Tahoe.

"I'm sure she'll call soon, begging for forgiveness."

"Yeah, wonderful. Call when you're heading back, would you?"

We hung up, and I chuckled all the way into Sacramento.

***

Fortunately, my humor subsided by the time I reached the Horvachek residence in an upper-middleclass Sacramento suburb. I wore a straight face when I knocked on the door, and when the General answered, he did nothing to encourage otherwise. The contrary, actually—he stared me down with a withering glare that made me think of the Marine colloquialism, *I'm gonna rip your head off and shit down your neck.* I subconsciously stood a little taller, thinking he might perhaps say, "At ease, soldier."

Instead, he said, "Dan Reno."

"It's *Reno*, as in no pro*blemo*."

His face tightened in a brief wince. "Come in, please."

I followed him past an immaculate kitchen and glanced down a hallway I assumed led to bedrooms. All with beds you could bounce a quarter off, I imagined. We went into a small room with a desk and a wall-length bookshelf. I measured the general at five-eleven and a hundred-eighty hard pounds. He lowered those pounds into a chair at the desk and told me to sit.

I opened a notebook on my lap and waited for him to speak. He studied me for a long moment, and I studied him back. His hair was military cut, the bristles gray and shiny. A thin white scar ran from the corner of an eye down to his square jaw. His skin, tanned and flared with wrinkles, was weathered but taut.

"I want to know why my daughter is dead." Voice flat, no emotion.

"You said the police in Nevada have hit dead ends."

"Correct. Both the Douglas County detectives and the Gardnerville police."

"You've lost confidence in them, I take it."

"Correct."

"Why?"

"One week, and they have no solid leads."

"Not all murder cases get solved in a week, General. Sometimes, it takes longer."

He paused, then swiveled his chair and pointed to a collection of photos tacked to a board above his desk. "I spent my entire career in the military, Reno. I assume you know that already."

I nodded.

"I spent five years as an MP. Did you know that?"

"No."

"That picture there," he said, reaching out to tap one with a pen. "That's me when I was about your age." The photo was of a man in the uniform of the military police.

"The point I'm making is, I have background in police operations," he said. "And I am not confident in the police agency investigating my daughter's murder. Is that clear?" The volume of his voice had not risen, but his enunciation had become more concise.

"You're more confident I can solve the case?"

"That remains to be seen. My confidence is something that must be earned. But I'm fully aware of your credentials."

"Other than a bounty hunting and PI license, I didn't know I had any."

"I have a complete file on you, Reno. I know everything you've accomplished in your career. That's what I mean by credentials."

"I wasn't aware a complete file on me existed."

"I'm a three-star general. I may be retired, but please don't underestimate me."

I didn't respond. He could have only been referring to my FBI file, something I'd never seen. It was hard for me to believe he was well-connected enough to access it. The FBI and the US military branches did not have a cozy relationship.

"You might have made a good soldier," he said.

"I was never big on taking orders."

His eyes flashed with anger, then his expression softened, and a certain wistful disappointment took hold of his face. Perhaps he remembered he was no longer a commander of men.

"Don't act like you're special," he sighed. "I've seen plenty like you. All piss and vinegar, and no respect for authority. Is that your deal?"

"I'm sorry you got that impression."

"Are you telling me I'm wrong?"

"I have no problem with authority, unless it gets in my way. I work for myself, and I do what it takes to get the job done."

He nodded and leaned back, seemingly content with my response. His rigid posture and wide shoulders relaxed into the chair, making him look a bit smaller and older. From a drawer, he pulled two manila folders and handed them to me.

"These are the case reports from Gardnerville and Douglas County," he said. "Look them over. Take your time. I have some work to do on my computer. When you're finished, tell me what you think."

"Okay," I said. He began typing on his keyboard as I opened the first file. Somehow, General Raymond Horvachek had acquired copies of the official police files on his daughter's murder. Or at least what I assumed were official files. They sure looked authentic, thick with graphic crime scene photos, coroner's reports, forensic comments, and interview transcripts.

The Gardnerville PD file consisted of only a few pages. While Gardnerville was the nearest city to where I'd discovered Valerie Horvachek's body, the location she'd been dumped was beyond the city limits. The bulk of the investigation, including the autopsy and any forensic tests, thus defaulted to Douglas County.

A Gardnerville detective had done some perfunctory work, probably well aware that Douglas County would soon have ownership of the case. The detective had canvassed a small neighborhood near Route 207, closest to the most logical entry points into the woods. He'd asked residents if they had seen or heard anyone on a snowmobile on the night in question. None had—not a surprise, as the neighborhood was almost a mile from the forest.

The Douglas County file was an inch thick, including the photos taken at the crime scene. Nick Galanis and his partner, a cop named Greg McMann, were the lead investigators. I flipped through the pages until I found the autopsy report.

Valerie Horvachek had been strangled to death, according to the medical examiner. The toxicology results showed she was drunk and had a fair amount of cocaine in her bloodstream at the time of death. She also had a large knot behind her ear, clearly the result of blunt trauma. The ME stated she was likely knocked unconscious before the murderer had cinched a rope around her neck and killed her.

The next pages I read attempted to chronologically account for the victim's whereabouts and activities in the hours before her demise.

She had arrived in South Lake Tahoe on December 23rd. With her were three friends, two men and a woman, all Sacramento residents in their early to mid-twenties. They checked into the Horizon Casino, the men in one room, the women sharing another. Around seven, they dined together at McP's Irish Pub, a popular hot spot for young partiers. They left before nine, planning to hit Vex's, a dance club at Harrah's. But first, they stopped back at the Horizon to 'freshen up,' which upon further questioning, meant breaking out the nose candy.

At ten, Valerie and one of men left the Horizon to walk to Harrah's. The other two had apparently become amorous and stayed behind.

Vex's was throwing a holiday promotion offering two-for-one drinks, and the nightclub was crowded. The two friends became separated, but Valerie was seen dancing with an older man. It was near midnight when she left with this person.

The man was identified as Nick Galanis.

I raised my eyes to the general. He stopped typing and looked back at me. "What?" he said.

"Nick Galanis?"

"Keep reading."

Galanis said he drove Valerie Horvachek to his lakeside condo, where they had sex until two in the morning. He said he then called a taxi to pick her up, and, wearing a heavy coat, she went to wait outside. He fell asleep shortly after she left his residence, he claimed.

I scanned a few more pages consisting of interviews with Valerie's friends. Then, I closed the file. "Having Nick Galanis involved in this investigation is a conflict of interest," I said.

"I know that."

"Actually, every detective in Douglas County reports to Galanis, so none of them can be trusted to be impartial."

"Correct," the general said, and I noticed he was squeezing what appeared to be ball of pliant wax in his left hand.

"So that's why you want to hire a private eye?"

"Douglas County P.D. should have assigned the investigation to an alternative police agency once they knew Galanis was involved," he said, his hand flexing as he spoke. "Galanis himself should have made the decision. The fact that he didn't renders him culpable."

"Maybe so," I said. "But that doesn't mean he was involved in your daughter's murder."

"I didn't say he was. But I can't trust him. Would you?"

"Nope."

He didn't smile, but the furrows over his brow became less deep. "It seems to me we're on the same page then, Reno. I'd like you to drop whatever you're doing and start immediately."

"That can be arranged."

"Good."

I handed the general a one-page contract and waited while he read it. So far, we'd avoided any direct conversation regarding his daughter's life. All I knew came from the emotionally sterilized, just-the-facts reporting in the police files. It told me that she seemed to enjoy nightclubbing, casual sex, booze, and blow. So did I, when I was her age. But I wasn't the daughter of a decorated officer, and I wasn't dead.

Coming next was the part I hated. They say losing a child is the most painful death a human can suffer. I had no desire to probe the general's psyche on the subject. But certain questions must be asked.

"General Horvachek," I said, once he'd scrawled his signature and returned the contract to me. "Tell me about your daughter."

He shifted the lump of wax to his right hand, his square-tipped fingers squeezing in a steady rhythm. "Valerie was the sweetest little girl you could imagine. I was older when she was born, forty-one. She brought a light to my life I can't describe. But my career did not allow me to always be there for her." His voice tailed off, then he fixed his eyes on me like anti-aircraft guns locking on a target. "Do you understand that?" he rasped.

"You were defending our country."

"Civilians never really know what that means. You never understand the sacrifices."

"I don't claim to."

He took a breath and closed his eyes for a moment. "In her teen years, my daughter became a wild child. My wife said to me once that her behavior was a means to get my attention. But by the time I retired and came home for good, she was already gone."

"Gone?"

"Yes. My little girl was no more. She'd grown into something I didn't know. The tattoos, the clothes, the makeup, the attitude. Almost like she'd become infected with a disease."

"It's not uncommon for people her age to be rebellious," I said.

"I kept hoping she'd grow out of it."

"Can you describe her lifestyle to me?"

"She wouldn't go to college. She couldn't hold a decent job," he said, his voice rising in intensity and edged with disgust. "She worked as a stripper. She ran around with a different guy every week. She got busted for drugs and drunk driving." He paused. "Some lifestyle," he muttered, the words thick in his throat.

"Did she have brothers or sisters?" I asked. If she did, I'd want their perspective.

"Her older brother was killed in action," he recited, staring at nothing. "Afghanistan."

"I'm sorry to hear that," I said. He didn't respond.

"I'll need to get contact information for her friends and her most recent places of employment."

"I've prepared that," he said, taking another manila file from his drawer.

"Excellent. This will be enough to get me started. I'll e-mail you updates on my progress every couple of days." I rose from my chair but paused when I heard a light knock. The door opened, and a woman looked in at us. Perhaps fifty, but fit and well-preserved. Hair dyed blonde, the tips touching her bare shoulders, the skin smooth and bronze. Her slacks and blouse not tight, but not hiding her athletic figure. A woman oozing vitality and health. Except her face betrayed her.

"Dan Reno—my wife, Marilyn."

"Pleased to meet you," I said.

She nodded and rested her glazed eyes on me for a sad moment. "Please bring to justice whoever ended our Valerie's life," she said. "We need closure."

"Yes, ma'am."

She stood aside, and I began down the hallway, but the general's hand shot out and grasped my forearm, the grip like a steel claw.

"Find my daughter's killer, Reno," he growled, his eyes boring into mine. "I want to see him burn."

***

Dark clouds were rolling in from the west when I drove away from the Horvachek home. The sky over Sacramento was low and overcast, the air heavy with cold. The first raindrops splattered on my truck's dirty windshield as I pulled into a strip mall on Folsom Avenue. I parked and went into an anonymous bar tucked between a pet store and a mini-mart.

I often worked in neighborhood lounges when I was on the road. This one was just what I was looking for, a long, narrow joint, no windows, a shuffleboard running opposite the bar, a pool table in the back. The lighting was dim and provided mostly by neon beer signs hanging from the walls. Three or four day drinkers sat hunched over draft beers and highballs, their murmured conversations lost in the jukebox's dulcet tones. This was a place where time meant nothing, where men came to escape cantankerous bosses, sullen wives, and the pressures of an unfair world. A place to pull up a stool, start with a shot and a beer, and wait for your troubles to melt away in the fuzzy clarity that usually came around the fifth drink.

I glanced at the chalkboard menu at the end of the bar, ordered a grilled ham and cheese, and took a table in a back corner lit by an Olympia beer display that had to be twenty years old. I sipped a nonalcoholic beer and told myself it was an acquired taste. My New Year's resolution was to cut out pointless afternoon alcohol. Nothing as drastic as total sobriety, of course. Just save some calories and keep my head clear, at least before dark. Probably a good thing for my relationship. Woman disliked drunks, I'd learned.

I settled into the warm glow of the corner and began rereading the Douglas County police file. I read slowly, resisting the temptation to skim sections. Some of the reports were handwritten, others typed, some by Nick Galanis, others by his partner, Greg McMann. As I read, I jotted notes on a separate pad.

The detectives had conducted thirty interviews, each transcribed on a form designed for that purpose. They had started with Valerie Horvachek's three friends. Next, they had interviewed bartenders and waitresses at Vex's nightclub. Then, they had spoken with Nick Galanis' neighbors.

When these interviews had failed to turn up an obvious motive or a witness, they changed angles. They'd concluded the dead body must have been transported by snowmobile (the coroner's analysis stated she had died before being dumped). There were three feasible starting points where a snowmobile might enter the forest and navigate to the site in question. The first spot was where I'd met Galanis and his deputies on Route 207. The second spot was more remote, a few miles deeper into Nevada, near a sand and gravel mine that was shut down for the winter. The final location was at the top of Kingsbury Grade, where a base lodge for the local ski resort operated. The area was densely built with vacation rental properties.

It seemed that Galanis had become disengaged at this stage, leaving Greg McMann to search for a witness to a snowmobile taking a body into the woods late at night. It was a job that potentially meant interviewing dozens of people. McMann had focused his energies at the base lodge location. He spoke to a number of permanent residents and ski resort employees. When that turned up nothing, he had posted flyers at all three sites, asking citizens to call Douglas County PD if they'd seen anything suspicious.

I got my sandwich and returned to my seat. I didn't yet have any sense of why someone would want to kill Valerie Horvachek. A robbery didn't seem likely. My impression was she was a party girl out for wild times, not someone who'd have much worth stealing. But that was just an assumption on my part.

Rape didn't seem part of the motive either; although she'd clearly had sex shortly before her death, there was no indication of forced intercourse, no trauma to the body other than the blow behind the ear and the ligature marks on her neck. No presence of semen either. I guess Nick Galanis believed in safe sex. *Good job, Nick. Very responsible of you.*

My fingers greasy, I turned back to the police report. There wasn't any mention of calls resulting from the flyers, but they'd only been posted two days ago. I wiped my fingers on a cocktail napkin and closed the file.

Maneuvering a 115-pound corpse onto a snowmobile and securing it in a reasonable fashion would be quite a trick. The perp would probably have to tie the body to his own, likely in front of him. It would be time consuming and make operating the snowmobile difficult, especially in rugged terrain. Someone would need to be both strong and a very competent rider.

Shit, very competent was an understatement, considering the killer would have been navigating at night. Riding a snowmobile on a marked trail in daylight was simple enough. But riding in the backwoods at night was something very few could do. Especially carrying an awkward, heavy object. And no one would have been fool enough to do it if they hadn't known exactly where they were going.

I scribbled some notes, reminding myself to check if snowmobiles required license and registration in California and Nevada. Maybe check snowmobile clubs, get a line on wilderness and adventure junkies.

Behind the crime scene photos, which were neatly glued four to a page, was a map showing the three starting points the cops had determined. The spot where I'd found Valerie was accessible from Route 207, but I wasn't sure about the other two locations. Did the detectives actually verify if routes to the body existed? Or did they just assume that by looking at a map?

I bound the police file with a rubber band. There was nothing in it that suggested procedural lapses by the Douglas County PD. There was nothing that made me overtly suspicious Nick Galanis was holding back or hiding information. On the other hand, the police work showed little creativity. For a murder case, I found their efforts uninspiring. I guess the general had drawn the same conclusion.

Before leaving, I glanced through the two pages the general had prepared on Valerie's friends and employment history. Then, I called Cody Gibbons.

"I'm going to be stuck in Sacramento for at least another couple of hours," I said. "What are you doing?"

"Losing money at the casino and slurping free drinks."

"You hear from Terr-Bear?"

"Nope, not a word."

"Hmm, that's too bad. Have you found a new broad yet?"

"I'm glad you find my personal life so entertaining, Dirt. Give me a break, I'm on the rebound here!"

"How long you gonna hang out?" I asked.

"My room's already booked for the night."

"I'll try to be back for happy hour."

"Well, hurry up, man. I'm going broke at this freaking place."

"Find some nickel slots."

When I left the warm confines of the bar, a freezing rainstorm greeted me, the downpour slicing diagonally across the pavement.

I zipped my coat and hustled to where the torrent was strafing my Nissan pickup. For a moment, I considered heading back east to try and beat the storm up 50. Spending more time in Sacramento meant risking major delays getting home—possibly a road closure, if the storm was severe.

"Screw it," I said. The general had hired me to do a job, and I wasn't about to put off my work because the weather posed a potential inconvenience. What would I tell him on my progress report? *Day One: It started raining so I went home.* I smiled as I imagined how he'd react to that.

I pulled out a street map, marked six different locations, and connected them with the shortest possible line. It looked like a big S, but fortunately, all the addresses were in the central area of Sacramento, nothing too far west.

The first address was in a residential area off Madison Avenue. It was for the home of Scott Church, one of the two men who traveled to Tahoe with Valerie.

It was a decent looking suburban home, not a bad rental pad for a twenty-three-year-old guy. I splashed up the driveway and knocked on the front door.

"Scott Church?" I said to the man who answered. Five-ten, 170, shoulder length dirty-blond hair, bloodshot eyes, jeans, tennis shoes, a black Motley Crew concert tee.

"That's me, man, what's up?" He smiled, his two front teeth unnaturally white compared to the others. I could smell the booze on his breath from three feet.

"My name's Dan Reno, private investigations. I've been hired by the Horvachek family to look into Valerie's death."

"Private eye, huh? Sure, come on in, man." I followed him to a large family room where two dudes were sprawled on couches watching football. Beer bottles and fast food wrappers covered a coffee table in the center of the room. One of the men was asleep, snoring quietly.

"Sorry about the mess. We had a party last night. Happy New Year. You want a beer?"

"Thanks, but I'm trying to stay sober."

"What a concept," said a voice from the cushions. Six-one, skinny, stringy dark hair, swarthy and unshaven. His legs splayed, one dangling over the edge of a couch.

"Kyle, this guy's a private eye, asking about Valerie," Scott Church said.

"You're Kyle Sheldon?" I said to the reclined man.

"The one and only."

Good, I thought. Kyle Sheldon was the second man in Valerie's group in Tahoe. A two-for-one deal.

"Take a seat," Scott said. He moved a pizza box from a wooden kitchen chair.

"Thanks," I said, mildly grateful I wasn't invited to sit on a couch I suspected was crusty with every variety of human bodily fluids. I'd lived in places like this when I was younger.

"How did you guys know Valerie?"

Scott shrugged. "She was just a local chick who liked to party. She'd come watch our gigs sometimes. We're in a band. Other people…"

"Other people what?" I said.

"Other People rock!" Scott and Kyle Sheldon said in concert. They high-fived and grinned.

"Other People is the name of our band," Scott said.

"Gotcha," I said. "Scott, you were the one who went with Valerie to Vex's?"

"Yup."

"Did you have a relationship with her?"

"He wishes," Kyle said.

"She was just a friend," Scott said. "Platonic."

"Did you go to Vex's, Kyle?"

"No, I hooked up with Val's friend, Christie. That was sweet."

"Old news, Kyle. Nobody cares," Scott said.

"Scott, tell me about what happened at Vex's."

"What happened? Not much, unfortunately. The place was a sausage fest."

"How did that work out for Val?" I asked.

"Shit, every guy in the place was drooling after her."

"Did anyone seem to be particularly persistent? Maybe paying more attention than she wanted?"

"Not that I saw. I wasn't really paying that much attention."

"What about the guy she eventually left with?"

"The older dude? Val took a liking to him, and they split together."

"What time?"

"Must have been around midnight or so."

"Did Val usually date older guys?"

Scott smirked and nodded his head at me as if ready to share an important revelation. "She was dating a friend of mine just recently. A good guy. But on the side, she was boning three different dudes. When my friend caught on, he asked why she was such a slut. She said she was tired of slumming it and was hooking up with a guy with a real job and a convertible Corvette."

"Was your friend pissed?"

"Naw. He knew what she was all about before they went out."

"He just wanted to get laid. He didn't care," Kyle added.

"Is your friend Max?" I said, hoping I remembered the right name from the general's file.

"Yeah," Scott said. "He'll tell you about her."

"What else can you tell me about her?"

"I need another beer. You sure you don't want one?"

"I'm sure, but thanks for asking."

Scott left and came back with a bottle of Bud. He took a long swig and said, "Valerie just had attitude coming out her ass. She could be a lot of fun, but I think she figured her big tits and nice ass would get her a free ride. Basically, she was pretty much a bitch."

"And," Kyle said, not taking his eyes from the television, "Max said she was a dead fuck with a box like the Grand Canyon."

"How long have you guys known her?"

"A year," Scott said. "Maybe a little less."

"What did she do for money?"

"Mostly waitressing. I don't know where. She never kept a job for long. She said she was considering a strip joint, where she could make good bucks working one or two nights a week."

"Okay. Scott, what time did you leave Vex's?"

"Around 12:30, I think. I walked back to Harrah's."

"That's right," Kyle said. "I remember because Christie went back to her room when he showed up."

"Did you guys go anywhere after that?"

They shook their heads. "Just went to sleep," Scott said.

On the TV, a player ran a kickoff back for a touchdown.

"Any idea why anyone would want to harm Valerie Horvachek?" I said.

The men thought about it for a moment, then they both said, "No."

***

Outside, the rain had slackened to a drizzle. I got in my truck and took the solid state recorder from my shirt pocket and hit stop. Another marvel of modern technology. Smaller than a pack of cigarettes, it ran on its own battery and could reliably record and store twenty hours of conversation. Later, I'd download the data to my PC and run a program that would transcribe the content.

A mile down the road, I found the address for Max Caselle in an apartment complex on Fair Oaks Boulevard. I knocked on the door of the first story unit, staying dry under the balcony jutting from the unit above. I heard footfalls and waited, staring into the door viewer and trying for a friendly expression.

The door opened the couple inches the security chain would allow. "Can I help you?" The man was five-foot-seven and had dark hair.

"I hope so," I said. I handed him a card.

"This is about Valerie?"

"Yes, it is."

He released the chain. "Come on in."

His apartment was tidy, the kitchen table clear except for neatly stacked sections of the *Sacramento Bee*. On a coffee table in the main room sat an open textbook and a laptop computer. We sat while he studied my card. His hair was straight, medium length, face shaved, sideburns just below the ears. Thick-rimmed glasses, a silver earring, a goatee. An edgy, modern guy.

"What would you like to know?" he said.

"Who killed her."

His eyes met mine, then he scratched his head. "Yeah, no kidding. You have any ideas?"

"Not yet. Do you?"

"No. Listen, I met her maybe two months ago. She came on to me at a party, a hot chick like that, then asked if she could move in here."

"Just like that?"

"Yeah. She needed a place to stay, and once she found out I had my own place, she just flat out asked to move in."

"Was she going to pay rent?"

Max laughed dryly. "Valerie? Not a chance. The chick was broke, man."

"When did she move out? Or did she?"

"About two weeks ago, I gave her the boot."

"What for?"

"She was running around, having sex with whoever. It didn't surprise me, but I wasn't going to let her stay here, if she was like that."

"Did you like her?"

He thought about that for a second. "She was all right. Not somebody I'd be interested in long term, if that's what you mean."

I was tempted to ask him if he let her hang around just so he could get laid occasionally. But I'd already drawn that conclusion, and I didn't want to put him on the spot.

"What did she do for money?" I asked.

"She had a few restaurant jobs, but she'd work a couple shifts then quit."

"Must have been hard for her to make ends meet."

"Yeah, she was always scrambling for cash. She mentioned she was thinking of becoming a stripper, soaking desperate chumps out of their paychecks. That's how she put it."

"So, you let her stay for free."

"Sure. I didn't mind the company, at least not at first."

"And then?"

"We had a minor romance going on, but that ended pretty quick. Then, she'd just show up to crash, do laundry, or chill out."

"Sounds like she was using you."

"No doubt. So, I told her to hit the road."

"Did the whole thing piss you off?"

He smiled. "I'm not that dumb. I mean, I knew how it was going to end. She had some major issues."

"Like what?"

He blew out his breath "Where to start? She split from her folks' pad because she wanted to live by her own rules, which was basically, Valerie does what whatever she wants, and if you don't like it, tough shit."

"Not exactly the ideal roommate, huh?"

"Yeah, she was pretty self-centered. But she had moments when was mellow and not bad to be around."

"How about drugs? Was she into coke or crank?"

"Sure, when she could get it. But she usually resorted to bumming it off people."

"Like from a guy in a convertible Corvette?"

"Who?"

"I heard something about her seeing a guy driving a Corvette."

"Oh. She mentioned that once, but I thought she was probably lying. Half of the stuff she said was bullshit."

I looked out his window and saw water spilling over a clogged gutter. The gray afternoon was growing darker.

"Why anyone would want to kill her?" I said.

"You got me. I mean, she may have been a bitch, but no one would kill her for that."

"Where were you December 23rd and 24th, Max?"

"What, you think I'm a suspect?"

"Are you?"

He shook his head. "I was here on the 23rd and at my parent's house all day Christmas Eve. I got ten witnesses that can verify it."

"Okay."

"Too bad Valerie wasn't with her parents for Christmas, huh?"

I thanked him, gave him my card, and asked him to call if he thought of anything that might help. He shook my hand and said, "No problem."

I drove off through the showery gloom. For the first time, I felt a real pang of sympathy for Valerie's parents, who were probably wondering what they did wrong to produce such a troubled daughter. At twenty-two, Valerie seemed like an angry teenager, acting out her emotions. But that was putting it politely. It would have been just as easy to say she was a selfish, manipulating bitch looking for a free pass. She didn't seem to be very good at it, though. A young, sexy woman could do all right if she played her cards right, but from what I'd heard, Valerie was scraping by.

Still, I was somewhat surprised that none of the men, including her former boyfriend, if he could be called that, expressed any grief she had died. And these were the people she had meant to spend Christmas with, two of them anyway. Pretty sad.

I almost missed the next turn, my tires spraying a shower of water as I jerked the wheel into a residential neighborhood about a mile from the general's house. Wide streets, big houses on big lots, BMWs and Range Rovers in the driveways. Posh, money-class suburbia.

Christie Tedford was the name of the young woman who had traveled to Tahoe with Valerie. The address I had for her was to a house at the end of a curved stone walkway lined with birch trees, the canopy thick enough to keep me dry as I walked to the door. I rang the chimes and waited until a woman with silver hair and a dour expression answered.

"Hello, ma'am," I said, offering my card. She read it and looked me over. She was old enough to be Christie's grandmother. But her eyes were hard and defiant, and showed no concession to age.

"The Horvachek family has hired me to investigate their daughter's murder," I said quietly.

"How does this have anything to do with me?" she said, the syllables dripping with emphasis—an uppity socialite talking down to the help.

"It doesn't, ma'am. But I would like to speak to Christie Tedford, if I could. Is she your daughter?"

"You needn't concern yourself with Christie. She's spoken to the police."

"I'm sure she has."

"So, she's already put this behind her."

"I'm sure we'd all like to put this behind us, but until whoever murdered Valerie—"

"Perhaps I've not made myself clear. Christie will not be speaking with you."

"And why not?"

"I don't owe you an answer, and I have other things to do. Good day." With that, she shut the door in my face.

"Thanks for your time," I muttered. I spun on my heel and walked back through the trees to my truck. Crotchety wench must have been having a bad day. If Christie was anything like Valerie, that might explain it. Not that it was an excuse to be rude.

It was 3:00 P.M., about two hours of daylight left. Driving the hundred miles over the snowy pass back home would be dicey, especially at night. There were three addresses left on my list. One was a medical center downtown, where the court had ordered Valerie to attend drug and alcohol counseling. The other two were her most recent employers: a TGI Friday's restaurant and a strip joint called the Suave Gentlemen's Club. Being New Year's Day, I assumed the counselor Valerie had seen would not be in. And I wasn't too eager to burn time visiting a restaurant where she may have worked only a few days. The strip club seemed more promising.

The Suave was conveniently located right off the freeway. It was a rectangular stucco structure that probably had once been home to a less conspicuous business. A red-carpeted walkway under a green awning led to an opaque glass door. Above the doorway was a black sign with glittery pink letters, and above that, a billboard rose thirty feet into the wet sky. *Sexy Dancers for the Discerning Gentleman,* it claimed. The advertisement was visible to everyone driving on the freeway.

Judging by the number of cars in the parking lot, the billboard was doing its job. I parked and trotted fifty feet through the steady rain, huddled in my ski jacket. In the parking spot nearest the entrance was a black convertible Corvette, a newer model. I paused for a second, then scrawled the license plate number on the back of one of my cards.

A bouncer standing at a podium inside the door said, "Ten-dollar cover." I paid him, he stamped my hand, and I waded into the dark place.

The seats along the rail of an elevated runway were all taken. A brunette in giant platform heels and a G-string was grabbing her ankles and shaking her ass. The men at the rail, none of whom looked like discerning gentlemen, waved dollar bills, drank, talked, and stared. Dance music boomed from speakers hanging from the ceiling.

I sat at a table away from the stage. Behind me, the walls were lined with booths, where strippers lap-danced for twenty bucks a pop.

A waitress approached, no heels, hair tied back, figure hidden by her clothes—probably a dancer pulling a waitress shift. "You get one free drink with your cover," she shouted.

"Black coffee," I yelled back. "Do you know Valerie Horvachek?"

"Who?"

She left, and I looked around for who might be in charge. There was no shortage of security. Big dudes everywhere in black polo shirts with pink emblems. No shortage of strippers, either—probably thirty or so patrolling the room.

I got up and took a walk. I went past a door labeled *VIP Room*. A great marketing ploy, luring men into a back room under the guise they were big shots. As far as the strippers were concerned, the only thing important about the VIPs was how much they were willing to spend for a quick blow job.

I stopped at the men's room, and while taking a leak, I could hear a tapping sound coming from a stall—someone chopping coke with a credit card on the toilet tank lid. I went back out and headed across the joint to a side bar, dodging girls trying to entice me into a booth.

The bar, like others I'd seen at strip clubs, was removed from the main action, tucked in a less noisy corner that offered no convenient view of the dancers. It was a small bar, six stools. It was small because customers rarely occupied the seats. Instead, it served as a place for employees to relax during breaks.

Two bouncers sat watching a basketball game on TV. Next to them, a frumpy, middle-aged woman was consoling a stripper who looked like she'd been crying. The seat next to the dancer was empty, and the last stool at the bar was taken by a burly man with a shaved head and a beard. He wore a black leather vest over a white T-shirt, his forearms scrolled with tattoos.

I sat in the single empty seat, feeling about as welcome as a pork chop at a Jewish wedding. The dancer shot me an unhappy glance and showed me her back, while the burly guy glared at me as if I was one word away from a good ass stomping.

The bartender, a skinny, prematurely balding fellow, asked what I was drinking, and I asked him if I could talk to the manager.

"Regarding what?" he said.

"Valerie Horvachek. She worked here, right?"

"Val? Blondie with big, natural knockers? Yeah, but I haven't seen her for at least a week."

"That's because she was murdered."

"What?"

"Hey," the burly guy said, injecting himself into the conversation as if his utter badness granted him the right to do so. "What the hell you talking about?"

I turned my head and looked at him. "I'm investigating the murder of Valerie Horvachek. Did you know her?"

"She's not dead. You're full of shit, man."

"Sorry to bring the bad news."

"I don't fucking believe you."

"Believe whatever you want. It's a free country."

Apparently, that stumped him. While he tried to formulate a reply, the bartender waved his arm and said, "Mike! Mike, come over here."

I turned and saw a tall man in dark slacks and a shiny blue button-down shirt stride toward us. His black hair hung to his shoulders, and his face was edged with a neatly trimmed seven-day growth. A silver chain rested on his chest where his shirt was unbuttoned. His skin was the color of tarnished copper. He was about thirty. An Arab, or maybe a Latino. Or a dark-skinned Italian.

"This guy says Val is dead," the bartender said.

"And you are?" the man named Mike said to me.

"Reno, private investigations. You're in charge here?"

"Yeah," he said, a hint of superiority creeping into his tone. "I own this club."

"I'm impressed," I lied. "Can we talk in your office?"

He looked at his watch. "I got five minutes," he said. Clearly, his time was important. He had a business to run. Probably had strippers to hire. He struck me as the type who would insist on up close and personal interviews.

I followed him behind the bar and down a short hallway. We went through a door on which a name was displayed in gold lettering: *Mike Zayas—President.*

It was a big office, a couch along one wall, a tiki bar in the corner, a big TV screen mounted across from the couch. A fancy desk was in another corner, which was where he sat. I stood until he motioned for me to sit in a chair opposite him.

"Looks like you're doing well for yourself," I said. "Business is good, huh?"

"There's a lot of money to be made in this industry. But you have to be smart. Most club owners go out of business."

"You're one of the successful ones, I take it."

He leaned back in his chair. "I won't comment on how much money I make. Let's just say, I could retire tomorrow if I wanted." He gave me a moment to process his remark, to let it sink in, as if surely I'd be jealous, and that would set the tone of our little encounter. I played along the best I could, keeping a straight face and resisting the urge to tell him I didn't give a rat's ass about his money.

"Now, what's this about Val?" he asked. Real casual about it.

"Dead. Strangled."

"When did this happen?"

"December 24th. How long had she worked here, Mr. Zayas?"

"A couple shifts," he said after a moment, measuring his response.

"Anything you can tell me about her?"

He shook his head and fixed me with a stare. 'I'm smarter and tougher than you,' it said. "Sorry, I never got to know her."

"Anybody else here get to know her?"

The stare again. "Not that I know of."

I crossed my legs and noticed my boots would need to be replaced soon. "Mr. Zayas, were you dating Valerie Horvachek?"

He laughed. "Where would you get that idea?"

"She told people she was seeing a man driving a black Corvette."

He laughed again, dryly. "Maybe she was having a fantasy."

"You're pretty choosy, huh?"

"Choosy? Yeah, I am. I don't bang every piece of trim who works here, if that's what you're getting at. Not that I couldn't if I wanted to." He nodded and smiled, a smutty glint in his eyes.

"Did you bang Valerie?"

"You know what? I really don't remember." The shine in his eyes faded. "Actually, it's none of your goddamn business."

"Why would someone want to kill Valerie?"

"I have no idea." He looked at his watch again. "Time's up, my friend." He stood and opened the door in dismissal.

"I'll tell Valerie's family you expressed your deepest sympathies," I said.

"You do that."

We walked out, and he left me on the main floor. I considered buying a few lap dances and questioning Zayas's stable of working girls. But it was too loud to have a conversation, and I wasn't in the mood to be titillated. So, I headed to the exit, but just as I reached the door, I was intercepted by the burly man I'd spoken to at the bar. I ignored him and walked outside. He came out behind me.

"Look, I was asking about Valerie because I liked her," he said, his tone conciliatory, like he'd made a very conscious decision to not hard-ass me. I stopped under the awning. The rain had paused.

"How long had you known her?" I said.

"Just a couple weeks, since she started here." He had tufts of brown hair rising from the back of his shirt, and held a black leather jacket in his fist.

"You work here?"

"No. Is she really dead?"

"Yes. Someone knocked her out and strangled her."

"Where?"

"Lake Tahoe."

"Was she robbed?" A drop of water fell onto his shaved head and ran down the side of his face. He wiped at it and shrugged into his coat.

"She was found naked. No clothes, no purse."

"So, whoever killed her took her stuff." He zipped his jacket against the cold, the leather tight over his barrel-shaped bulk.

"Looks that way," I said. "You think she had much worth stealing?"

He took a pack of smokes from his coat and lit up. His goatee was thick and long and probably dyed to hide the gray. He blew a stream of smoke into the damp air and squinted as if pondering some dilemma. "Strippers can make a lot of money," he said.

"Did Valerie?"

He studied the curls of smoke rising from his meaty fingers. "She didn't share her finances with me."

I didn't say anything. He took another drag off his cigarette, then flicked it out onto the wet pavement.

"Damn cold out here," he said, and walked back into the building. As he went in, I turned and checked the lettering on the back of his coat. *Blood Bastards*, it read.

***

There was little traffic heading east, and I made good time for about thirty miles. But just as it started getting dark outside of Placerville, it began to snow. The snowflakes swirled in my headlights as I slowed on a long stretch of straight highway notorious for speeding tickets.

The information I'd gathered on Valerie Horvachek had provided insight into her personality and lifestyle, but I still had no clue why she was murdered. Many things were possible if I exercised my imagination, but for now, I was grasping at straws.

I drove along, my tires crunching over the snow building up on the road. Most murders were motivated by money or love. Was it possible a jealous lover had killed her? Sure. Attractive and promiscuous woman meets fatal attraction. Could have even been a customer at the Suave Gentlemen's Club.

Most strip joints were crime-ridden holes, teaming with prostitution and drug abuse. A fair percentage of the clientele were criminals—some there to do business, others just to affirm their sexuality by basking in the attention of young, naked women. The biker in the Blood Bastards clan could have been there for either reason, or both. His interest in Valerie might have been strictly romantic. But I doubted she would have chosen him as a sugar daddy. Seemed like she was more interested in types like Nick Galanis, or Mike Zayas. Regardless, I didn't consider the biker a suspect, because I'd be the last guy he'd want to talk to if he killed her.

But that didn't mean the biker might not have had a financial interest in Valerie. For all I knew, he might have been pimping her. Or using her as a drug mule.

The same could also apply to Mike Zayas, a man who wore his self-importance and greed like a bad cologne. He acted like owning a men's club was the holy grail of business achievement. What he didn't admit was he was taking a fat cut from every act of prostitution performed in the back room. I also thought he was likely tapped into whatever drug trade was occurring at his establishment. Smart businessman, making a lot of money—as long as he stayed out of jail.

An orange Caltrans snowplow pulled onto the highway, and I swerved around it. I wanted to make time while I could. It would be full dark soon, and that meant thirty miles per hour in these conditions. I'd need to drive to Sacramento again soon to talk with Valerie's friend Christie, and maybe to revisit the Suave Gentlemen's Club. Next time, I'd wait for the weather to cooperate.

I called Candi and told her I'd be late, and before we hung up, I heard the beep of another call coming in. It was Cody.

"Dan, I'm in Marcus Grier's office," he said, his voice oddly subdued. "They found Terry's body on the beach down near Camp Richardson."

"Her *body*?"

There was a long pause, long enough for me to anticipate his next words.

"She's been murdered."

4

It was 8:00 P.M. when I came off the grade into South Lake Tahoe. I'd driven through the teeth of the storm, at times barely able to see. Near Echo Summit, I'd lost control on a patch of black ice, my four tires spinning futilely until catching traction an instant before I would have slammed the guardrail. A bulletin on the radio announced the pass had just been closed. If I'd left much later, I'd still be out there, maybe until morning.

The cellular reception had died before Cody could tell me anything more, and now, his phone was going straight to voicemail. I hadn't had dinner, and my stomach kept telling me to stop and eat, but I drove straight through town until I reached the sheriff's complex.

Snowflakes danced silently in the dome of light above the parking lot. The visual effect reminded me of a snow globe I played with as a child. I walked through the flurry, the flakes melting on my face.

"Marcus Grier, please," I said to the receptionist behind the bulletproof glass partition separating her from the empty lobby.

"Who's asking?"

"Dan Reno."

I sat and waited. My relationship with Sheriff Grier was good, but at times uncertain. I'd come to know him well in the three years since I moved from the rat race of San Jose to South Lake Tahoe. Our paths crossed frequently as a result of my investigation and bounty hunting business. Somehow, we'd managed to avoid the resentment and friction that often exists between the police and private eyes. The reason, I believed, was we both despised the individuals that made up the worst of society's criminal element.

Grier's dilemma, like any cop's, was taking down the bad guys while staying within legal boundaries. Although we never spoke of it, over time, he'd found it quite convenient to rely on me to cross the lines that he could not. This had become our unspoken alliance, one that served, to some extent, as a basis for our friendship.

As for Cody Gibbons, Grier originally hated him. An ex-policeman himself, Cody lived his post-cop life like an exuberant teenager on summer vacation, skirting legal convention and waging a no-holds-barred war against criminals unfortunate enough to find themselves in his sights. Cody viewed the Lake Tahoe area as a home away from home, a perfect retreat when things got too hot, or a bit too boring, in San Jose. While I stretched the rules, when Cody came into town, as he sometimes did to assist me on cases, he outright ignored the law if it impeded his vision of justice. Cody's approach created obvious problems, but after a bloody affair last fall, I think Grier had begun to see Cody as an asset. A volatile one, but one that was also useful.

Grier opened the squad room door. He appeared at a truce in his ongoing battle with his weight. Five-ten and once 240, I now put him at 215.

"Dan," he said, weariness plain on his face. He was a nine-to-five cop, and I knew he wanted to get home to his wife and two daughters.

"What's going on, Marcus? Are you holding Cody Gibbons?"

"No. He's free to go."

"He's still here?"

"Yeah. Come on back. There's someone you should probably meet." I followed him past the empty desks to an office. We went in, and Cody was sitting against a wall, talking to a tall, slender man with silver hair and a face that looked like it had seen two lifetimes of sun.

"Dan Reno, Bill Worley," Grier said. "Bill just came aboard to head up our plainclothes team."

"How's everthan', Dan?"

"All right. Yourself?" I reached out and shook his hand. The skin was dry and cracked.

"Oh, fair to middlin'."

"Your accent—Texas?"

"That's right," he drawled. "El Paso."

"You'll find the winters up here a bit chilly."

"You don't say." He smiled. He had to be at least sixty.

The room became quiet for second, then I said, "What happened to Terry?"

"Someone hit her behind the head and strangled her to death," Cody said.

I felt my mouth drop. "Strangled?"

"Yeah."

"Any suspects?"

"No, sir." Bill Worley's blue eyes peered at me from under his leathery brow.

I sat in the single empty chair in the room. "Valerie Horvachek was the name of the girl strangled a week ago and dumped in the Nevada backwoods." All three men stared at me.

"Two women strangled," Worley said.

"A serial killer?" Grier ran his fingers over his stubble-like hair.

"I've just been hired to look into Valerie's death," I said. "The father wasn't happy Nick Galanis admitted sleeping with her and is still lead investigator on the case."

Worley stood. "Lordy. Reckon we ought to call Douglas County first thing in the morning."

"And say what?" Cody said.

"If we're searching for the same killer, it only makes sense we work together."

I saw Grier wince. "Gibbons," he said, "I'd like you to stay in town for a day or two. We'll probably have more questions."

Cody stuck his hands in his pockets. I didn't know what was going through his mind—grief or remorse over Terry's death, or maybe some sense of guilt, or maybe even relief that the relationship was over.

"I'll stick around," he said.

***

I drove Cody across the state line and a couple miles into Nevada. I pulled into Chuck's Place, a dark, funky bar with the best tacos and French fries around. I did my best thinking over tacos and French fries. Good fuel for the brain, especially when I was starving. Add a margarita on the rocks and I could solve the world's problems.

"How'd the cops know to call you?" I asked.

Cody poured a beer from the pitcher he'd ordered. "They found Terry's purse in a trash can in a picnic area about fifty yards from her body. Her cell phone was in it. They saw I called her a bunch of times." He rubbed his eyes with his fists and groaned.

"You all right, partner?"

"Yeah. This just ain't the way I planned to start the new year."

"Did Grier or Worley consider you a suspect?"

"Sure. But I cooperated fully, and if they really thought I did it, they'd have found a reason to hold me."

"You'll be eliminated as a suspect tomorrow anyway."

"Why? You sure the killer is the same one who killed Valerie whoever?"

"Cause of death was the same. Both sexy blondes. Seems pretty obvious."

"A serial killer in Lake Tahoe?" He wiped his mouth with the back of his hand.

"Why not?"

He swallowed and put down the huge cheeseburger in his paw. "They usually like big cities. It's harder to be anonymous in a smaller town."

"I don't know if the killer lives here. He could have just been in town for a week of vacation."

We were silent for a bit, then Cody said, "Terry told me she forgot her meds when we got here. She wasn't a bad person. I should have driven her straight back to San Jose when she told me that."

"Did she ask you to?"

"No."

"Don't blame yourself for this, Cody."

"I was her enabler."

"No, you weren't. She was a grown-up. She made her own decisions."

"She had chemical imbalances. The doctors gave her pills to control her emotions. I took her to Lake Tahoe without her meds to booze it up. I probably deserve to be jailed."

"Nonsense. Take it easy, man."

"Jesus Christ," he breathed. He motioned to the bartender. "Double CC, straight up."

I put my hand on his shoulder and squeezed the mass of muscle. "Her problems didn't have anything to do with you."

The bartender set the glass of whiskey on the bar, and Cody held it in his fingers for a contemplative moment before draining it with a flip of his head.

"You gonna hang around and help me work the case?" I said.

When he looked at me, there was a heated light in his green eyes, as if a harnessed fuel had been lit. "Yes, I believe I will," he said.

***

The skies were clearing when we left the bar, the clouds moving fast in the black sky. The temperature had dropped—the cold after the storm. My windshield was caked with frozen snow, and I gave up trying to scrape it off. Cody and I sat in my cab waiting for the defroster to melt the buildup. Every minute I hit my windshield wipers, until finally sections of ice began breaking apart.

We drove two miles down the dark, plowed highway back to the casinos. The parking lot at Pistol Pete's was nearly empty. Looked like all the partiers had packed up their hangovers and dragged themselves home.

Inside, the casino floor showed no sign of the previous night's festivities. The gamblers were sparse, mostly locals. The volume of the slot machines seemed turned down to a pleasant level, almost like backyard chimes.

Starting at the end of the casino floor, we began questioning the dealers, cocktail waitresses, and bartenders. The good news was all of them had worked last night. The bad news was the place had been so packed and chaotic that even someone dressed like Terry could have escaped notice.

It wasn't until we reached the roulette wheel in the center of the casino that a croupier recognized her.

"Sure," the man said, his thin mustache from a bygone era. He stared into the picture on Cody's cell phone. "She was here for a while." His jaw worked a piece of gum, his hands busy stacking chips.

"Was she with anyone?" I said.

"Hard to say, woman like that. She was surrounded by men."

"Anyone in particular you remember?" Cody said.

He paused and adjusted the green visor on his head. "Naw. Not that I saw."

We moved to the craps table, where a short Asian stickman was raking chips off the board. Half the table was occupied, mostly low stakes at play.

"Yah, her. I saw her." He grasped Cody's hand and angled it so he could see the phone screen better. "Loud lady, big bosoms, small bets."

"She have a man with her?" Cody said.

"Many men."

"Was there any man paying more attention to her than the others?" I asked.

"Ah. Maybe one. Chopper guy. Like Hell's Angels. Staring and staring."

"Describe him."

"Hair long. Tied in back. Blond guy. Not young, though."

"How old?" I said.

"Maybe forty-five. Tattoo of tear on his face." He touched the corner of his eye.

The dice clattered on the table, and he began paying bets and raking in the losers.

"How tall?" Cody said, and we waited until he'd made the table right and shoved the dice to the shooter.

"I don't know. Taller than me, shorter than you. Average."

"Call me if you remember more. It's important." I handed him my card. The dice tumbled across the board and came up craps, ending the round.

"Bad luck, guys," the stickman said. We walked away.

"Let's try over here," I said, turning toward a large bar area adjacent to the gaming tables. A neon sign above the bar advertised it as the *OK Corral.* There was a stage and perhaps thirty cocktail tables.

The bartender and two waitresses didn't recognize her picture. But a younger guy who came out of a backroom did.

"Oh, yeah," he said, his hands on a dolly stacked with cases of beer. "I saw her last night."

"Was she with anyone?"

"Some guy was buying her a drink."

"Describe the guy," Cody said.

The kid looked to the ceiling and tilted his head. "Jeez, I don't remember."

"But you remember her," I said.

"Hell, yeah. Was she a call girl?"

"Outstanding," Cody said.

It was ten o'clock. We went back out to the card tables, and I looked up at the series of dark spheres protruding from the ceiling. The eyes in the sky, the casinos called them, all equipped with security cameras recording the events below.

"First thing tomorrow, I want to talk to security here about viewing the tapes," I said

"They'll tell us to go pound salt."

"Not if we get Marcus Grier involved."

"*He* might tell us to pound salt."

"Have a little faith, man. I'm gonna go get some sleep. You should do the same."

"Aye-aye, Captain."

I headed for the exits, but stopped short and saw Cody standing where I had left him, like a six-foot-five, 300-pound Sasquatch pondering his next move. He looked at the elevators across the casino, then sighed and trudged to the bar as if pulled by an undertow he was too weary to resist. I went into the men's room, came out, and made it almost all the way to the exit before I shook my head and turned around. I didn't want my buddy drinking alone. I wanted to get home, but I would not desert Cody. Not tonight. I owed him that.

5

My head was foggy the next morning. I probably could have slept ten hours but woke after just six, drank a cup of coffee, and went outside to shovel the driveway. Need to snap out of it after a late night? Try clearing a foot of snow off your driveway in ten-degree weather.

I came back inside, sweating, and drank more coffee while waiting for Candi to get out of the shower. I was tempted to join her. We were still in the stage where I couldn't get enough of her body. We were also still in the stage where she hadn't yet uttered a single complaint; not even the slightest disparaging remark about me or my habits. But I knew that wouldn't last. She was only human, and so was I.

Still, I was committed to not give her anything to be unhappy about. So far, it hadn't been that hard. I'd trained myself to be tidy over the years. I stayed in good shape, I owned my place free and clear, and I managed to make a decent living. And I'd curtailed my boozing to a large degree.

As far as her habits, the only issue I had was her rearranging the kitchen to the point that half the time I couldn't find what I was looking for. I'd always kept a bottle of vitamin B and a container of concentrated protein powder next to my coffee pot. Now, I was searching through the cupboards, wondering where she could possibly have hidden them.

"Try the drawer beneath the coffee pot, ding-a-ling," Candi said from the hallway, stark naked except for a towel on her head.

"Huh? Oh, okay." I found the articles and smiled. Just like her to flash me and redirect my blood flow when I knew she had no time for sex. I think she did it so I'd think about her while she was at work. An effective strategy, if that was her intention.

An hour later, she was gone, and Cody pulled into my driveway, his diesel motor rattling loudly. I met him at the door. He wore a sky-blue beanie pulled low above his eyes and a thick, army-green winter coat. Steam poured from his mouth as he clapped his hands against the cold.

"Enjoying the weather?" I asked.

"Next year, I'm going to Cabo for Christmas. I swear to god, it's eighty and sunny down there right now." He went and stood near my stove.

"You sleep all right?"

"Not really. I think I need to quit trying to make sense of my life." He stared into the swirling fire behind the stove glass as if the solution might lie within. Then, he saw me looking at him, and said, "Don't worry about it, I'll be fine. Let's get to work."

I'd moved an easel from Candi's studio out to the main room and pinned up a three-foot square pad of drawing paper she used for sketches. I sat on the arm of the couch and began writing with a black felt tip pen.

"Early December 24th, Valerie Horvachek knocked unconscious and strangled. Body found in the mountains." I wrote it out toward the upper left.

"New Year's Eve, Terry Molina, strangled, body found on Lake Tahoe shore New Year's Day." I wrote it on the right-hand side of the pad.

Under Valerie, I wrote, *cocaine, booze.*

From the couch, his elbows on his knees, Cody said, "Put the same for Terry."

"Okay," I said. "From what I heard, Valerie had money problems." I wrote *money issues* in her column.

"Terry wasn't working. Put the same for her."

"The meds you said Terry was taking—"

"I don't know exactly. Some form of bipolar, she said."

Under Terry I wrote, *mental pills.*

"Was Valerie taking anything?" Cody asked.

"Don't know. I'll e-mail her father."

I paused, then wrote *promiscuous* under Valerie. I looked at Cody. He shifted his hulk, leaning back on the couch. "Same for Terry," he mumbled.

Next, I wrote *Sacramento* in Valerie's column. "Terry was from San Jose," Cody said. "I don't think she ever lived, or spent much time, in Sacramento."

"Do you know where she went to high school?"

"No."

"What did you two talk about when you went out?"

"Not about where she went to high school."

"Let's find out," I said, making a note under Terry.

Back on Valerie's side, I wrote, *biker.*

"What's that about?" Cody asked.

"A biker at the strip club where she worked asked me about her. Seemed a little more than a casual interest."

"And the dice man said a biker type was hounding after Terry," Cody said. I added *biker* to Terry's side.

Cody stood and looked out my big window facing the mountains. The trees in the meadow beyond my property were hunched under the weight of the recent snowfall. A birch had snapped at the trunk and its tangle of gray branches lay half buried in the powder. "So, we got two gals with a few things in common," Cody said. "Where does that get us?"

"Nowhere, yet. It's a starting point." I reached over and made one more notation under Valerie: *Nick Galanis.*

"Cop probably wishes he'd kept his pecker in his pocket," Cody said.

"Maybe. No one seems to consider him a suspect, though."

"Does he have an alibi?"

"Nope. Just his word."

I joined Cody and stared out at the landscape. The sky was an icy blue over the ridges, the sun thin and distant.

"Maybe we should go have a chat with old Saint Nick." Cody's lips curled in a tight smile.

"Not yet," I said.

***

We drove to Harrah's, South Lake Tahoe's largest casino. Harrah's was owned by a publicly traded conglomerate that also owned Harvey's Casino, and had recently acquired Pistol Pete's. I knew the person who oversaw security for all three operations, a rawhide-tough black woman in her fifties named Joan Wallace.

We went to the security booth at Harrah's and asked to speak with Ms. Wallace. Thirty minutes later, a security guard escorted us into the back offices. He led us to a door and knocked quietly.

"Yes?" barked a voice.

The guard opened the door and peeked in. "The private detectives, Ms. Wallace."

"Let them in, please."

Joan Wallace did not greet or acknowledge us when we came into her office. Her eyes were locked on her screen, her fingers clattering on the keyboard. She was not a large woman, nor was she diminutive. Her black hair was threaded with gray, her lips thin for a woman of her race, and her brown skin had a dusty texture to it.

She hit a final key and turned toward us. "What's this about, Mr. Reno?" She pronounced my name correctly, though we'd only met twice before, and only briefly on those occasions. Her memory was good, as was her attention to detail, both attributes I appreciated. She was someone whose time I didn't want to waste. Not that she would let me.

"Ms. Wallace, my partner, Cody Gibbons."

"I remember you, Mr. Gibbons," she said, her voice flat as yesterday's beer.

Before Cody could reply, I said, "You may be aware a guest at Pistol Pete's was murdered the night before last."

"I am."

"We have reason to believe the murderer also killed a woman here on Christmas Eve."

That got her attention. Her eyes sharpened, and her hands became still. "Why do you draw that conclusion?"

"Two attractive blonde women, both knocked out with a blunt object and strangled."

She nodded. "Go on."

"We know the latest victim, Terry Molina, was gambling at Pistol Pete's from roughly 8:00 P.M. onward on New Year's Eve. We think it's possible the killer made contact with her there."

"And?"

"We'd like to review your security tapes. We confirmed she was at a roulette table and a craps table and also at a nearby bar, the OK Corral."

"We only share our video content with police agencies, at their request." She turned back to her monitor.

"I understand. We can return with Marcus Grier, if you like."

"You're working with Grier on this?" Her eyes snapped back to me.

"Yes, ma'am."

"I'll call him to verify."

"Please do. In the meantime, my goal is to get a serial killer off our streets as soon as possible. I think that benefits everyone."

"A serial killer?"

"Two women were murdered in the same fashion, a week apart."

"Has the press been informed of the killings?"

"Not that I know of. Not by me."

She picked up a pen and tapped it in her palm. "Christ, this is the last thing we need," she grumbled. Lake Tahoe had been hit hard by the recession. One casino had closed last year, along with a number of restaurants. The hard-fought-for tourist dollar would dwindle even further if reports of multiple murders showed up in the papers.

She turned toward me again, her face resolute. "Go ask for Chris Davies at Pistol Pete's. He'll give you access."

"Thanks for your cooperation, Ms. Wallace."

"In return, please do what you can keep this quiet."

"We'll be discrete."

"Good."

She pressed a button, and a faint buzz sounded. A moment later, the door opened. The guard who had escorted us stood waiting. We rose from our chairs.

"Mr. Reno?" Ms. Wallace said.

"Yes?"

"I hope you're as good as they say you are."

"Like a starving dog on a bone," Cody said, clapping me on the shoulder.

For a second, she showed a hint of smile, then she nodded her dismissal. The guard walked us down the hall and let us out the door back into the casino.

"Well done," Cody said, as we walked past the card tables. "I could hear the attorney in you."

"Maybe I'm channeling my old man."

"Yeah? I didn't know you were the spiritual type."

"Me neither."

"Well, whatever it takes. Nice job with that dried up old crow."

"What, she's not your type?"

"She's not anyone's type that I know of. Anyway, I'm staying single for a while."

"You should consider celibacy. Make your life less complicated."

"That's a sobering thought, and I haven't even had a drink today."

"And it's already ten A.M. Congratulations."

We opened the casino door to a blast of frigid air and hurried down the block to Pistol Pete's. Before we got there, a gust of wind whipped down the street and pelted us with tiny bullets of ice. I hunched in my coat and ducked my head against the onslaught.

Inside Pistol Pete's, a man with sandy hair and a surfer's tan waited for us under the *SECURITY* sign next to the cashier's cage. He wore a short sleeve shirt and a necktie. Average height and a lean athlete's body. A skier or snowboarder, no doubt.

"Chris Davies," he said, shaking hands. "This way, gentlemen." We followed him up two flights of stairs to a white room lined with racks of electronic consoles and computer monitors. In one corner, the screens were arranged in a semicircle around a keyboard and a high-backed chair. Davies sat there and looked up at us.

"Tell me the timeframe you want to view."

"Eight P.M to one A.M., December 31st," Cody said.

"Our systems were upgraded last quarter," Davies said, his fingers clicking on the keyboard. "We now have twenty cameras recording twenty-four-seven."

"How do you store the data?"

"We download to external drives daily and keep a twelve-month repository." He pointed to a screen showing an overhead diagram of the casino floor. Camera locations were marked with a blinking red arrow indicating the direction the lens was pointed. "Which views do you want to see?"

I studied the diagram and asked, "Where is the OK Corral?"

"Here."

"These three, then," I said.

He picked up a phone and gave directions, and five minutes later, a kid with a face bumpy with acne brought out a stack of six disks.

"Three hours per disk, eighteen hours of viewing pleasure," Davies said. "You can set up at those two terminals." He pointed to a foldout table along a far wall.

"Any chance we can take these home?" I said.

"No, sir."

We walked across the room, and I sat in a plastic chair and inserted a disk into the computer in front of me. An overhead view of the roulette table flickered onto the screen. The resolution was grainy, and the people around the table moved in jerks and starts, as if frames were missing.

"Arnold, can you instruct them on the commands?"

"Sure," the kid said. He pushed his thick-rimmed glasses up on his nose and knelt between where Cody and I sat. "You're in a default setting now. The video will run at high speed, so you can view an hour in about forty minutes. We also use a compression mode on these disks, which is another reason the image looks poor. But here's the good news: if you see something you want to examine in more detail, click here. You'll get a menu that lets you slow to real time, freeze, zoom in, and improve resolution. Try it."

"Any audio?" I asked.

"Nope," Davies said. "Too much ambient noise for a mic to isolate anything but gibberish."

We spent the next few minutes familiarizing ourselves with the commands. Then, Davies and the kid left us, and we settled in to examine the hours of monotonous video.

Two hours later, we'd covered from 8:00 to 11:00 P.M. with no sign of Terry. I leaned back and uncrossed my legs, one of which had fallen asleep. No cop or investigator I'd ever met enjoyed the tedium of surveillance. I rubbed my eyes and turned my attention back to the monitor. Cody suggested lunch, and I was ready to agree when he said, "There she is."

He turned his screen so we could both see it. A big head of blonde hair was at the craps table. Cody slowed the video stream and zoomed in. We could only see her from the back, but when she turned to talk to someone, it was clearly her. We spent the next thirty minutes watching her play craps. Over time, a group of men congregated around her, displacing couples or females who I imagined found Terry annoying. Apparently, the men didn't care what was coming out of her mouth as long as they could get a glimpse of her cleavage.

"Pause it," I said. A man with hair tied in a ponytail had worked his way next to Terry. I could see a clear profile of his smiling face, his lips moving in conversation. He wore a black T-shirt advertising a motorcycle shop.

"Zoom in on his right arm," I said, pointing. "I want to see if I can read that tattoo."

Cody moved the mouse and clicked until the screen showed nothing but a blurred blue smudge. He then sharpened the focus until I could make out two capital letters, both Bs, over the vague shape of a skull.

"This is as clear as it gets," Cody said.

I looked up and saw Davies coming toward us.

"Can we print this?" I asked him.

He thought about it for a second, his lower lip thrust out. "Don't see why not. Hit file and print, and it will print over there." He pointed to a large multifunction machine near his desk.

"Great, thanks."

"You guys want me to pick you up a sandwich?"

"Hey, that's damn good of you," Cody said, standing and pulling a twenty from his wallet. "Roast beef for me."

"Turkey," I said. "No mayo. I'm watching my weight."

"I'm not," Cody said. "Can you get me a couple bags of chips, too?"

Davies left the room, and we printed a dozen copies of the ponytailed man's face, along with a close-up of his tattoo. Then, we went back to watching the craps table, but a couple minutes later, Terry walked away. Ponytail stayed for another minute, then he moved out of the picture.

I returned to my screen and fast-forwarded to 11:30 P.M. Terry promptly floated into sight at the roulette table. Within a few minutes, Ponytail arrived at the opposite end of the table, giving me a good view of his body. Hard to say without seeing him in person, but he looked about five-ten, 200 pounds, more fat than muscle.

Then another man appeared next to Terry. His back was to me, and I couldn't see his face. He had a full head of dark, curly hair, and wore a blue sports coat. Within a minute, he had his hand on Terry's back.

Terry turned toward him and smiled and spoke. Ponytail stared at them from across the table, his face pinched, his lips set in a scowl. Less than five minutes passed before Terry whispered in the man's ear, and they walked away from the table together. When the man turned, his face came into full view.

"Oh shit, oh dear," I said.

"What?" Cody craned his neck to see my screen. "Who is that?"

"Captain Nick Galanis."

***

It was past three when we left the casino. We had spent the hours after lunch watching the view from the camera above the bar, where Galanis had bought Terry a drink. When the clock had struck midnight, they had shared a long kiss while the place erupted in celebratory bedlam. Five minutes later, they had walked away hand in hand. We also viewed the remaining footage of all three cameras, until they ended at 1:00 A.M. Neither Terry nor Galanis appeared after they had left the bar. The ponytailed man had also disappeared shortly after Terry had left the roulette table.

I left a note of thanks for Chris Davies, then we walked outside and began hiking down the frozen sidewalk.

"You think we should go chat with Galanis?" I asked Cody.

"Someone needs to. He was with both women before they died."

"I doubt he'd talk to us." I stepped onto a snow-covered strip of grass where the footing was more certain. "Anyway, we need to tell Grier and Bill Worley."

Cody grimaced and bowed his head against the cold. As a general rule, cops didn't like private investigators involved in their cases. Some didn't tolerate it at all. I'd seen the inside of a few jail cells as a result. The best any private detective could hope for from the police was a passive ambivalence. My history with Marcus Grier afforded me that, and maybe a little more, if I played my cards right.

"You think South Lake Tahoe PD will tiptoe around Galanis?" Cody said.

"Hard to say. I doubt they'll break his balls, if it comes to that."

"Why not? There's no love lost between Douglas County and South Lake PD, right?"

"They still have to cooperate and work together."

"What about Galanis? I've heard most of the Douglas County force thinks he's an asshole."

"Don't know that he has a lot of friends, but he's in a position of power," I said.

"We could put a tail on him, see what comes up."

"That's an option."

"You got a better one?"

"Yeah. Grier's always been straight up with me. So, let's propose a fair exchange."

"Meaning?"

"We put him on to Galanis, and in return, he shares with us what Galanis has to say."

"You have a lot a faith in your fellow man, don't you?"

"Maybe it's a spiritual thing."

Cody laughed. "Gimme a break. Grier will probably tell you to blow it out your ass. And besides, ol' Tex is the chief detective."

"Grier is still the top cop in South Lake. Bill Worley is new."

"Hell, Dirt, it's your town. You call the shots."

We made it to my truck and drove out to 50 and back into California. The crow's feet splayed from the corners of Cody's green eyes were deeper than I had remembered, and I saw the first hints of gray in his beard. I wondered if the wear and tear of his lifestyle was catching up with him. He'd been my closest friend since high school, during a time when he was kicked out of his home and lived on the streets. Despite the challenges of his situation, he'd never missed a day of school. At eighteen, he had gone to college in Utah on a football scholarship, and starred as defensive end before returning to San Jose to begin his career in law enforcement.

Cody's stint as a San Jose cop had ended after seven years of insubordination and mayhem that had somehow never landed him in jail. His termination came after he testified against a ring of corrupt plainclothesman estimated to have pocketed a million dollars in drug money over a six-month period. Cody's final goodbye to SJPD came in the way of an affair with his boss's wife, who Cody claimed hated her husband so much that cheating on him turned her into a nymphomaniac.

When Cody had opened shop as a private investigator, I was skeptical he had the discipline and organizational skills to run his own business. My doubts turned out unfounded. Despite his outward disregard for the law and a personal life that ran like a demolition derby, Cody was quite successful as a businessman. He'd even confided he'd saved a considerable sum for his retirement, which was fairly amazing, given his spending habits.

A retired district attorney, a friend of my late father's, once offered his perspective on Cody's situation: "San Jose lawyers know where to go for certain types of cases. Few private eyes will engage to the degree Gibbons does in dangerous situations. Gibbons knows this and charges triple rates."

We bounced up the curb to the police complex and sat in the parking lot while I dialed Grier's cell. He picked up after a couple rings, his voice deep as a kettledrum.

"Hi, Marcus. You in the office?"

"No, why?"

"Cody and I are in your parking lot. We've got some things to share with you."

"All right. I'm on my way in. Ten minutes."

Cody rolled down his window and lit a cigarette. "What else do you know about Nick Galanis?" he said.

I watched a solitary blackbird take flight from a tall pine. "When the previous police chief retired last year, Galanis wanted the job. It was between him and a career cop from Carson City, a guy everyone knew was just putting his time in."

"So Galanis didn't get the job."

"Right. But he was promoted to captain. All the Douglas County plainclothes report to him."

"What else?"

"Rumor has it he was offered a job as a TV weatherman, but became a cop instead."

"Is he a good cop?"

"As a detective, yeah."

"That's not what I meant. Is he clean?"

I was hoping Cody wouldn't take the conversation this direction. He hated crooked cops, and felt his firing from SJPD was mostly due to his taking a stand against the corruption that riddled the force.

"Somewhat, I suppose." I felt Cody's eyes like lasers on my face.

"What kind of answer is that?"

"He probably ain't the shiniest fork in the drawer," I mumbled, pretending to be distracted by a deer that had come out of the woods to pull leaves off a low tree at the edge of the compound.

"I'm looking forward to meeting him," Cody said.

"Hey," I said, "You already got a personal stake in this because of Terry. Let's not rush to any conclusions on Galanis' character. We need to keep it in low gear."

"I'm cool." Cody smiled and winked.

"You sure?"

He flicked his cigarette out into the snow. "Absolutely, partner. There's the sheriff." I looked out the driver's side window and saw Grier pull up in his squad car. We got out and met him, walking gingerly on the slick pathway to the entrance of the building.

"Something quick, men?" Grier said. "I'm hoping to get home on time for a change."

"Shouldn't take long, Sheriff," Cody said. Grier led us inside and to his office.

"We reviewed security video at Pistol Pete's, Marcus," I said, standing in front of his desk. "Terry Molina was last seen having a drink shortly before midnight with a man I think you'll recognize." I handed him a copy of a screenshot I'd printed.

Grier's eyes widened, and he looked at me like I'd just told him he was due for a proctology exam.

"So, Nick Galanis had a drink with her," he said. "He sure gets around. Any indication she left the casino with him?"

"No. But Pistol Pete's has cameras on the exits. Shouldn't be tough to confirm."

He rubbed his face and picked up his phone. "I'll tell Bill Worley."

"Hey, Marcus?"

"Yes?" He held the phone, his finger poised to dial.

"We'd like to interview Galanis, but I don't want to screw things up for Worley. I have no problem backing off, if you'll share what Galanis has to say."

He set the phone down. "This is now an interstate police matter. It's going to get damn sensitive."

"I know it will. That's why I want to be cautious. Otherwise, I'd drive over and talk to Galanis right now."

"You really think you'd get anywhere?"

"Yeah," Cody said. "I really do."

Grier hung up the phone and picked up a blood pressure monitoring device he kept on his desk. He strapped it to his wrist, then changed his mind and removed it.

"I don't like to be leveraged, Dan. Don't push it."

"I'm just trying to do the right thing."

He shifted his unhappy gaze to Cody. "As for you, Gibbons, you might find this is a good time to head back to San Jose."

"I thought you wanted me to stick around, Sheriff. Now what, this town ain't big enough for the both of us?"

Grier smiled. "Don't cause me any grief, Gibbons. I'll arrest you before you can spit."

"On that happy note, we'll let you get back to work," I said. "Take it easy, Marcus."

He nodded and attached the blood pressure gizmo to his wrist again.

***

"That went about as well as I thought it would," Cody said.

I shifted the transmission into drive and idled out of the lot. "Grier will support us. He's just not always thrilled about it."

"We'll see. Where to?"

"Ski Run Boulevard."

"What you got in mind?"

"I want to see if I can find somebody at the ski resort familiar with the back country."

The weak sun hovered low over the lake as I parked at the California base lodge. The sky was colorless. From the parking lot, the lake looked gray as weathered asphalt. A few skiers were still straggling to their cars, but most had already departed. We walked past the ticket windows into the lodge, and down a hallway of lockers that led to restaurant and shops.

"Well, I'll be goddamned if it ain't happy hour," Cody said, spotting a bar. "Why don't you come get me when you're done?"

"All right."

Cody peeled off to the lounge, and I continued to the back of the building, where the ski patrol had a small counter next to the rental area. But no one was there.

I looked around and saw a man in a red jacket marked with a broad white cross come in through the rear doors. Sunglasses, a skier's tan, not a youngster, but far from over the hill. Competent looking.

I walked up to him as he set an armful of steel poles in a corner. "Excuse me," I said. "Got a question for you."

"Shoot, Luke, the air's full of pigeons." He stood straight and winked.

I smiled back. "How familiar are you with the back country in Nevada?"

"Been skiing here all my life."

I opened a trail map I'd picked up on the way in and pointed to the Nevada base lodge at the summit off Kingsbury grade.

"From here, can I get to Got Balls Bowl?"

"Nope. Easiest way to Got Balls is here." He pointed to the area where I'd ducked the rope the day before Christmas.

"Yeah, I've done that before. Actually, I want to see if I can get to a glade to the right and probably a thousand feet below the bowl."

"Over here," he said, and I followed him to a counter. He produced a worn topographical map crisscrossed with ballpoint pen marks. "Show me where you want go."

I traced a path to my best guess at the location where I'd found Valerie Horvachek's body. "I want to see if I can get there from the Nevada lodge."

"Why? There's no decent skiing along that route."

I handed him a business card. "I'm investigating the murder of a girl who was found there."

"No shit?" he said, round-eyed.

"Yeah. You think someone could have transported a body from the Nevada lodge?"

He rubbed his chin and thought about it for a moment. "From behind the lodge, you can traverse along the ridge for about a mile, if you stay high. If you drop down too early, you're in trouble—this area is a deep gorge." He tapped his pen on the map. "When you reach this point, you have to drop down, but you'll be clear of the gorge."

"So, I'd be below Got Balls. Could I get to where I want to go without hiking?"

"Yeah. Probably."

I studied the map. "Do many people use this route?"

"Hell, no." He shrugged. "No reason to."

"Do snowmobilers ever go out here?"

"Snowmobiles? Not that I've ever heard of. I thought you meant a skier transporting a body on a rescue toboggan."

I met his eyes.

"You know, a gurney sled," he explained.

***

The ski patroller told me to keep his map, said he had plenty of copies. By the time I herded Cody out of the bar, it was twilight. We drove back toward Pistol Pete's, Christmas lights twinkling on the buildings and trees along the road.

"Tomorrow morning, can you drive me up Kingsbury grade?" I said.

"Sure."

"I'm going to try to ski back to where I found the body. Then, I'll need you to pick me up on route 207 in Gardnerville, about a mile north of Waterloo Lane."

"I'll check a map. What are you looking for?"

"Any sign the killer took the route from the Nevada base lodge."

"Big Dan, the mountain man."

We hit a stoplight. "As far as Terry," Cody said, "I want to canvass the nearest houses and businesses to where she was dumped."

"Let's do it in the afternoon."

"Okay." The light turned green, and we drove in silence for a minute. "You going to spend a quiet night with Candi?" he asked.

"Yeah."

"All right."

"Want to come over for dinner?" I looked at Cody, but he was staring off.

"Nah, I'm good. I'll come get you in the morning."

"You sure?"

We crossed into Nevada, and I followed his eyes to two women on the sidewalk in furry boots and tight jeans.

"Right as rain," he said.

"Okay, partner."

I steered into Pistol Pete's and dropped Cody off at the hotel entrance. I watched him walk inside, his stride powerful, his jacket stretched tight around the shoulders. He looked charged with energy and purpose—to what end, I was unsure. Cody Gibbons was my best friend, and I knew him like a brother, but at times, his behavior was a mystery to me. I'd learned I could no sooner predict or influence his actions than I could convince a dog to not chase a cat. The best I could hope was that he wouldn't do anything irreparably self-destructive.

Conceding that Cody would do what he would, I drove back home, where my house was lit with the single strand of Christmas lights I'd hung over the garage. Inside it was warm, and Candi was cooking in the kitchen.

"Hey," she said. "Long day?"

"Yeah," I said, sitting at the kitchen table.

"Mix you a drink?"

"I'd love one, doll."

She poured me a whiskey-seven and joined me at the table. From her purse, she pulled a plastic container holding a glass pipe and a baggie of marijuana. She lit up while I took a big slug off my drink. Our nightly happy hour ritual. Candi didn't drink much, and I rarely smoked dope—a clear distribution of vices.

"I've never seen you this busy. What's going on?" She knocked the ash from her pipe and refilled it.

"The murders of Valerie and Terry are definitely related. They both were with Nick Galanis."

"That perv screwed both of them?"

"We don't know that about Terry."

"Do you think Galanis killed them?"

"I don't know. I doubt it."

"What a crazy deal."

"It's strange." I shook my head, then said, "It's a nuthouse out there."

"You just think that because you're sane."

I laughed. "You think so?"

"Yes. I do."

I finished my drink and helped her make a salad to go along with the chicken and rice she'd prepared. After we ate, we went to her art room, and she showed me a painting she'd begun, a surrealistic rendition of the meadow and mountains visible from my backyard.

"Groovy, baby," I said.

"This is a serious work," she admonished. "I've taken pictures of this scene every week since I've moved in, capturing the change of seasons. The sky, the trees, the grass, the mountains, all in a continual state of flux."

"Very cool."

She took my hand and backed her body into mine, her head tucked under my chin. "I love it here," she said, staring out the big window into the night.

"Me too," I said.

I closed my eyes, and we stood silently, her soft curves against me, her hands holding mine around her waist. Then, the moment was interrupted by the blare of my cell phone.

"Goddammit," I muttered. I waited for it to ring again and gave Candi a final squeeze before picking it up.

"Dan, it's Liz. There's a man here at Zeke's who wants to talk to you." Her voice was shrill.

"Who is he?"

"He wouldn't say. But he acted like he expects you to get right over here."

"Tell him that's not going to happen. If he wants to see me, he can make an appointment."

"Dan," she said, her tone hushed, "I think he's a member of those bikers that came in."

"Why?"

"He's got a Nazi tattoo, and he rode up on a Harley. Some people left when he came in. He's bad news. You want me to call the sheriff?"

"No." I checked my watch. 7:00 P.M., a busy hour at the restaurant. "I'll be there in a few minutes."

"What's up?" Candi said.

"There's someone at Zeke's I need to have a few words with."

"Is it trouble?"

I paused for a moment. "If it is, I'll put a stop to it." I smiled. "Nothing to worry about, should only take a few minutes."

I hurried out to the garage and started my truck, but before I backed out, I unlocked the steel toolbox welded behind the cab. I removed my bulletproof vest, my .40 caliber automatic, and a spring-loaded sap I called 'Good Night, Irene.' Moving quickly, I shrugged into the vest and my shoulder holster and hit the gas out toward 50. The single traffic light for the turn onto the highway was green, and I gunned it through the intersection and, a minute later, banged into Zeke's parking lot.

The Harley was parked next to the steps to the main entrance. It was low slung, the tank red, the rear tire fat between chrome pipes. I looked for an empty spot and took a lap around the packed lot before parking in the handicap stall next to the bike. Then, I stepped out of my cab and went through the front doors.

The only empty seats at the bar were to either side of a man who wore black boots, jeans, and a jean vest with a patch of a growling, red-eyed dog sewn on the back. His torso was linebacker wide, and his shoulders and biceps looked ready to blow out the seams of his T-shirt. A black swastika stood out in the maze of tattoos on his upper arm. His forearms and hands were so densely covered in blue ink, I couldn't make out individual tattoos.

I walked up and sat at the stool to his left. "You wanted to see me?" I said.

He turned slowly and rested his eyes on mine. There was no hair on his head or face, save for scant eyebrows, above which some indecipherable German words were tattooed. His pale blue eyes were shadowed by the thick, jutting ridge of his skull. His nose was bent and flat like a boxer's, his jaw thick and square. A thin white scar ran from aside his nostril down over his lips.

"I hear you're part owner of this joint." He smiled with his mouth, and his eyes were like pinpricks of light.

"What do you want?"

He looked away, scanning the bar, and when he looked back at me, his thin smile was gone. "To meet the man who sent my three partners to jail."

"You're looking at him."

He took stock of me, his eyes deliberately roaming up and down my person as if I were a product on a shelf. "That black hair of yours. You ain't a Jew-boy, is you?"

"What's your name?"

"I'm Jake Massie. But you don't need to know that, because I won't take your check. I only take cash money."

"Sorry, you've lost me."

He chuckled deep in his throat. "You owe me."

"Regarding your partners?"

"That's right. It's ten grand a head, my friend, to cover expenses. Cash money, like I said."

I felt the lump of the sap in my coat pocket, and for a long moment, I considered cold-cocking Jake Massie right there and then. But I didn't want another altercation in my place of business.

"Let's go out back, talk about it over a smoke," I said.

"It's tempting, but no, thanks. Your beer garden is covered in snow. You ought to get it shoveled."

"Our conversation is finished, then."

"Good. I'll meet you here ten tomorrow morning. That should give you enough time to get to your bank."

This time, I chuckled.

Massie's brow creased over one eye, and his lips pulled back from his teeth. "You think this is funny? You won't, if I don't get my money. That's a promise."

I reached in my coat pocket, grasped my sap, and said, "If I see you again, you'll be joining your friends in jail. Or worse. That's my promise. Now get the fuck out of my bar."

He smiled again, but his eyes stayed hard and fixed on my face. "I heard you were a tough son of a bitch. Maybe next time, we'll meet at your house. Just around the corner, right?"

"I see you around my property, and that includes this restaurant, you'll regret it."

"I'll regret it? Let me spell something out for you, toadstool. I'm a busy man, and I'm not sure you're worth my time. But I have plenty of friends who'd love to meet you. The brotherhood is only a phone call away."

"The Aryan Brotherhood?"

He grinned, his teeth glistening. "You're not so fucking stupid after all, are you?"

With those words, he shrugged into his leather coat and walked out, his gait bow-legged and cocksure. The words *WAR DOGS* were stitched across the back of his jacket.

Liz hurried over, her nipples scribbling under her blouse, and stared at me with unblinking eyes.

"If you see him again, call me," I said.

6

Cody called at eight the next morning, his voice thick and groggy. "Hey, Dirt, I overslept."

"When can you be here?"

"You better drive up Kingsbury yourself. I'll meet you in Gardnerville around ten thirty."

"You get in any trouble last night?"

"Nothing unusual."

"Well, take some aspirin and vitamin B."

"Yes, doctor."

He hung up, and I gulped the remainder of my coffee and went into bathroom where Candi was in her bra and panties, putting on her makeup.

"I don't want you to worry about what I told you last night," I said. "Just call me if you see anyone on a Harley on our street. Or at the college."

"I keep my gun loaded, you know."

I looked at her and realized she was serious.

"It's hidden in a cupboard in the kitchen," she said.

"You're not going to have to shoot anyone, babe."

"Don't think I won't if someone messes with us."

I shook my head and went to the garage and loaded my truck. Skis, boots, poles, and a pack complete with binoculars and a compass. And also, a collapsible metal detector that I'd bought years ago. Used it once, and it had collected cobwebs ever since.

After double-checking my gear, I backed out of the garage. Then, I stopped in my driveway and dialed Marcus Grier.

"First thing in the morning, huh?" he said.

"That's right. Sorry to start your day off with this, but I was paid a visit last night by a man named Jake Massie. War Dogs member, claims to be Aryan Brotherhood."

"Go on."

"He told me I'm responsible for his three buddies landing in jail, and I owe him thirty grand for it."

"He was serious?"

"Afraid so. Said the AB was backing him up."

Grier exhaled. "I'll pull up a mug shot on him. If I see him, I'll bring him in."

"On what charge?"

"Doesn't matter. I'm going to let him know he's not welcome here."

"All right. One other thing. Could you send a squad car by my house every couple hours? And maybe one by the college too? Massie said he knows where I live."

"Great. Anything else?"

"Not at the moment."

"I'd say you owe me a steak dinner, but I don't take bribes."

"I'll buy you one anyway. Thanks for your help, Marcus."

***

There was little traffic, and it only took fifteen minutes to reach the crest of Kingsbury at 7800 feet. I followed a brief line of cars past rows of condos and fancy vacation homes along the curvy road leading to the ski lodge. The sun had just peeked over the ridge, and the sky was clear and bright, the blue void split by a brilliant streak of white jet exhaust rising from the east and slowly making its way across the expanse.

It was twenty-two degrees, according to the digital readout on my dashboard. Visibility excellent, a perfect day for recon. I parked, wedged into my boots, and assembled my gear. Beanie, goggles, gloves, all accounted for. I zipped my jacket, slung my skis over my shoulder, and hiked to the near side of the lodge. Once on the snow pack, I clicked into my skis and sidestepped up a tall berm until it leveled out. I skated from there to the back side of the lodge, which overlooked a long stretch of thickly forested flatland flanked by a granite headwall about half a mile away.

There were no tracks leading out, but it had snowed twice, heavily, since Valerie Horvachek had been murdered. I didn't see any sign of anything resembling a trail, so I pushed off and let gravity pull me, my skis slowly cutting through the dense snowpack until I reached the woods. The snow was firmer under the trees, and I poled my way to the right until I began to coast along the tree line.

I kept my head up and scanned for any evidence this path had been taken recently. The grade steepened, and my speed picked up. Even in a straight line, it was difficult snow to ski, water heavy and grabby, threatening to catch a ski at the slightest adjustment in balance. I concentrated on keeping my weight neutral over both legs. My thighs had started to burn by the time I reached the headwall. I looked back the way I'd come. It would have been easy going for a snowmobile, far less so for a skier towing a gurney.

Ahead of me, a logical path cut across the bald mountain side. I followed it, careful to stay high and not drop down into the deep valley below. The snow became variable, heavy in parts, and then thin enough for my edges to scrape along the hard-pack beneath the surface. I steered into the mountain, going just fast enough to keep momentum.

I traversed the hill for ten minutes, above cliff bands and around jutting boulders, until ahead of me and to my right, the terrain turned uphill. Now about a mile deep in the backcountry, there was no option but to go left, down the mountain. I pulled the map from my jacket pocket and estimated I was on course. If I could proceed straight, I'd run right into Got Balls Bowl, but like the patroller said, I'd be forced to go below it.

I headed down into a maze of trees. It was steep and jagged conditions, very difficult to ski fluidly. I made jump turns and skidded over low branches and the occasional rock. Every couple turns, I stopped to reset. Then, I realized I was going about it wrong. I'd seen plenty of patrollers bringing sleds down a hill. They used the oldest trick in the book, the first thing taught to every beginner skier.

I widened my stance, brought my tips together, and flexed my ankles inward. "All right, then," I muttered, and skidded down the slope in a classic wedge, the good old snowplow. Slow and steady, good speed control, no need to turn. It was then that I noticed a broken branch half buried in my path. Maybe it was nothing, but I saw two more.

Stopping again, I surveyed the trees around me. A few broken branches were no kind of evidence, and there was nothing else to indicate anyone had been here. I snowplowed to the bottom of the slope, turned right, and picked my way through some more trees until I looked up and saw I had passed beneath Got Balls. Another half mile or so to where I was going, I estimated. I found a bit of clearing and made a few turns until I came out of the trees and saw the banked slope I had skied the day I had found the body.

Back on familiar terrain, I resisted the temptation to speed up, instead falling back into a wedge and looking for any sign of passage. I reached the trail to the glade and proceeded slowly. A foot or two beneath my skis were my tracks from ten days ago, and maybe other tracks. Unfortunately, there was no way to dig down like an archeologist for clues. Once new snowfall obscured old tracks, they were lost for good.

At the entrance to the idyllic glade, I paused and scanned the area. I skied on and saw the yellow police tape, now broken and scattered and partially buried.

It was a little after nine, leaving me an hour before I needed to ski down to meet Cody. I found the sunken area where Valerie's body had once lay and took the metal detector from my pack. Then, I released my ski bindings and jammed my skis into the snow, the tips crossed and pointed toward the sky. From there, I began walking outward, sweeping the snow in six-foot sections. Forty feet out, I stopped after the surrounding brush became tangled and thick, then returned and began again. In this manner, I covered a circle, eighty feet in diameter, from the site of Valerie's body. The metal detector did not register a single blip. I then surveyed the area beyond the perimeter of the glade. Much of it was rough terrain, and there were plenty of places where a clue might be hiding within the dense trees and deadfall. I spent thirty minutes searching, my boots often breaking through the crust up to my knees.

I finally stopped and switched off the metal detector and took a long swallow from my water bottle. My hopes that the killer may have discarded a bungee cord, or maybe even a sled, had not panned out. Worse, I now doubted more than before that anyone would take the route I'd just navigated at night. But someone had taken some route, in the dark, through difficult terrain. That much was certain, and it suggested the killer was an accomplished backwoodsman.

Sweating, I yanked off my beanie and guzzled more water. When I finished, I wiped my mouth, and my eyes settled on a tree at the far end of the glade. There was a brief flash of pink on a branch. I squinted, then knocked the snow from my boots, clicked back into my skis, and glided to the tree. It was a small, snow-covered pine. I reached out with my pole and tapped the pink object. The snow covering it fell away. Among the pine needles hung a purse.

"Bingo," I said. From my pack, I pulled a pair of rubber gloves and forced them over my callused hands. Then, I gingerly lifted the purse by the strap. It was medium-sized as purses go, faux leather, shiny. The vinyl had begun to curl away at the edges. It was zipped shut.

I stepped out of my skis again and sat where the snow was flat and arranged the skis in my lap to provide a surface. I set the purse down and unzipped the main compartment. Inside were keys, a woman's wallet, a cell phone, and a plastic bag containing various makeup items and a couple of condoms. Also, a lighter, a pen, a few business cards, a bracelet, and a pair of sunglasses.

An inner side compartment was bulging, the material tight. I tugged the small zipper open and saw a smooth lump of clear plastic. I eased it free with my fingertips. It was a double-layered baggie of white powder. Too big to be her personal stash. At least an ounce. I opened the first Ziploc, then the second, licked my little finger and tasted a few tiny particles. Cocaine. Not flaking or rocky, but mostly powder. Probably heavily cut with baby laxative. Weak, street grade blow.

I replaced the coke, closed the purse, and fit it into a plastic evidence bag in my pack. "Shit," I said, looking at my watch. I was behind schedule. I got back on my skis, fit my goggles on my face, and pushed out of the glade into a steep section that required my full attention. My skis chattered like jackhammers over the rough conditions as I pounded my way down, muscling through crud and over boilerplate and nearly losing it on a patch of harbor chop. When I reached the flats leading to the road, I was hot in my coat.

I skated to the road and called Cody. A minute later, he came along in his red truck. He stood and waited while I opened his tailgate, stowed my skis and boots, and took a pair of jogging shoes from my pack.

"Find anything?" he asked. His face looked bloodless, the skin dry and cracked around the lips, his beard like rusted wire.

I pulled out the plastic bag holding the pink purse. "Hanging from a tree," I said.

Cody lowered his head and eyeballed my find. "Missed it the first time?"

"I wasn't looking for evidence when I was there before."

"I meant the cops."

"Oh. Yeah, apparently, they missed it."

"Did you find her driver's license?"

"I haven't gone through all the contents yet."

"Check and see if her license is there." Cody sat on the tailgate with me. The rear shocks hissed and conceded a few inches.

I set my ski gloves aside and stretched the rubber gloves over my hands again, then carefully removed the wallet, a lime green unit with a metal clasp. I snapped it open and checked the compartments. "Credit cards," I said, "but no license."

"Just like Terry's," Cody said. He stood and lit a cigarette.

"Her license was missing too?"

"They're souvenirs for the killer." Cody stared down the road and blew a stream of smoke from the corner of his mouth. "He can pull them out and relive the killings, get a little thrill whenever he wants."

I removed my beanie and ran my hand through my hair. "Leaving the purses where they could be found. Like saying, here's some evidence, catch me if you can."

Cody took another drag from his smoke, then flicked it out onto the road. "It's more than that. This guy wants to be caught."

"Why do you say that?"

"He's making some kind of statement. But he'll eventually need to let everyone know it's from him."

"That's an interesting take."

He blew into his hands. "Let's go."

I sat in the passenger seat while Cody hung a U-turn, gravel spitting and popping beneath his tires. "I need some food to settle my gut," he said. "Maybe a Bloody Mary."

"There's a few joints in Minden. Take the next right."

"Okay," he grunted. He drove hunched over the wheel and kept squeezing his eyes open and shut. Outside, a barbwire range fence ran parallel to the road, and beyond it, flatlands coated in frost stretched eastward toward a long, snow-capped escarpment along the horizon.

"I got drunk last night and drove to Carson," Cody said. He rolled down his window, coughed, and spit a wad of phlegm into the slipstream.

I started to ask him what for, then realized there could only be one reason. "The cathouses?"

"Yeah."

"Have a good time?"

He took his eyes from the road and looked at me. "Yeah, I did."

"Well, good."

"Look, is it too much to ask for a drama-free piece of ass every now and then?"

"Not in my book. Turn at the stop sign."

He rolled through the sign and stomped the gas pedal. We roared toward a cluster of buildings visible a few miles away.

"So, there were two bikers sitting at the bar at one of the ranches," Cody said, "and there's nowhere else to sit, so I'm right next to them. I ask how they're doing, just being friendly, and they got nothing to say to me. Who cares, right? I start talking to a few hookers, just buzzed and having a good time, then I see this black-haired girl come out of the back. She's got this incredible body, all tits and ass and a face like Angelina Jolie. So, I snag her and go back to her room. I'll tell you, I had a rod a cat couldn't scratch before we even got there."

"Very proud of you," I said.

"Thanks. Anyway, we sit on her bed, and she tells me one of the bikers from the bar was just in her room, and he was a bad trip and said some ugly shit, and then, he couldn't get it up, and she gave him his money back just to get him out of there. She's kind of freaked out and asks, do I mind if she takes a couple hits off a joint to calm her nerves. So, I get stoned with her, and she starts telling me what he said."

We came to a stoplight at the edge of town. I pointed at a restaurant across the street.

"She said the biker was jacked on speed and babbling a mile a minute about a stripper his best friend fronted an ounce of blow to. He said she got herself killed, and now, his buddy is on the hook for sixteen hundred, and his gang thinks he's a pussy-whipped douchebag. He thinks a rival gang may have killed her for the drugs, and he says he's gonna get to the bottom of it and fuck up whoever's responsible."

I stared at Cody, incredulous. The light turned green, and we rolled across the intersection and parked at the diner. "You had this conversation for real?"

"I shit you not."

"Did you get a chance to talk to the bikers again?"

"I went out to the bar as soon as she told me, but they were gone."

"Sounds like the biker was talking about Valerie," I said. "There's an ounce of coke in her purse. But whoever killed her didn't take it. She even has a few bucks in her wallet."

"She was carrying an ounce?"

"Yup.

We walked through the thin sunlight into the diner and sat at a booth looking out at the parking lot.

"Hmm. I thought he might have meant Terry," Cody said. He scratched his ear and glanced at me with bloodshot eyes.

"What? Terry was dealing?"

"No. I mean, I don't know. She had coke, so anything's possible."

"Was she a stripper?"

"Not recently."

"How long had you known her?"

The waitress came, and Cody ordered bacon, eggs, potatoes, and toast, and a double vodka tonic. I got an omelet and a Coke.

"We went out, what, four or five times."

"So, she could have been dealing."

"I suppose. But I never saw any sign of it. It's not like her cell was ringing off the hook, or she was running around making deliveries."

"Why did you think he meant Terry, then?"

"The hooker told me the biker had the same tattoo as the ponytailed guy ogling Terry at the craps table. Double Bs, Blood Bastards."

I stared at the scratched surface of the table. "The same as the biker at the strip joint in Sacramento."

"Huh?"

"Valerie worked at a strip joint called The Suave. I went there, and a biker wearing Blood Bastards colors quizzed me about her."

"Really? Describe him."

"A shade under six feet. Fortyish. Shaved head, long goatee."

"Huh. Might have been one of the guys at the bar."

The waitresses brought our drinks, and Cody took a long guzzle. "Jesus, that's strong."

"It's noon somewhere."

"Goddamn right it is." He took another swig, rattled the ice cubes, and drained the last drops.

"Did the hooker mention the name of the rival gang?"

"I asked her," Cody said. "The biker didn't get that deep into it."

I wiped at the wet ring my soft drink had left on the table and folded the damp napkin in a neat triangle. "Two victims, both holding drugs, both potentially involved with the Blood Bastards, and both fraternizing with Nick Galanis."

The color had returned to Cody's face. His green eyes cleared, and he smiled. "I think Galanis is probably involved in things he shouldn't be," he said.

"That would be a hard point to argue," I replied.

***

We finished eating, and I made a phone call. Then, instead of driving back over Kingsbury, I told Cody to drive north to Reno.

"Who's this guy you want to see?"

"An old friend of my father's named Albert Bigelow. Teaches sociology at the university in Reno."

"He's the one who used to ride with the Hells Angels?"

"Yeah, about thirty years ago. The old man offered him a plea bargain on a murder rap, probably saved him twenty years, in return for a promise to quit the gang."

"A district attorney would never get away with that today."

"The old man was quirky that way. He'd find a way to break the rules if he thought it served justice. Occasionally, guys caught a break, but most of the time, he prosecuted the hell out of them."

Cody didn't respond, and we drove in silence for a while. My father had died when I was barely a teenager, ambushed outside his

San Jose office by a paroled killer with a vendetta and a shotgun. A great orator and a fierce presence in the courtroom, Richard Reno was loved by cops, and despised and feared by the criminal community. Eventually, one of his enemies—a convicted rapist and murderer who never should have been released—caught up with him.

Outside his job, I remembered my dad as a zany and easygoing parent, rarely strict or heavy-handed, more interested in good times and nutty humor and the occasional off-color remark, much to my mother's consternation. He never took his work home with him, as if he realized every day with his family might be his last.

Earlier in my career, after a series of shootings had resulted in the death of a handful of criminals, a court appointed headshrink had claimed I was subconsciously seeking revenge for my father's murder. I never gave that analysis much credence. Then again, I didn't have much tolerance for violent criminals, particularly those who, in their amoral quests, destroyed lives and families with no more remorse than most people assigned to throwing out yesterday's newspaper.

"Bigelow reformed himself, I take it?" Cody said.

"And then some. He earned a PhD at Berkeley, and his dissertation on biker culture was published by a commercial house. Pretty interesting stuff."

"Yeah, but how can he help us?"

"He spends a lot of time tracking biker gangs, especially those in the western U.S. Had you ever heard of the Blood Bastards before?"

"No."

"I'll guarantee you he has."

We drove up 395, shadowed on the left by the snow-covered eastern flank of the Sierras. To our right lay the Great Basin Desert of Nevada, the sparse landscape barb-wired and marked by occasional barns, livestock pens, and feed silos. In fifteen minutes, we reached the outskirts of Carson City and passed a mile of hotels and strip malls before turning onto the newly built freeway.

It allowed us to bypass the bulk of the commercial thoroughfare and the crumbling casinos in Carson's dreary downtown. We made time and reached the University of Nevada campus a little after noon.

The campus was larger than I remembered, and we drove around for a few minutes before Cody jerked to a stop, and I asked a student to point us toward the social sciences building. We parked and walked down a sidewalk bordered by dry grass and leafless trees, past a couple large brick buildings, until we saw a smaller, single story structure. We went through the glass doors and down a scuffed white hallway that eventually brought us to the professor's office. I knocked and peered in the window at the man behind the desk. He looked up and motioned for us to come in.

Dr. Albert Bigelow was stout and thick as an ox, still an intimidating physical presence in his sixties. His face was meaty, his eyelids weighted, his bushy Fu Manchu mustache gray as raw iron. Hair of the same color, straight and full, fell over his forehead as if he were a much younger man. He removed his reading glasses and smiled with his eyes.

"What's it been, Dan, a couple years?"

"About that. Albert, this is Cody Gibbons."

"Oh? The name sounds familiar." He fit his glasses back on his broad nose, and we sat while he typed on his keyboard. "Ah. Ex-San Jose PD. You worked for Russ Landers." Bigelow looked up over his glasses.

"Landers fired me," Cody said. "Do you know him?"

"Not personally, but I know of him."

"He was a real asshole."

Bigelow's eyes crinkled in humor. "That's what I've heard." He turned to me. "Dan, what can I do for you?"

Since getting his doctorate in criminology, Albert Bigelow had published three books on organized crime. The first was on the Russian mob, the next on Columbian and Mexican drug cartels, and for his third, he chose a subject near, if not dear, to him: biker gangs. He had connections with cops as well as a loose network of crooks, all with whom he traded information. Over the years, he had compiled an ever-growing database of gang activities and members.

"Are you familiar with the Blood Bastards?" I asked.

"Sure," he said, fingers typing away. "Based in Sacramento. What are those scoundrels up to?"

"Two women were found strangled near Lake Tahoe. Both on coke, and one was dealing. I think one, or maybe both, is involved with the gang."

"Murder, drugs, bikers. As American as mom, baseball, and apple pie." Bigelow typed like a pro, his beefy fingers deft and quick, then he hit a final key, and his printer whirred and clicked and began feeding pages.

"Now, what else can you share?" he said.

I gave him Valerie and Terry's names, and described the Blood Bastard I'd spoken to at the Sacramento strip joint, and the dude we'd seen on the casino video. Cody added a brief accounting of what he'd heard at the cathouse. Bigelow typed it into his database as we spoke.

"Here's a bonus for you, Albert," I said. "I had a run in with another group of bikers, unrelated to Blood Bastards. Three members of a gang calling themselves War Dogs stirred up some shit at a bar in South Lake Tahoe. They were all arrested and charged with felonies by South Lake PD."

"War Dogs? They operate out of Stockton, I believe." He typed some more, then studied his screen. "They're not exactly unrelated to the Blood Bastards."

"What? How so?"

"Jake Massie is the War Dog's head honcho. He used to belong to Blood Bastards, but in 2008, he had a falling out with his brother, Virgil, the top dog in Blood Bastards. After that, Jake founded War Dogs."

"Good to know," I grunted.

"I'm printing you what I have on both gangs."

"Thanks."

"You have any more I can add to my files?"

"Here's one," I said. "A guy named Mike Zayas. Runs the Suave Gentlemen's Club in Sac. Possibly affiliated with Blood Bastards, likely involved in drugs and prostitution."

Albert typed some more, then said, "I've got nothing on him."

"I'll let you know what else I find out."

"Please do. My database is like a starving dog, always hungry."

I thanked him, and we left his office and drove off the campus. I sat in the passenger seat, half a dozen pages clutched in my hand.

"Let's get back to Tahoe," Cody said. "It's been more than 48 hours since Terry was killed. We need to check if anybody saw anything."

"Take 80 through Truckee. It's faster."

Cody turned onto the interstate and hit the gas, his tires humming on the course pavement. We left the city limits and sped across the high desert flats, reeling in the miles of westbound highway. I took the time to read the entirety of what Albert Bigelow had provided.

The Blood Bastards gang had formed about ten years ago. The membership was originally made up of disenfranchised Hells Angels and Mongrols. Ex-Mongrol Virgil Massie had founded the clan and was still in charge. Their riders were a mix of Mexican and whites, fifty strong, and their primary revenue source was drugs, mostly methamphetamine, but they also brought cocaine in from south of the border. On various occasions over the years, they'd had scrapes with the Hells Angels and Mongrols, who viewed the Blood Bastards as defectors. But Sacramento was a considerable distance from the Mongrol stronghold in Southern California, and was also outside the Hells Angels' primary stomping grounds in the San Francisco Bay Area, so the conflicts had lessened over time.

But it was not geography alone that had allowed the Blood Bastards to survive. In their skirmishes with the other gangs, the Blood Bastards let it be known they would make no concession and grant no quarter to their enemies. If death or imprisonment was the result, so be it. Realizing they had more to lose than gain in an all-out war, their larger adversaries focused their energies elsewhere.

Not long after the gang was formed, Jake Massie, younger brother to Virgil, was convicted of assault with a deadly weapon for stabbing a Hells Angel. He served five years at San Quentin, and during his incarceration, he joined the Aryan Brotherhood. When he was released, he came back to Sacramento, tattooed with swastikas and dual lightning bolts and carrying a copy of Mein Kampf. Jake made no attempt to hide he'd become a hardcore racist, and he tried to convince Virgil to purge the Blood Bastards of all but whites. Soon afterward, Jake narrowly averted an attempt on his life. He fled south to Stockton at that point.

The War Dogs were reported only fifteen strong, barely large enough to be considered a motorcycle gang. In truth, not all their members even owned bikes. They seemed to be a hybrid organization, part skinheads and part bikers, brought together by criminal interests and their belief in white supremacy. Apparently, Jake Massie had brought from the Blood Bastards his meth cooking expertise, because the War Dogs were big into labs.

The pages also contained a list of names and criminal records, and an accounting of arrests and incidents. I glanced through them and reread the page on Jake Massie, which was one of the few that included a mug shot. His face stared back at me, his eyes barely visible under his knotted brow.

I drew in my breath and called Candi on her cell.

"Hi, there."

"Everything okay, Candi?"

"Sure. I'm having lunch over at the pizza place near the school. Why?"

"Nothing. I'm just calling to say hello."

"Well, hello to you."

We hung up as Cody steered into a series of sweeping turns near where the desert transitioned to forest, right past the

California state line. Barren hills glazed with ice became steep pine-covered ridges covered in white, the snow piled high along the roadside. Fortunately, the weather was clear, because we were in an area where the Highway Patrol commonly slowed traffic to a crawl if any snow was falling.

I glanced at Cody. I'd not yet told him of my encounter with Jake Massie. I turned my eyes back to the passing scenery. It was not my habit to withhold information from him, but in this case, I was hesitant. The problem was, Cody would view any threat against me as a personal threat against himself.

Nonetheless: "The guy Bigelow mentioned, Jake Massie."

"The leader of The War Dogs, right?" Cody held the wheel tight into a turn.

"Yeah. He came by Zeke's last night to talk to me."

Cody stared at me. "What about?"

"Watch the road, would you? I told you about the War Dogs coming into Zeke's and getting hauled off to jail. Apparently, Massie's not too happy about my role."

"And?"

"He wants me to pay him thirty grand to right the situation."

He barked a short laugh. "You tell him to fuck off?"

"Yeah. He said if I don't pay, the Aryan Brotherhood will get involved."

Cody didn't say anything. "I think he's probably bluffing," I said.

"You didn't call Grier, did you?"

"Yeah, I did."

"Because throwing Massie in jail is no solution. The AB is a prison-based gang. They're as dangerous behind bars as on the street."

"Massie knew I own a stake in Zeke's. He also insinuated he knows where I live. Pass this guy, would you?" Cody had slowed and was tailgating a semi that was crawling along in the right-hand lane.

"Where does Massie operate out of?" he asked.

"Stockton. Why?"

Cody shrugged. "Because."

We passed through Truckee, and I saw Cody eyeing the bars, but we drove on, turning onto 89 heading due south, past Squaw Valley and Alpine Meadows ski resorts and into Tahoe City. From there, we drove around the west side of the lake, buzzing along until the tight curves above the sparkling turquoise of Emerald Bay forced us to slow. Twenty minutes later, we stopped at the entrance to Kiva Beach, just north of the South Lake Tahoe city limits.

Cody parked near a steel gate painted green. It was open, but the road to the beach had not been plowed, and a two-foot wall of compacted snow blocked the way.

"You want to hike?" Cody said.

I looked down the road at the Forest Service Visitor Center, a small one-man building that existed primarily to collect parking fees. The window was dark.

We left Cody's truck at the entrance and walked over the snowpack toward the lake. Beyond the visitor center was an empty parking lot, and beyond that, a scattering of picnic benches sat half buried amid the pine trees. A quarter-mile out, we came to the snow-covered beach. The snow was crusty, and our feet sank. Across the midnight blue water, I could make out a few of the taller hotels in Tahoe City. Behind them, the snow-capped mountains formed a jagged horizon.

There were no buildings visible down the curve of the shoreline to our left. A ways to the right, I could make out a flash of crime scene tape.

Cody followed me as I crunched along, sinking to my shins. The water lapped at the shore, sandy particles eating away at the snow. When we reached the spot where Terry's body had been found, Cody pointed toward the tree line at a metal trash barrel chained to a picnic bench. "That's where they found her purse."

I stood for a minute, staring at the trees that spread back to the highway. Farther down the beach, another hundred yards or so, stood the Beacon Bar and Grill, its back deck facing the lake. Next to it, a couple buildings served as a marina. A few small docks and a longer one stretched over the water.

I waved my arm at the restaurant, at the marina, and at a couple dozen cabins I knew were hidden back in the trees beyond. "Camp Richardson," I said. "Popular in the summer and spring, but I think mostly vacant in the winter."

"Let's start at the restaurant." Cody took off at a determined pace, and I trudged behind, scanning the scene and trying to imagine a nameless man dragging a body in the darkness.

We reached the front entrance to the Beacon, blowing steam into the fading afternoon. Inside, I asked for the manager, and a prematurely balding man with pale blue eyes and a nervous twitch on his lips presented himself at the hostess stand.

"We're investigating the murder of the girl found out there," I told him.

"The police were here yesterday. I gave them the names of everyone working New Year's Eve. We closed at eleven."

"How about at the marina?" Cody said. "Would anybody have been out there after you closed?"

"I doubt it. The marina's shut down for the winter."

"The cabins back there—are many rented?"

"A few, maybe. We're too far from the ski resorts and casinos to attract many winter tourists."

Cody stared off and shook his head imperceptibly.

"Where would I go to make a room reservation?" I asked.

"The main hotel. Just follow the road back to the highway."

"Come on," Cody said, and we ambled out of the place. A plowed road led from the parking lot. In the forested area next to the road sat a number of cabins, but the paths leading to them were snowed in.

"Why would the killer pick this place to dump Terry's body?" I said.

"Except for the restaurant, it looks pretty deserted. Maybe just a safe, convenient place."

"Dumping Valerie in the mountains sure wasn't convenient."

"Maybe our assumption it's the same guy is wrong."

I stepped around a patch of ice. "I think I'll call Jack Meyers."

"Who?"

"South Lake Coroner."

"The old guy who swills whiskey?"

"Yeah."

I punched numbers in my cell as we neared the Camp Richardson hotel, a two-story stone and wood structure hidden from the highway by a swath of pines. I got Meyer's voicemail and left a message.

We climbed the split log stairs to the entrance and went inside, where a fire was crackling in a huge river-rock fireplace. The lobby was large and sectioned by thick timbers supporting the ceiling. In the corner, a young blonde woman stood behind a counter.

"Hello," I said.

"Good afternoon and welcome," she said, her smile from a toothpaste ad. She had blue eyes, shiny hair, and a slender, athletic body.

"Hi there," Cody said, handing her a card. "We're looking into the body found on the beach New Year's Day."

"Oh, my god." Her eyes fell open as if horrified by the mention of it.

Cody put his elbow on the counter and leaned forward. "We're trying to find a witness. Were you working New Year's Eve?"

"No. That would be our night manager."

"Can you tell us how many rooms, or cabins, were rented out that night?" I said.

"Well, yes. I could tell you that." She smiled again, happy to help, and added, "We don't see much business this time of year. Winter is our slow season." Her eyes scanned a screen. "We had four rooms occupied here in the hotel, but only one cabin, one of our biggest. A two bedroom, sleeps eight."

"Are they still there?" Cody said.

"No, they left New Year's Day."

"How about any of the hotel occupants? Any still checked in?"

She typed for a minute, then looked up at us, an apology in her eyes. "No, they all left already."

"Dear, could you write down the names and phone numbers of the guests?" Cody said.

"Well, I probably should ask permission."

"We won't tell anyone it came from you."

"Promise?"

Cody winked. "Cross my heart and hope to die."

She showed off her teeth again, and in a minute, we left with a page she had printed for us.

We began back toward Cody's truck, hiking parallel to the highway on a bike trail the hotel kept cleared of snow. Ahead of us, someone was sitting on a bench along the trail. When we got closer, I could see it was a local homeless man known as Saint Alphonso.

He was a large black fellow, his steel wool beard partially hidden by the collar of a once white coat pulled up high around his face. The wrinkles beneath his red-rimmed eyes were deep and looked caked with soot. Next to him sat a battered red backpack fitted with a pair of wheels on an aluminum frame.

"What's happening, Alphonso?"

He gave me a startled look, then blinked in recognition. "Hullo, suh. How you?"

"Good. What are you doing way out here?"

He shrugged and didn't answer.

Cody pulled out a pack of cigarettes, and Alphonso watched him light up.

"Ah trouble you for a smoke, suh?"

Cody gave him a Marlboro, and Alphonso took it between his tortoise-shell fingernails.

"You have somewhere to stay nearby?" I asked. I took the lighter from Cody's hands and gave Alphonso a light. His lips were cracked and scabbed over.

Alphonso shut his eyes and inhaled. "Ah doin' awright."

"Two nights ago, a man dumped a woman's body on the beach out there." I pointed behind him.

"Ah knows that."

"You do?"

"Yes, suh. Ah seen it."

"What did you see?" Cody said.

"Just what you said."

"Can I sit here, Alphonso?" I pointed to his backpack. He looked at me, then moved the pack.

"Suit yourself."

I sat in a cloud of smoke. "About what time did you see this?"

"Oh, two or three in da mornin'."

"Where were you?"

"In my campin' spot. Ah seen da man's pickup a comin' wit no lights. Den he stop and take her and dump her off like a sack a trash, drag her out dere."

"Did you get a good look at the man?" Cody said.

"Nah. He was a piece away an' it was dark dat night."

"Was he short? Tall?"

"Ah say, medium."

"Think, Alphonso," I said. "This is important. Are there any details of this man you remember?"

Alphonso closed his eyes again and took a deep drag and exhaled slowly from his nostrils. "He was wearin' a beanie on his head. Ah could see da shape."

"How about his truck? Could you see the color?"

"No, suh."

"Was it a big truck? Or a smaller one?"

"Ah say, medium."

"Shit," I said.

"Was it a diesel engine?" Cody said. "You know what a diesel sounds like?"

"Ah dint hear no diesel. It was a regular motor."

I stood. "Ah help you more if ah could. Ah dint like seein' dat."

I took a card from my wallet, and on the back wrote, *free lunch and a beer*, and initialed it.

"Stop by Zeke's next time you're hungry, Alphonso. They'll take care of you.

"Yes, suh."

"Please call me if you remember anything about the man or the truck."

"Ah do that."

***

Cody declined my offer to stay for dinner and dropped me off where my truck was parked at the ski resort. The sun fell behind the western ridges as I drove down the grade, and a low moon glowed radiant in the dimmed sky. When I got home, I put away my ski gear in the garage and brought Valerie Horvachek's purse inside.

Candi heard me and peeked out from her art room. "I hope you won't be mad at me," she said, her face uncharacteristically sheepish.

"Why would I?"

"I brought you home a little surprise."

"You did?"

She stepped from the room and, in her arms, was a ball of gray fur. I walked over and saw she held a kitten. It looked at me with lime green eyes and meowed.

"You told me you liked cats," she said.

"I do, but..."

"Isn't he cute?"

I reached out and petted the kitten's head. It was a long hair variety, its fur billowy and gray as oil smoke. "He's quite a fluffy guy," I said.

"I think he's adorable." She held him up and touched the kitten's nose with her own. "Here," she said, handing me the furry ball.

It was small enough that I could cradle it securely in one hand. "Where did you get him?"

"A lady in front of the grocery store had a litter in a box. When I saw him, I couldn't resist. His name's Smokey."

I sat down, and the kitten meowed and licked my knuckle.

"Oh my," Candi said. "He likes you."

"We'll need to keep him inside, at least until he's bigger," I said. "Coyotes hunt out there in the meadow."

Candi took the kitten from me and put it in a cardboard box lined with blankets. Smokey promptly climbed out and began exploring the family room. I let Candi tend to our new pet while I boiled water for pasta and made a green salad. While the spaghetti cooked, I poured myself a tall whiskey seven, and Candi joined me at the table with her ceramic pipe and baggie of pot.

"How's the investigation coming?" She plucked a clogged screen out of the pipe bowl with her fingernails and replaced it with a new one.

"Too early to say. Making progress, but not sure where it's heading."

"Cody is still staying at Pistol Pete's?"

"Yeah."

"Is he okay?"

I took a long sip. "I think so."

"Has a funeral been scheduled yet?"

"Cody and Marcus Grier contacted her family. I imagine her parents are making arrangements."

She exhaled a hit through a window she had cracked open. "Is Cody going to the funeral?"

"We haven't talked about it."

"Do you think he should?"

"I think his focus is on finding who killed her."

"Oh." She studied her pipe and began reloading it. "How long do you think it will take?"

I put down my glass and smiled at her. "Honey, it's impossible to say."

"Tell Cody to join us for dinner tomorrow. He shouldn't be grieving alone."

"I invited him tonight, but he said no, thanks."

"Well, tell him I insist for tomorrow, okay?"

"I'll tell him."

***

We finished eating, and Candi was tending to the dishes, when my cell rang. It was Jack Myers, the coroner, returning my call.

"What is it you want, Reno?" he said, his crusty voice no doubt exacerbated by a lifetime of booze and cigars.

"Evening, Jack. I'm investigating the murder of Terry Molina."

"Good for you."

"Have you done the autopsy yet?"

"Just the preliminary, if it's any of your business."

"It is my business. Like I said, I'm investigating her murder."

"Are you being a smartass with me?"

"Not intentionally, Jack."

"Your intentions can kiss my ass. You can kiss my ass too."

"What did I say to deserve that?"

"Everything."

"How about if I buy you a drink?" I said.

"Jesus Christ, am I that easy?"

"You're never easy."

"Fine, you big bastard," he grunted. "Meet me over at the King's Head."

He hung up, and I told Candi I'd try not to be long. I put on my coat and went out to the garage and, ten minutes later, pulled up to South Lake Tahoe's sole British pub, a Tudor building next to a condo complex on a side street off 50. When I got out of my truck, I saw Jack Myers grunting his way from his sedan, leaning heavily on a cane as he swore and grimaced.

"Need a hand?" I said.

"What, I look like a cripple?" His blue eyes glared at me from under his bushy gray eyebrows.

"No, you look like a gymnast ready to hit the parallel bars."

"Hilarious. Get the door for me, would you? It's my cursed spine again."

I opened the door to the bar and held it while Jack hobbled forward. He'd had a knee replaced recently and was considering back surgery. After a long career as a coroner in Houston and San Francisco, he'd moved to Tahoe to retire, but reconsidered after going crazy with boredom. He now said he intended to work until he was no longer physically able. By the looks of him, that might not be too far off.

We sat at the bar, and Jack groaned and ordered a scotch rocks. "My daughter and her kids came by yesterday. My grandson, the surly punk, shot his mouth off, and I had to kick his ass."

"Your grandson? How old is he?"

"Six. The tough little son of a bitch made me wrench my back."

"Maybe you should pick on guys your own age."

"What a thoughtful comment. You'll see what it's like to get old one day, if you're lucky. Are you gonna order something, or am I drinking alone?"

I got a cocktail, and Jack and I chatted for a while, over the drone of a British commentator calling a soccer game on TV. Our history went back a few years to a violent case that had involved the uncovering of a corrupt county sheriff's activities. Jack claimed the flurry of autopsies he did as a result caused the beginnings of his back problems.

"What do you want to know about Terry Molina?" he said, after ordering a second scotch.

"How did she die?"

"She was strangled with a rope."

"Was she knocked unconscious first?"

"Appears so by the contusion behind her ear. But she was awake when she was strangled."

"How do you know?"

"Traces of smelling salts in her nostrils. Also, her fingernails were broken, likely trying to claw at her assailant. There's skin under her nails. My guess is whoever killed her woke her first. Wanted her to know what was happening."

I swirled the watery dregs of my highball. "Did she have sex that night?"

"Depends if you use the Bill Clinton definition," Jack said with a chuckle.

"Huh?"

"She gave someone a blow job. There were still traces of semen on her chin."

"Oh. Any sign she was raped?"

"No. Rapists usually don't risk getting their dongs bit off."

I was struck with a lurid image of Terry performing oral sex on Nick Galanis. Maybe Galanis asked for a blow job to give him a break from Terry's blather. I tried to ignore the thought, but couldn't avoid a smile.

"How about the rope, Jack? Any idea what type it was?"

"Half inch variety. Appears a tight nylon weave."

"Like a mountaineer's rope?"

"Possibly, yeah."

"Have you seen Douglas County's autopsy results for Valerie Horvachek, the strangled girl in Nevada?" I asked.

"No. I'll compare notes with them tomorrow, after I finish the full autopsy."

I leaned forward on my elbows. "What else, Jack? Who do you think did this?"

"Son, I've been studying murders since before you were born. But that don't mean I've got a crystal ball. All I can tell you is it was a sadist. The type who looked into her eyes as he snuffed her, wanted her to know he had the say whether she lived or died."

"Okay, but what's the motive? Money? Love?"

Jack was quite for a moment. "Maybe hate," he said. "But that's your job to figure out, not mine."

The bartender brought more drinks, but I had a busy night ahead and couldn't afford the luxury of a three-drink buzz. Fifteen minutes later, Jack ordered another and I left the bar, my glass still full. A drizzle of snow had frosted my windshield, and I drove slowly on the slick roads. When I got back home, Candi was in bed playing with the kitten.

I went to my office and spread a clean sheet of Candi's sketching paper over a folding table. I removed and photographed every item from Valerie's purse. Keys, makeup, credit cards, sunglasses, condoms. In her wallet, I found a business card from the Suave Gentlemen's Club with a phone number handwritten on the back. I copied the number, then reassembled the purse with each article, including the baggie of cocaine in the inner compartment. The only thing I left out was her cell phone. It had died, but fortunately it used the same charger as mine. I plugged it in, and it came to life.

In the address book were thirty-six entries. It took half an hour to type every name and number into my PC. One of the names was Mike Zayas, owner of the Suave. The only others I recognized were the three friends she traveled to Tahoe with, and her ex-boyfriend, Max, from Sacramento.

I stood and stretched, then sat back down and began typing a progress report for the general. Twenty minutes later, Candi called for me, and I said I'd be there in a minute. The report grew lengthier than I planned, and I realized I was using it as a means to organize and track every detail I'd uncovered. I continued, knowing I'd have to reduce the version I'd e-mail. Another twenty minutes passed before I heard Candi walk up behind me. She leaned her head down next to mine, her perfume fresh and vaguely tropical.

"Almost finished?"

"Yeah, just about."

I felt her flesh on my face and turned to see she was naked.

"Come to bed," she said.

That concluded my work for the day.

7

When the sun rose in the morning, the sky looked sandblasted clean, the blue massive brilliant and without error. The horizon was so sharp, I could make out individual trees on the ridge a mile away. I went outside to get the newspaper, and along my eaves, rows of silver icicles sparkled in the early light.

After Candi left for work, I stood staring out the large window looking over the meadow. There was a path running across the white flats and up the mountainside to a waterfall that was now iced over. The trail wasn't passable past a certain point in the winter, but in the spring, I'd put on a weighted pack, jog the couple miles up to the waterfall's base, and watch the snowmelt gush from a slick, granite ledge, a hundred feet above.

I put my coffee cup in the sink and went to the garage to a storage cabinet, where I kept a climbing rope and carabiners and a pair of crampons. The rope hung neatly coiled on a peg. I took it and wrapped a length around my fist and jerked it taught, the nylon chafing my skin. I stood there for a while, my hands clenched around the rope, then went back inside.

The information I'd gathered so far on the murders of Valerie Horvachek and Terry Molina had grown to the point where I needed to make decisions on where to focus the investigation. The possible involvement of biker gangs in Valerie's murder, if not Terry's, was something I could not discount. But the more tangible evidence led in a different direction, to a prolific womanizer who was also the chief of detectives for Douglas County PD.

Marcus Grier hadn't been thrilled with my request he share whatever Nick Galanis said about his time with Terry. Although

I considered Grier a friend and even an ally, I couldn't blame him. The relationship between the police forces on either side of the border was awkward. The two sides cooperated out of necessity, but because priorities and loyalties rarely lined up, conflict often resulted.

The fact that Galanis was with Terry the night before she died meant the South Lake Tahoe police had to consider him a suspect. Add to the mix Galanis' history of corrupt activities, and the implications became even more serious. If Galanis was somehow involved in Terry or Valerie's murder, the potential for fallout was enormous. Those with allegiances to Galanis might find their careers in jeopardy, while others stood to benefit. As for Grier, he would tread cautiously—it was his nature.

To compound things, I was now in possession of a critical piece of evidence; Valerie's purse. I suppose I could simply hand it over to Grier, or take it directly to Nick Galanis. But the purse had value, and I wasn't about to give it up without something in return.

It wasn't quite 9:00 A.M. that I called Cody, and when he didn't answer, I left him a message saying I'd come by Pistol Pete's later in the morning. Then, I picked up the plastic bag containing Valerie's purse and drove to the South Lake Tahoe Police station.

I parked next to a wall of dirty snow, left the purse in my cab, and went into the lobby. "Hi, Helen," I said to the receptionist, a hard-looking woman on desk duty after injuring her leg while chasing a shoplifting suspect. "Is Marcus in?"

She looked up with blunt eyes. "I'll see," she said.

A minute later, Grier opened the door and motioned me in. "What is it?" he said.

"What happened to 'good morning'?"

"Not much good about it so far," he muttered.

"Maybe I can change that. I've found Valerie Horvachek's purse," I said to the back of his head as we walked down a hallway, then into his office.

He turned before he sat, his eyes bulbous. "Where?"

"In the woods, near where she was found."

"That's a crime scene."

"Give me a break, Marcus. I didn't see any sign Douglas County has been there since I found the body."

"Where's the purse?"

"In my truck."

Grier pushed a button on his phone. "Bill, would you come in here?"

I heard the knock of heels on tile, and Bill Worley's craggy face appeared in the doorway. He wore a blue jean shirt and a bolo tie.

"You remember Dan Reno?"

"I surely do. Howdy, Dan."

"Hello."

"Bring in the purse, please," Grier said to me.

"You gonna let me in on what Galanis said?"

The two cops looked at each other. "Don't see the harm," Worley said.

"Hmmph," Grier snorted. "Get the purse."

I walked out through the lobby, and when I returned, the receptionist hit a buzzer and let me back into the squad room. Grier and Worley halted their conversation when I entered the office. I set the purse on Grier's desk. Worley lifted the bag by the corner and looked it over.

"You already went through it, I take it?" Grier said.

"Everything's still there," I replied.

Grier looked at me for a long moment, then nodded to Worley.

"Nick Galanis said he took Terry Molina to his place, where they engaged in consensual sex until about two in the morning," Worley said. "Then, he called her a cab. Said she went outside to wait for it."

"Why would she go wait out in the cold?" I said.

Worley sat with his boots flat on the floor and his veined hands on his knees. "Galanis said they had words, and she stormed out."

"Words about what?"

"He said she asked for money. Said he told her he'd never have touched her if he knew she was a whore."

From behind his desk, Grier said, "The lovey-dovey basically came to a halt at that point."

"I imagine it would." I lowered myself into the chair opposite Worley. "Did you call Tahoe Taxi?"

"First thing we did. They confirmed the call. The driver showed up at 2:20 A.M. He waited ten minutes, reckoned he'd been stood up, and left."

"Someone must have been lying in wait for her," I said.

"What kind of nut would kidnap a woman from in front of a policeman's house?" Grier said.

"Someone not afraid of the police," Worley answered.

Grier's phone rang, but he hit a button and muted it. "Or maybe someone *taunting* the police," he said.

"Could be someone who wants to get caught," I said. The two cops looked at me like I was crazy. "Is Galanis considered a suspect?" I asked.

Grier opened his mouth, but Worley spoke first. "I consider him one. He could have killed both women in his condo."

"What would be his motive?" I looked at both men and neither responded. The room grew silent. "Are you going to get a warrant to search his home?"

"If it comes to that," Grier said.

"Marcus, Nick Galanis is a crooked cop. He may not be a murderer, but I'd say he's in this up to his eyeballs. Valerie, and maybe Terry, were somehow involved with a biker gang called the Blood Bastards, who deal coke and meth. These bad boys were at Pistol Pete's for New Year's, and Cody saw them again just the other night."

Grier walked from behind his desk. "What are you saying? That Galanis is linked to these bikers?"

"They could be paying him off to deal drugs in the area."

"Do you have any evidence of this?" Worley said.

"Not yet I don't."

"Listen," Grier said, stepping forward and standing over me. "Our deal is you would back off from Galanis if we shared what he had to say."

I looked up at Grier. His face was shiny, his eyes wide in their sockets. "So it is."

"Good. Whatever Galanis' role, we'll get to the bottom of it. In the meantime, I don't want you in his face. Understood?"

"Loud and clear."

"Then, we're done here."

"I take it you haven't found any witnesses?" I said.

"Not so far," Worley drawled.

"Have you?" Grier said.

"A homeless man named Saint Alphonso—"

"I know who he is," he said.

"He was camping near Kiva Beach, and said he saw a pickup stop between two and three, and a man dragged a body out to the beach. But it was too far for him to make out any detail."

Grier sighed. "If you're still waiting for a 'good morning' from me, forget about it."

***

I drove away from the police complex and headed east on a two-lane lined with columns of spruce and fir, each tree as different as they were the same. I called Cody and this time he answered.

"I need to get back to San Jose, Dan. I got called for a deposition tomorrow."

"You're heading back right now?"

"Soon as I pack and check out."

"I'll be there in five minutes. Meet me at the coffee shop near the elevators."

"All right."

We hung up, and I waited at the stoplight where Pioneer Trail intersected Highway 50, a block from the state line. Fancy resorts had recently been built at the border, one boasting a gondola rising to the ski slopes. Smaller, less expensive hotels were razed to make room for the new developments. Despite the recession, South Lake Tahoe was rapidly transforming into a high-end tourist destination. With the increase in visitors came more money and more crime.

Marcus Grier had spent his early years as a peace officer in a medium-sized city in the Deep South. It was a place where flying the Confederate flag was commonplace, and the status of the black population had not evolved much since the early 1960s. The whites were content to have the blacks serve as cab drivers, cooks, janitors, bellmen, and clerks. Mobility beyond that level was rarely available. Grier's job as a patrolman was granted as part of a plan for the white police force to have at least one 'inside man.'

The ghettos Grier had patrolled were caldrons of crack and heroin addiction, prostitution, and every form of sordid violence. Street walkers infected clients with AIDS, pimps slit the throats of their girls and left the bodies in gutters, abandoned babies were found in dumpsters, and drug gangs shot children during drive-bys.

Grier had quit after his two daughters reached school age and moved out west to Tucson. He had spent some years there as a deputy sheriff before landing his job in Tahoe. He'd confided to me after we became friends that, as a young man, he had wanted to join the ministry, but took a job as a cop because he needed the money. He said he moved to Tahoe to escape the rampant crime that plagued the cities where he'd worked. This conversation had occurred over a long night of drinking after the murder of an elected Tahoe official concluded a case that had left four local criminals dead.

Originally seduced by the natural beauty of the Lake Tahoe region, Grier had assumed South Lake Tahoe's crime rate would be on a lesser scale than he was used to. What he didn't know was that, for years, Pistol Pete's Casino had been run by a Mafioso who'd exploited the demand for recreational drugs among both the residents and the hard-partying weekend visitors. Under mob management, the drug trade around Lake Tahoe had flourished to the point that coke and meth traffickers now recognized Tahoe as a key dealing and distribution hub. Of course, this would not have developed without payoffs to certain cops.

Eventually, though, the mob got too greedy, and the Nevada Gaming Commission forced them out of Pistol Pete's. That left a vacuum in the drug trade, one that was currently filled by rogue Mexican gangs and, possibly, bikers.

I parked and went into Pistol Pete's. I found Cody sitting in a booth at the casino diner, an unopened newspaper and a cup of black coffee on the table. He was staring at his cell phone.

"Hey," I said. "What's up?"

"I just got a call from Terry's brother. He sounds like a real dipshit."

"Why?"

"He says he talked to a detective at SJPD about Terry's murder, and when he brought up my name, the cop brought in my ex-boss."

"Landers?"

"Right. The brother said Landers told him I should be considered a suspect, and SJPD wants to talk to me as soon as I'm back in town."

"What did you say?"

"I told him he needs to pull his head out of his ass, because Landers is on the take, and the police in Lake Tahoe have already cleared me."

"And?"

"Then, he goes off on a tangent, saying his sister was bipolar and not responsible for her actions and needed stability instead of a douchebag like me who obviously just wanted to get his dick wet. I told him he's wrong, and he said bullshit, I'm just the last in a long line of assholes who used her, and now, she's dead, and she didn't deserve it, and he hopes I feel warm and fuzzy about the whole thing, and on and on. I finally hung up on him."

The waitress came by, and I told her I wasn't hungry. When she left, I looked at Cody, and his eyebrows were creased in a V on his reddened face.

"Sounds like Terry's brother is looking for a scapegoat. Don't buy into his bullshit, Cody."

"I'm not. Before I hung up I told the prick to find some other outlet for his grief."

"Good."

"When I get back to San Jose, I'm going to interview a few friends of hers. Find out if there's anything to the biker and blow angle."

"Yeah? I was thinking of heading to Sac and looking into that myself."

"Oh?"

"You got any free time this afternoon?" I asked.

"Sure, why not? I think I can carve out a few hours."

"You ready to roll?"

Cody smiled. "Let's go."

***

It was early afternoon when we came off the freeway. We'd driven separately, and Cody followed me into the Suave Gentlemen's Club's parking lot. The spots nearest the entrance were taken, but the bulk of the lot was empty. Next to the black Corvette that belonged to club owner Mike Zayas was a line of Harleys. The weather was beautiful for winter, sunny and nearly seventy, a perfect day for a ride. The bikers inside apparently preferred the scenery in the strip joint over the open road.

Instead of parking in front, Cody drove to the side of the building. I followed him and stopped behind his Dodge.

"What are you doing?" I said, walking to where he sat in his cab. He was shrugging his arms into a bulletproof vest.

"What's it look like?" On the passenger seat, the butt of his .357 protruded from a shoulder holster.

"Slow down, Cody. We're just going to ask some questions, not start World War III."

"Just a friendly conversation with the law-abiding citizenry, huh?" He looped the holster over his shoulder, pulled up his pant leg, and began securing a sheath holding a survival knife.

"We'll get nowhere if we front these dudes. How about a little restraint, okay?"

"Are you going to suit up?"

"No," I said. "I'm not."

He chuckled. "And you've been in this business how long?"

"Too long. Why don't you relax, have a cigarette?"

"I just had one."

"Give me one, then."

"You quit, remember? Look, no worries, Dirt. I just like to be prepared. These guys are supposed to be the genuine article. They throw around their weight, we need to be ready."

"Promise me you won't stir up a shit storm."

"Scout's honor." He saluted with two fingers. "Now, go get your gear. You're not doing yourself any favors walking in there with your dick in your hand."

I turned and looked out toward the freeway. Above the rush of cars, the sky was a benign blue laced with wisps of orange and white clouds. For some, it would be a day for picnics on the grass, tossing a football, or just a quiet stroll in a park. But I was working and probably deluding myself if I thought I could waltz into a biker hangout and get anywhere with a smile and a handshake. On the other hand, bringing Cody was a dangerous tactic, and not one that guaranteed results.

"Fuck it," I muttered. Valerie Horvachek and Terry Molina were both potentially involved with the Blood Bastards, and now, they were dead. It was time to get some answers.

I opened the steel box behind my cab, strapped on my body armor, and snapped a ten-round clip into the freshly oiled Beretta .40 caliber automatic I'd owned since I had gotten into the business. I fit a three-million-volt palm-sized stun gun into my vest pocket, along with a spring-loaded sap, and put on my black coat, its roomy fit hiding the hardware.

"Maybe you should get a lap dance," I said to Cody as we approached the front door. "They got some real babes here."

"Not in the mood for it."

I withheld comment. We walked inside, and the bouncer behind the cash register took my twenty and stamped our hands. On the main floor, the music was turned low, a murmur compared to the thumping rock I'd anticipated. I stopped near where the central runway split the room. There was no dancer on stage and only a few girls lounging in the dark corners.

"This place is deadsville," Cody said.

I shrugged. "Midweek, two o'clock. Must be a slow time."

We moved to a booth against the wall. A couple tables away, a stripper was performing a lap dance for an unshaven fat man in a T-shirt that clung to his bulging gut. At the runway, two fellows in baseball caps, barely drinking age, chugged bottled beer. A dancer came out from behind a curtain, surveyed the clientele, scowled, and disappeared.

"Hi there," said a girl who'd approached from the side. "Would you like a lap dance?"

She was a Latina, wearing the prerequisite platform heels that created the illusion of height, but I doubted she was five feet tall. The red lingerie hugging her body left little to the imagination. Her small breasts were perky, and her body was naked below the waist except for a G-string that disappeared between the cheeks of her round ass.

"No, thanks," Cody said.

"How much?" I asked.

"Twenty."

I took a bill from my wallet and gestured for her to sit.

"*Cual es tu nombre?*" I said.

She looked at me in surprise. "*Celestina,*" she said. She had a mole under her eye and small white teeth and red lips bright against her brown skin. If she was eighteen, she hadn't been for long.

"I think I saw you in Tijuana once," I said in Spanish.

"I used to live near there, in Rosarito."

"Now you live in Sacramento?"

She hesitated, then said, "For now."

"You like it here?"

"It's okay." She put her hand on mine and began scooting out of the booth. "Are you ready for your dance?"

"Let's talk for a minute, okay?"

She looked at me with doe eyes. "Okay."

"Are you sending money home to your family?"

"What does that matter?"

"Here." I passed her a twenty and took another from my wallet, along with a picture of Valerie.

"Do you recognize this girl?"

She studied the picture. "She worked here."

I nodded. "Did you know her?"

"I saw her, but we never spoke."

"Did she have any friends? Boyfriend or girlfriends?"

"Why are you so interested in her?"

"It's better you don't know, Celestina."

Her lips twitched, and she looked away. I saw a brief shudder in her shoulders.

"What about her friends?" I said.

"The motorcycle man with the bald head had a thing for her. That's all I know."

"He got a name?"

"They call him Roscoe."

"How about Mike Zayas? Did he have a thing for her?"

Her face froze. "I have to go," she said, sliding her bare cheeks off the seat. I pushed the second twenty over the table to her, but she hurried away without it.

"How about a translation?" Cody said.

"She said a biker named Roscoe liked Valerie. When I asked about Mike Zayas, she boogied."

"I saw the color go out of her face."

"Zayas is probably not a warm and fuzzy boss."

"You think he's pimping her?" Cody's lips looked bloodless, a tight line over his jaw.

"Or worse."

"Let's go have a word with him."

"I want to see if Roscoe is here. I think he's the one I talked to before."

We got up and walked around the vacant stage, past a pair of bouncers who eyed us. I felt Cody hesitate, and I prodded him with my elbow. "Keep walking," I said.

Around a corner and toward the back of the place, the stools at the small bar were full. Two Hispanic men in black Suave logo golf shirts sat next to two bikinied dancers. A pair of bikers wearing vests stitched with the double Bs occupied the stools at the far end.

The bartender was the same man I'd seen when I was here last, his shoulders narrow and his chest sunken over a small potbelly. Cody and I stood and waited for him to stop surfing the channels with the TV remote.

"Hey, bub, how about a beer?" Cody said.

The heads at the bar turned, the faces displaying varying degrees of annoyance. Then, they turned away and back to their conversations—all except for the biker I was looking for, the bald man with a billy goat beard. He swiveled on his stool, and our eyes locked.

The second biker, a large-knuckled dude with greasy hair who looked like he'd dry shaved, ignored us until the biker I assumed was Roscoe said to me, "I was hoping I'd see you again." Then, the second biker also turned and regarded Cody and me. His body was all sinew and muscle, his jawline dented and ridged with knots.

"Well, I couldn't stay away from this place, Roscoe," I said.

He gave me a sharp glance, then eased off his stool. "Join me for a smoke?" he said.

"All right."

"I'll keep your seat warm," Cody said, wedging his frame next to the other biker.

I followed Roscoe toward the front, but he peeled off to the far side, to the VIP room. He punched in a code on a keypad next to the door, and we went in.

The lighting was dim, and I could barely make out the rows of curtained nooks. From behind one of the curtains, a man's voice breathed, "Yeah, that's good. Suck it, mama."

We went behind a curtain and sat in two chairs. It was a small alcove, about six feet square. The scent of disinfectant didn't quite hide the musk of stale body fluids.

"You still investigating Valerie Horvachek's murder?" Roscoe said.

"Yeah."

"Making any progress?"

"Some. You got anything that might help me?"

He leaned forward on his chair, his fist propping his bearded chin. In the scant light, I could see a puckered scar glowing on the dome of his head.

"Maybe I do," he said. "Valerie was a nice girl, a good kid. She didn't deserve to die."

"Who does?"

"Whoever killed her." His lips curled around his chipped teeth, and he stared at me bluntly.

"And who's that?"

He peeked outside the curtain, the skin around his features tight, and he lowered his voice to just above a whisper. "Valerie was holding drugs, enough someone might kill her for it."

"Who?"

"There's a ragtag gang out of Stockton. White supremacists."

"Why do you think they're involved?"

He leaned back and scratched at an eyebrow. "There's bad blood between us and them."

"How does that relate to Valerie?"

"I dug the chick, all right?"

"So, what, your enemies killed her because they knew you liked her?"

"That, and also to steal her stash."

I sat with my elbows in my lap and studied the man across from me. He had dark bags under his eyes, and his nose was oily with blackheads. His lips were pursed in an uncertain expression, as if he was trying to gauge whether his words were believable.

"The gang from Stockton," I said. "Their name?"

"War Dogs," he rasped.

We stared at each other in the small space. The air had turned warm and a fetid odor rose from the carpet.

"Why are you telling me this?" I said.

"Look, man, I'd go after these cocksuckers myself, but I got to act within my gang."

"They tell you to lay low?"

"It's a timing thing."

"So, you think sending me after them is the solution?"

He blinked. "I thought you were investigating her murder."

"I am."

"Then, do as you see right, man."

It grew quiet again, then he shuffled his feet and peeked out the curtain. "I'll go out the back way," he said.

"You really liked her, huh?"

He sighed and dropped his eyes. "Fuck, I thought I loved her."

I shook my head as I watched him leave the alcove, and after a moment, I went out toward the front exit. I was nearly there when a fat man stumbled from a behind a curtain, a black stripper on his arm. He giggled and put his squat hand on her jiggling ass. I fell into the shadows and tailed them out to the main floor.

As I headed back toward the bar I caught a glimpse of the young Latina watching me with round eyes from a doorway. Then, the crash of broken glass and a loud thump sounded, followed by angry shouts.

"Shit," I said, and ran around the corner to see Cody standing in front of the bar and covering up as the biker he'd sat next to whipped a flurry of punches at his face.

A stream of blood ran from Cody's eye into his beard. The biker's face was split in a maniacal grin as he relentlessly hooked and jabbed, his fists moving in a blur. Then, Cody stepped forward and threw a short upper cut into the man's gut. It didn't look like much of a punch, but the biker's smile vanished and his mouth went round. He gasped and keeled over, and Cody grabbed his hair with both hands and slammed his face into the bar top with a sickening crunch. The biker's face erupted in a burst of red, and he collapsed to the floor.

In a second, one of the bouncers at the bar rushed Cody, and the other came at me. He tried to tackle me, but I side-stepped him and popped him across the back of the head with my sap, not hard, just enough to sit him down and take the fight out of him.

Cody was not as charitable with the bouncer foolish enough to try to take him on. The man was big, maybe 250, but his attempt at a tackle barely budged Cody, who wrapped his huge arms around the man and squeezed. I watched as the poor fellow went red in the face, then purple.

"Let's get out of here," I said, but then, Mike Zayas came out of the door behind the bar. Behind him were two bikers, bearded, tattooed, wearing dirty jeans and stomp-ass riding boots, one holding a knife, the other with a set of brass knuckles on his fist.

Zayas wore slacks and pointy shoes, and his shiny black hair fell onto the white collar above his dark sports coat. Cody turned toward him, still holding the bouncer in a bear hug. Zayas stopped, but the man with a knife came at Cody.

I pulled my stun gun and leapt forward. The knife arced toward my face, and I tried to catch the man's arm, but the blade sliced through my coat and cut deeply above my left wrist. I thrust the stun device into the man's midsection, and his body went rigid, his hair on end, the knife falling as his hands splayed. I held the device to his ribs until smoke started to rise from my fist. Then, before he could topple, I reared back and hit him as hard as I could in the jaw.

The biker with the brass knuckles had stepped in front of Zayas as if to shield him, but now he turned to me, his face bunched in a mask of fury. He fainted to his right, and I danced back, blood dripping from my arm. At that moment, Cody rushed forward, pinning Zayas against the bar with the nearly unconscious bouncer in his grip. Zayas yelled and squirmed, then lost his footing and fell to the ground under Cody and the bouncer's mass.

"Maybe you'll bleed out, bitch," brass knuckles said to me. He faked a punch, then pounced from the left, going for my injured limb. I caught him with a snap kick to the solar plexus, and he stopped as if he'd hit a wall. He opened his mouth, but no sound came. I swung with a right, and he made a feeble attempt to duck the punch, but I connected just under the ear, and he went down like a skid row whore.

Cody pushed himself upright, and Zayas struggled from beneath the dead weight of the bouncer, who was blinking and lying flat.

"Sorry about this," Cody said, glancing my way. "I was just trying to have a beer."

Zayas rose to his feet, his clothes scuffed with dirt and his hair in his face. He smoothed his pants and jacket, then his hand went inside the coat.

"Wrong move, Rico," Cody said, his pistol suddenly trained at Zayas' forehead.

I went to Zayas and removed a .25 automatic from his breast pocket, popped the clip, and tossed the gun behind the bar. My arm was soaked in blood, and it was falling in fast drops off my fingers.

"Take off your shoe," I said to Zayas. "Take out the shoelace."

"This some kind of joke?"

"Do it, asswipe," Cody said.

Zayas did as I said, then I had him tie a tourniquet around my forearm. When he was done, we backed around the corner, and two more bouncers wearing Suave shirts came hustling at us from the other side of the joint. They stopped when Cody waved at them with his piece.

"There's a big mess at the bar," Cody said. "Get some brooms and mops and go help your boss wipe the shit off the floor."

The bouncers froze, incredulous, and we went out the front door. Roscoe was sitting on a Harley smoking a cigarette. He flicked his butt away and started putting on his helmet, then he saw us. He swung off his bike and stared, his face frozen in disbelief.

"What the fuck?"

"Your buddy at the bar has anger management issues," Cody said.

"You ought to find yourself some smarter friends," I added.

Roscoe started for the door, then stopped, his hand on his chin. We continued to the side of the building where we'd parked. My arm was beginning to throb, but the blood flow had ebbed. I hadn't looked at the cut, but I knew it would need stitches. I grabbed Cody and stopped him.

"Care to tell me what we accomplished? Besides announcing to everyone there that we're the enemy?"

"Be happy to, Dirt. Bear with me." He opened his truck and took something from the glove box, then knelt down and stuck his hand into a shrub growing along the stucco wall.

"What are you doing?"

"It's a receiving unit. I stuck a bug to the back of Zayas' belt when I took him down."

I paused and looked back the way we'd come. "Really? How effective is it?"

"Very. You really need to study up on your gadgetry."

I didn't argue the point. We climbed into our trucks and drove out to the main lot and toward the frontage road. I looked over and saw Roscoe watching us. He stood at the edge of the awning where the green carpet led into the Suave, and he was still there in my rear-view mirror when I hit the gas and followed Cody down the street.

***

The emergency clinic in Sacramento was nearly empty, but it still took two hours to get six stitches in my arm. When they released me, it was almost five, and the street was crammed with rush hour traffic. Cody leaned against his truck, squinting into layers of orange smog that spread across the horizon and muted the sun.

"How's the arm?" he said.

I peeled back the bandage, clenched my fist, and watched the stitches tighten across the skin. The flesh was numb.

"Have you heard anything on the bug yet?" I said.

Cody studied his mobile phone and punched a few buttons. "Nope. There's typically a delay in the download. It's not instantaneous."

"I don't buy Roscoe's story on the War Dogs."

"Why not?"

"For one, whoever killed Valerie didn't rob her. She still had her stash. And two, a gang wouldn't go after a rival's girlfriend. That would be a chickenshit thing to do."

Cody grunted and shook a smoke from a pack of Marlboros. "Maybe it was a crime of opportunity."

"What opportunity? She wasn't robbed or raped. We're dealing with something different here."

"Why did Roscoe put you onto the War Dogs, then?"

"He doesn't know Valerie wasn't robbed. Maybe he really thinks they did it."

"Or maybe he just wants us to go hassle them."

"What for?" I said. "Give me a cigarette, would you?"

He tossed me his pack. "To piss them off. Or distract them."

I lit up, took a drag, and studied the blue eddy of smoke twirling into the afternoon. "The Blood Bastards and War Dogs were both in South Lake Tahoe during the timeframe when Valerie and Terry were murdered," I said. "My theory is one of the gangs, if not both, is in bed with Nick Galanis, paying him off. The question is, how do we find out?"

Cody looked at me, a smile on the corner of his mouth. "Just a matter of asking the right people the right questions. Maybe we should start with your buddy, Jake Massie."

"Where do you think that will get us?"

"Who knows, Dirt? I'd just like to meet the dude. He sounds like an outstanding citizen." A nurse had washed the blood from the cut on his forehead and applied a butterfly bandage. She had missed some blood, which had dried in the crow's feet spreading from his eye.

I stared out at the hazy sunset and watched a stream of cars crawl by. "If we leave now, we can be in Stockton before full dark," I said.

"On the road again," Cody hummed.

***

We crawled through a couple lights, but once we hit Highway 5, it was open road, fifty miles straight through the agricultural heart of the San Joaquin Valley. Rows of green crops spread from either side of the highway, stretching toward mountains distant and dwarfed by a purple sky. Cruising at eighty, we reached the outskirts of Stockton just as the first stars appeared.

I passed Cody's rig, and he followed me to a brewery offering American food, strong beer, and wireless internet access. I gathered my computer bag, and we went in and took a table in the lounge near a crackling fireplace.

A pretty waitress in a short dress and a pushup bra came to take our orders. Cody flirted with her while I powered up my PC and connected to the internet.

"And for you, sir?"

I looked up into her bedroom eyes and lush cleavage and felt a sudden reminder to get home to Candi tonight, hopefully before she fell asleep. "A light beer, and how about the fish tacos?"

"Great choice." She took our menus and pranced away, her ass swaying under her skirt.

"Fish tacos?" Cody chuckled. "Is that a Freudian slip or what?"

I smiled. "Who knows what lurks in my subconscious?"

"I do—a horn dog. Maybe we should bag this and go on a trim hunt."

"I'll pass. Besides, I thought you were gonna take it easy on the broads for a while."

"I said that, what, two days ago? I think that counts as a while."

"I'm sure for you it does."

"You're right. And I remember the days when you were no different."

"That was when I was in my twenties."

Cody started to say something, then stopped. He stared off, flames from the fireplace dancing in his eyes.

"What?" I said.

"Those were good times back then. And you tore off more pieces than I could count. I couldn't keep up with you."

"That was right after I got divorced. I was drunk most of the time."

Cody sighed, a sadness taking hold on his face. I suppose he missed the days when we used to drink and chase women together. Those had been wild, irresponsible days, drunk and hungover, broke and confused, and the sordid cases we worked in San Jose often soaked in blood. I knew how many men I'd killed, but I doubted Cody kept his own accounting. If he did, he never spoke of it. He'd certainly killed more than me, among them rapists, child molesters, drive-by murderers, cartel assassins, and devil worshippers. All scumbags the world was better off without, but that had not absolved us from certain legal entanglements. Over the years, I'd used up more than my fair share of favors, from both my father's ex-law firm partners and a handful of sympathetic cops and public officials. Whether or not I'd run that well dry was something I hoped not to find out.

"You might as well read up," I said, handing Cody the file Albert Bigelow had provided on the Blood Bastards and the War Dogs. I kept the page listing the known members of the War Dogs and began entering their names into a site I subscribed to. I started with Jake Massie. An address for an apartment in south Stockton came up. I wrote it down and entered the next name on the list.

The waitress brought our beers, and by the time our food arrived, I'd compiled a list of addresses for ten War Dog members.

"Entertaining stuff," Cody said, handing me the file. He took a long sip off his beer. "Not much of a stretch to imagine either gang buying off a corrupt cop if it allowed them to expand their business."

"It's possible." I shook an inadvisable amount of Tabasco on a taco, took a huge bite, and washed it down with half a beer. "We'll get to the bottom of it soon enough."

"I don't think talking to Massie is going to help us get to the bottom of anything," I said.

"The guy's a shitbag ex-con who tried to extort you out of thirty grand. Who said anything about talking?"

"Three War Dogs are in jail because of me, Cody. I don't want to rub salt in the wound, right?"

Cody tilted his beer, drained the last of it, and wiped his mouth. "Ten-four, good buddy."

"I'm serious," I said.

"I realize busting him up won't help us solve the murders, okay?"

The waitress came by, and Cody ordered another 24-ounce beer. "You see my handsome friend here?" he said to the waitress. "He may look like the all-American boy, but he's the most bad-ass bounty hunter you'd ever want to meet."

The waitress turned to me, her eyes shiny. "Really?"

"Not a word of that is true," I said.

"He's modest. Cute, huh?" Cody winked, and she smiled and bent lower, affording him a view down her low-cut blouse.

I shook my head and concentrated on my food, and when she left, I told Cody to do the same. "We got work to do," I said.

Fifteen minutes later, we drove off in my truck, leaving Cody's conspicuous red rig at the restaurant. We headed south for ten minutes and found the address for Jake Massie's apartment just off the freeway, on the edge of Stockton's black and Mexican ghettos. Gang graffiti was everywhere, scrawled across fences and stucco walls and covering a derelict Ford sedan resting on its rims.

A group of *cholos* on the corner stared us down as we drove past, their pants baggy and low on their hips, red bandanas tied around their heads.

"Not exactly where you'd expect a white supremacist to live," I said.

"Not unless he has a death wish."

I stopped in front of a row of apartments facing the street. The window for unit 190 was dark.

I didn't know if my conversation with Massie at Zeke's had convinced him to abandon his notion I would pay him. Criminals were an unpredictable lot. I had no way of knowing if I'd ever see him again. But he said he knew where I lived, and that was something I couldn't ignore. Taking an idle approach to Massie's threat was an uncertain approach, or at worst, a weak approach. Massie was a predator. Had I invited him to escalate his game? Letting Massie walk away may have been stupid on my part. I could have followed him out of Zeke's and taken him down, hurt him bad, let him know he'd never get a dime from me, and made sure he understood that if I saw him again I'd kill him. What then? Would that be the end of it, or the beginning of something worse? Factor in Massie's ties to the Aryan Brotherhood, and the potential for trouble was exponential. But the AB, like any gang, existed primarily to make money. Would they come after me just to avenge a one-on-one beating?

I sat staring at apartment 190, and for a moment, I regretted ever mentioning Massie to Cody. He would not tolerate Massie's threat against me, and I knew this when I told him of the situation. So whatever happened next was of my own design.

We got out of my truck and knocked on the door to Massie's unit. I stood to the side, my lead-filled sap in my fist. Cody had his hands in his pockets and looked no more concerned than a neighbor looking to borrow a cup of sugar.

When no one answered, I peeked through the window, but it was entirely blocked by a curtain. I tried the doorknob, and it was locked.

"You want to go in?" Cody said.

"Let's try a neighbor." I walked to the next door, where a light shone in a window.

A Mexican woman as wide as she was tall answered my knock. Her face was acne scarred, and she wore an apron over a print dress. Her feet were crammed into flats that looked ready to burst, and her ankles were the size of softballs.

"Stockton PD," I said, flashing a badge. "We're looking for Jake Massie." I jerked my thumb to the right.

"You not the police," she said.

"Why don't you think so?" Cody said.

"Because the cops know that creep moved two months ago."

"You know where to?"

"Maybe. What's in it for me?"

I produced a twenty. "You have an address?"

She reached out a pudgy brown hand, took the bill from my fingers, and left us at the door, then returned with a scrap of paper.

"Peters? Where the hell's that?" I said.

"East. Take Highway 4."

"How do you know where he moved?"

"My husband drives a tow truck. The city told Massie to get his car off the street." She pointed behind us at the junker Ford at the curb. "He called the company my husband works for. He wanted the car towed to his place in Peters."

"Thanks," I said.

"My husband told his boss he wouldn't go out there."

"Why not?"

Two high-pitched voices rose inside, a skirmish between children. She barked at them in Spanish, then said, "I have to go." The door closed.

We walked back to my truck. "Not much east of here. Farmland, mostly," I said, and entered the address into my GPS.

I drove back out to 5 and cut over to Route 4, and within a few minutes the city lights disappeared behind us. It was a dark night, the moon a sliver in the black sky. The narrow two-lane rose and fell, and there was no one on the road except us. Ten miles out, a low split-rail fence appeared on the left, and a mile later, I turned at the dim sign for Hewitt Road, drove north for a couple miles, past a gas station and a few closed stores on the main drag. Another couple turns and we were out in the farmland. My GPS said the destination was on the right. I pulled onto the dirt shoulder and parked under a large tree. Cody and I squinted at a house perhaps a quarter mile out. The windows were lit, and I could see where a gravel road led from the house to near where we'd stopped. There were no other lights visible from our vantage point, just blackness.

"Typical," Cody said.

"What?"

"White trash criminals love these type of small town, remote areas. Cheap land, small police presence. A perfect place to get off the grid."

"We're only twenty minutes from Stockton."

"Might as well be a hundred miles. I bet Stockton PD is drowning in gang activity."

I started my truck and drove a mile up the road to the next intersection. There was one other farmhouse, but that was the only building we saw. We turned around and drove back.

"Park here," Cody said, pointing to a clump of oaks off the road.

I stopped, and we got out and waded into the trees, to a spot with a clear view of the house where Jake Massie supposedly lived. I peered through a pair of binoculars at a row of Harleys and a couple cars parked in the dark driveway. Shapes moved inside the windows. I adjusted the focus and saw it was mostly men, but at least one woman.

"You hear that?" Cody said.

"Music?"

"Yeah. Sounds like Guns N' Roses."

"Here," I said, passing him the binoculars. "Looks like they're having a party."

Cody studied the house for a minute. "It's seven o'clock. Wonder how long it will go on?"

"Maybe all night."

"Someone will probably leave sooner than that. Go on a beer run."

"When they do, let's hope they turn toward town. We'll look mighty suspicious parked here."

He grunted and handed me the binoculars. In the dim light, I saw peeling paint around the windows and the warped garage door, and a plastic tarp covering a section of the roof. Further back from the house, I could barely make out a separate building, possibly a shed made of aluminum siding.

An hour went by. I called Candi and told her I was three hours from home, and to not wait up. "I'm on surveillance. It could take a while."

"Are you with Cody?"

"Yeah."

She paused. "Just come home in one piece, okay?"

"Don't worry, doll."

"Call me when you're heading back. I don't care what time it is."

"I promise."

When I hung up, I balled my hands in my coat pockets. The thin daylight heat had left with the sun, and the night air was sharp with cold. Not a single car came down the road. It was dead still, no rustling wind, no crickets chirping. The only sound was the faint bass notes coming from the house. We stood in the trees, passing the binoculars back and forth.

"They're coming outside," Cody said, the lenses pressed to his eyes. I saw light from the front door and heard a brief shout, then more voices and the shrill of a woman's laugh.

"They're getting on their bikes."

A moment later, a motorcycle headlight pierced the dark, followed by the rumbling throb of its engine. Another headlight flashed, and soon, the open land in front of the house was crisscrossed with beams of light. A car backed up and made a Y-turn, its headlights scanning the field just short of us. Within a minute, eight bikes and two sedans caravanned up the gravel road leading from the house. They rolled onto the street a hundred yards from where we were hidden in the lee of the trees, then they hit the throttles and roared off, black figures hunched on mechanical beasts, some steering one-handed, others low over the bars and accelerating, the sedans following behind as if relegated to the rear.

"We could follow them," I said as their taillights faded, "but this is too good to pass up."

"Great minds think alike," Cody said on his way back to my truck. He grabbed his gear bag, and I did likewise, then we set out at a jog toward the house.

No one had bothered turning off the lights—the place was fully lit. We came to the front door and stood in the yellow light from a naked bulb. The door was locked, so we went around to the back door. Also locked.

"Let's try the garage," I said. Along the side of the house was an obstacle course of strewn junk, the rusting guts of a dishwasher, car batteries, particle boards from a destroyed book case, dented propane tanks. The ground was soft, and I tried to stay on the weeds and not muddy my boots.

We came around the front, and I pulled on the corner of the garage door. The wood was rotted with termites, and the paint flaked off in my hand. Cody walked to the opposite side and heaved, and with a wretched screech, the door swung partially open. I clicked on my flashlight and ducked inside, where a gray Chevy pickup was parked. Around the truck were unpacked boxes, motorcycle parts, an upended bed frame, and a garbage container overfilled and reeking of spoiled food.

I looked into the open window of the pickup and saw dusty seats and a maze of spider webs strung between the steering wheel, dashboard, and door handles. "Is it open?" Cody said, pointing to the door to the house. I reached forward and turned the doorknob. Light spilled into the garage. Cody pulled the garage door shut and followed me inside.

My concern over leaving footprints became moot when I saw the old linoleum flooring was a mosaic of muddy tread marks and scuffs. The walls were in worse shape, the paint battered and streaked with grime around a series of fist-sized holes in the sheet rock. We walked into a kitchen and were greeted by roaches skittering across the floor and around the beer cans and overflowing ashtrays on the counters.

"A real five-star kind of guy," Cody said. "You see a telephone in this shithole?"

"Over there." I pointed to a room where a couple of torn couches faced a television.

Cody opened his bag. "I've got four bugs left," he said.

"I'm gonna see if I can find a computer." I walked down the hall and opened the door to a bedroom where a mattress lay on the floor, and the only furniture was a dresser with drawers half opened. Dirty clothes littered the room, and next to the mattress was a scattering of porno magazines, *Butt Fuck-o Rama, Anal Intruder*, and one titled, *Grab Your Ankles, Bitch!*

"What we got?" Cody's shadow fell over me from the doorway.

"Someone just can't get that prison sex out of their system, looks like."

"Nice," Cody said. He knelt down and stuck a bug under the dresser.

Across the hall was another bedroom, and this one was a bit less dismal. Someone had made a half-assed effort at making the bed, and the worn carpet was clear of laundry. A pair of black boots was tucked under a desk, atop which sat a notebook computer. I pressed the enter key with my knuckle, and the screen came to life. A shirtless Jake Massie on his Harley, his muscled torso covered in blue ink, a topless woman in cut-off jeans posing next to him.

I unzipped my bag and removed a wallet-sized black box with a thin USB cord attached at one end. I plugged the connector into the port on Massie's computer.

"What's that?" Cody said.

"External hard drive, software rigged to download the entire content on the PC."

"And I thought you weren't a gadget guy. How long will it take?"

"Depends. Twenty minutes, maybe longer." I opened the desk drawer and began leafing through a pile of papers. Bills, coupons, a white power pamphlet, a default notice for failure to make payment on a 2004 Chevy truck.

"I'm gonna go check on that shed in the back. Stick this under the desk somewhere." He handed me a tab not much larger than a penny.

"All right."

When I heard Cody go out the back door, I stood and scanned the contents of a closet on the other side of the room, found nothing interesting, then walked out to the main room. The carpet was stained, and the fireplace was filled with broken beer bottles. A bong sat on an end table next to a small glass pipe. I lifted the couch cushions and found bottle caps, a cut soda straw, and a used condom stuck to the frame.

In the kitchen, a window above the sink had a direct view to the two-lane highway. All was dark, the low horizon indecipherable from the fallen sky.

I went back out to the garage and shined my flashlight over its entirety. There was nothing to suggest Jake Massie or whoever else lived here had any interest in wilderness activities. No skis, backpacks, ropes, nothing of the sort. The only thing of interest was the gray pickup. Saint Alphonso had said a man in a dark, medium-sized pickup had dumped Terry Molina's body at Kiva beach. Problem was, this truck probably hadn't been driven for weeks, based on the spider webs coating the interior.

The single bathroom in the home was comparable to a construction site outhouse for cleanliness. I held my breath and checked the medicine cabinet. Nothing.

Just as I was wondering what was taking Cody so long, the back door banged open. "We got company, Dirt," Cody said. "Let's move."

"Shit." I quick-stepped over to the kitchen window and saw two bikes turn from the highway onto the gravel road. They hit the gas and the low rumble of their motors became audible. Swearing, I hurried to Massie's desk, disconnected my device from his computer, then ran out the back door behind Cody.

Staying low, we moved to a cluster of trees near the shed in the back. Once safely out of sight, we stopped and waited. But the two bikes did not continue to the house. Instead, they halted halfway along the gravel road.

"What are they doing?" Cody said.

I pulled my binoculars from my bag. I couldn't see much in the glare of their headlights, but then I saw one point with his hand, and they began turning around.

"I think they saw my rig." They had approached on the highway from the same direction they had left, so it was possible that, through the trees under which I'd parked, they'd caught the reflection off a taillight.

We both still wore shoulder holsters. Cody pulled his .357, the big bore oiled and shining in the moonlight.

"Go," he said, then we sprinted out of the brush, leapt a narrow culvert, and ran full out down a faint trail bordered by tall grass. The highway was a quarter mile away, by my estimate, a distance I ran in just over a minute in college.

It didn't take us much longer than that to reach the trees along the road. The two motorcycles had pulled up thirty seconds previous, their lights facing down the highway in long streaks. Through the branches, I saw the silhouette of one man, still one second, holding a blade the next, then he was gone behind my truck.

I pulled my Beretta as I crunched through leaves and twigs, then fired into the sky. A second later, Cody fired, the blast from his pistol shaking the ground.

One of the bikers had not dismounted, and bent low over the bars, he grabbed his throttle and roared off. The second man, who I suspected was about to slit my tires, rose into view and ran for his bike. Just as I reached my rear bumper, his motor choked to life and gravel spit from his rear tire. He hit the paved road, and I fixed him in the sights of my automatic and felt my finger tighten on the trigger.

"Whoa there," Cody said behind me, panting. He reached out and pushed my straightened arm downward.

8

We headed away from that small town toward Stockton and ran into no bikers on the way. Wherever they were, we saw no sign of them. Good for us, I suppose. Confronting Jake Massie alone was one thing. If he was surrounded by his gang, a different story. Maybe bad for us, maybe bad for him and his gang. Probably bad news for everyone.

"You weren't going to blow that guy off his bike, were you, Dirt?"

"I considered shooting his tire."

"Best you didn't. Better to wait and see what we learn from the bugs and that computer."

I took the entrance to 5 heading north. "Do I hear the voice of restraint?"

Cody lit a cigarette and rolled down the window. "It's a matter of choosing which tactic makes the most sense. I don't get in anyone's face unless there's something to be gained."

"Really."

"Yeah, really. That's the difference between us. You're just as violent as me, maybe more. But you need to get mad first. And then, you're out of control."

I glanced over, and Cody was staring out the windshield. "And you have perfect control of your temper?"

"Nope, never claimed that."

"What are you saying, then?"

"Massie threatened you. It's only natural to be pissed."

"I wasn't going to shoot the biker."

"You had that look on your face."

I shook my head. "Next subject," I said. "What did you see at that shed?"

"It was locked up like Fort Knox. No windows. Smelled like ammonia and rotten eggs. So thick I could taste it. Made my eyes burn."

"A meth lab."

"No doubt."

"You get a transmitter down?"

"Yeah, in one of the shrubs near the house. I'll e-mail you the audio files tomorrow when they come through."

Cody rolled the window down farther and flicked his cigarette into the slipstream. His hand was covered with dried mud, dirt caked under the fingernails.

"What did you do, bury it?"

"Huh? Bury what?"

"The transmitter."

"Oh. No, I just hit some mud when I planted it."

We drove in silence for a few minutes, the freeway a swirling river of red and white light. "You want to stop for a drink?" Cody said.

"No. I've got a long drive in front of me."

"So do I. Why don't we get a hotel, drink some beers, blow off some steam? You look like you could use it."

"Not tonight."

"Why not? You worried if you get drunk you'll want to go back to Massie's house and wait for him?"

I shot a sharp glance at Cody, and he looked back and chuckled. "I know you better than you think, Dirt."

I shrugged and widened my eyes, trying to relieve the tension across my forehead. He reached out and patted my shoulder. "Go home and be with your woman tonight. Get a good night's rest. And if you see Jake Massie in Tahoe again, call me."

I pulled into the restaurant where Cody's truck was parked. He collected his gear and got out.

"You promise me that. If you see him, call me." Cody stood outside my window, peering in, his head like a buffalo's. His amused expression was gone, his eyes hard as rivets under the V of his brow.

"Okay, partner," I said.

***

By the time I reached Sacramento, my eyes kept closing, and I turned the radio up loud and drove with the cold wind blowing in my face. Finally, I pulled off the freeway to a gas station and bought a large coffee. I sat in the parking lot, sipping from the steaming cup. The painkiller the doctor had injected hours ago had worn off, and the wound on my arm was a stinging ache.

I closed my eyes and felt myself drifting off. I didn't fight it, and sleep came quickly. Almost immediately, I dreamt. Twenty minutes passed before I woke, the dream still vivid in my mind. I was in a bar, my ex-wife on the edge of my vision silently chiding me, and at a table sat a doctor, my father, and Cody. I felt their conversation was of little consequence, then my father was next to me. He didn't look distorted as he sometimes did in my dreams. His face was just as I remembered it, his nose broad and straight, the mustache below black and just beginning to gray. When he spoke, his dark eyes became almost square where the skin creased at the sides.

"Never let them get behind you, son," he said. I waited for more, but he was gone.

Fully awake, I spent some time staring out my windshield at nothing. Then, I gulped my coffee and hit the gas into the black night. I drove hard, and my mind was clear. I did not invest myself in conjecture over what the bugs Cody had planted on Mike Zayas and at Jake Massie's house might reveal. Nor did I worry about the threat Massie and the Aryan Brotherhood posed. As if a child, I felt safe and secure by my father's presence. For reasons I wouldn't consider, I no longer felt grief over the fact he'd been ambushed and murdered. Instead, a quiet calm replaced the sense of loss. And behind that, something else, something deep and relentless and ugly and accessible not at my request but accessible nonetheless, and waiting, always waiting.

***

When I woke the next morning, the bed was still warm where Candi had been sleeping. I sat up and saw it was past eight o'clock. From the kitchen, I heard noises, then Candi walked into the bedroom. She was wearing tan slacks, low heels, and a purple turtleneck sweater. Probably pretty standard apparel for a teacher, but on her, it looked sensational.

"Waking up, sleepyhead?"

"Yeah." I yawned and swung my legs out from the blankets.

"I made coffee."

"Thanks, babe."

"You're really putting in some hours."

"I know. I could use a break."

"My god, what happened to your arm?"

I touched my forearm where the bandage covered the stitches. "Nothing. Just a little cut."

"Are we still going skiing tomorrow?"

I stood, pulled on a pair of sweats and a T-shirt, and remembered it was already Thursday. "Absolutely. Then, I'm taking you to dinner."

I went to the bathroom and brushed my teeth, and when I came out to the kitchen, she had gathered her purse and coat and was on her way to the garage. She stopped and set down her things down and wrapped her arms around me, her head on my shoulder. Then, she looked up, her eyes on mine, and said, "I know you said not to worry about you. But I do."

"We'll have fun this weekend, I promise."

I walked with her to her car and watched her back out and drive away. When she was gone, I took a cup of coffee and walked the perimeter of my property. I hiked through the snow along the fence bordering my neighbor's house and followed it past the meadow and to the opposite side of my home where I'd stacked cut firewood under an awning I'd built. I continued through my side yard out to the driveway and picked up the plastic-bagged newspaper lying there. A few flakes fell from the sky. The air was gray and heavy. Two houses down, a truck backed from a garage and drove past where I stood. Once the sound of the motor faded, the neighborhood was quiet. After a minute I went inside.

Two cups of coffee later, I was lifting weights in my garage, alternating sets of bunch press and curls with a ninety-pound bar. When I went back inside, my cell was ringing.

"Check your e-mail," Cody said. "I sent the audio files. I'm on my way to the courthouse. Didn't have a chance to listen to them."

"Okay."

"Any sign of Massie?"

"No, but I wouldn't expect there to be. He's probably at home sleeping off a hangover."

"Keep your eyes open. Don't give him the benefit of the doubt."

"I'm not."

We hung up, and I went to my desk and saw the e-mail Cody had sent. There were two attachments, one titled *Zayas* and the other *Massie's dump*.

For the next two hours, I listened to the sounds picked up by the bug Cody had stuck to the back of Mike Zayas' belt. The program allowed the option of skipping past periods without decipherable voices, but I decided to just let the tape play. I listened to Zayas display his proficiency at both Spanish and English profanity as he ripped into his hired help for letting a couple of gringo amateurs kick their asses. He fired one of the men, who I suspected was the big fellow Cody had put in a bear hug and squeezed nearly unconscious. A few minutes of silence went by, then there were some clinking noises followed by loud gaseous eruptions punctuated by splashes and grunts and sighs. This went on for what seemed like a long time, until I was laughing and drying my eyes and thinking how I might use the section for a prank phone call on Cody.

Finally, the toilet flushed, and thumping music replaced the bathroom comedy. Then, a door closed, and the music became faint. Next, the distinct beep of a cell phone.

"Have you sold your inventory yet?" Zayas said.

The reply came back scratchy and barely audible. Zayas had the phone on speaker mode. I paused the program and adjusted the volume and tone controls, experimenting until I could just make out the other voice on the call.

"The market's flooded with cheap drugs. The spades downtown are stocked up and not buying."

"What about Del Paso Heights?"

"Same story there, and in south Sac."

"And you think it's coming from Stockton?"

"Pretty goddamn sure. Two different sources report seeing them in town. My brother made it clear last time we talked he'd fuck me any way he could."

"A big shipment arrives tomorrow, and one more next week," Zayas said. "We need to keep the cash flowing. That's what I committed to the cartel. You understand what that means, don't you?"

"We need to fix the problem."

"That's right, my friend. And fix it permanently."

"I'll see what I can do."

"No, Virgil, you *do* what you have to do."

"I hear you. As a plan B, we also know some people in the Tahoe-Reno area."

"Good, but don't let that distract you from fixing the problem *here*."

"It will be taken care of."

"It better," Zayas said, and the conversation ended.

A few minutes of dead time passed before a knocking sound broke the silence.

"Come in."

"*Señor Zayas*," a male voice said.

"*Si?*"

The voice continued in Spanish. "I want to let you know about the biker, Roscoe."

"What about him?"

"He was talking with the men who were here. Before the trouble, Roscoe went with one into the VIP room. After, he spoke with them outside, before they left."

"You saw this yourself?"

"I did."

"What did he say to them?"

"I don't know, boss. But I think it's about Valerie who used to work here. That's all he talks about."

Zayas grunted. "Is there anything else?"

"That's all."

"Go then."

The door closed, and the cell phone beeps sounded again.

"One more thing, Virgil," Zayas said. "Your boy, Roscoe."

"What about him?"

"He got all sweet on one of the dancers here. Then, she went missing. Turns out she was murdered up in Lake Tahoe."

"So?"

"A couple private investigators came here asking questions. Roscoe's been talking to them."

"So what?"

"So, since she's got killed, Roscoe's been worthless, and he's got diarrhea of the mouth."

"I'll talk to him."

"No, you retire him. I can't afford to have anyone with a big mouth involved in my business."

"You won't see him again."

"Good."

Zayas sighed, and papers shuffled for a few minutes before I heard a clunking sound and a different style of beeps.

"Send Celestina in here," Zayas said.

Thirty seconds later, a quiet knock, and Zayas said, "Come in." A pause, then, "Such a pretty little thing. Come here, around my desk."

"What would you like me to do?"

The sound of a zipper. "I want you to wrap your pretty red lips around my cock and suck it. And then, I'll take you to the couch and spread your legs wide, and I'll fuck your tight pussy. Are you ready to get fucked?"

"I…if that is what you wish."

"You don't sound too enthusiastic, Celestina."

"I'm sorry, Mr. Zayas. I'm on my period."

"I don't care. Get on your knees."

I didn't have it in me to listen and began fast forwarding. The program stopped at small bits of voice. At one point, Zayas instructed her to lick his balls, and at another told her, "Don't just lie there, wrap your legs around me." After twenty minutes, the recording ended abruptly. Maybe the bug fell off Zayas's belt and was damaged, or perhaps the battery died or the time maxed out.

I rose and checked my watch. It was noon. The air in my office felt fouled, and I was struck with a sudden urge to be outdoors. I went out to my deck and stood on the redwood planks and looked out over the meadow. The day was crisp with cold, and the sky had cleared above the 5000-foot tall, snow-covered ridge circling the valley. After a few minutes, I locked my house and drove out to 50 toward Zeke's.

The lunch crowd looked good for a Thursday. Waitresses hurried in and out of the kitchen, juggling plates of barbequed chicken and brisket sandwiches smothered in hickory sauce. The dining room was noisy, and folks were eating at the bar and the small cocktail tables. The big TV in the corner was tuned to a basketball game, the drone of the commentators lost in the hubbub.

I said hello to Liz and Ron, a young bartender I skied with occasionally. He brought me a nonalcoholic beer, then I walked back to the kitchen and waved at Zak Pappas, who was still carefully sober and drug free and working hard running the place.

"I'm gonna look over the bar receipts," I said.

"Go for it." He moved sizzling meat around the grill with a pair of tongs, his motions fluid and precise. The fire-pit smoked and crackled, the fan above sucking the smoke into an aluminum cowl.

I retrieved the ledgers from Zak's upstairs office, the furniture and cluttered shelves unchanged from when his father Zeke owned the establishment. Down the creaky stairs and back at the bar, I took a seat in the shadowy nook under the TV and spent fifteen minutes checking the numbers.

Satisfied the tills weren't being tapped to any large degree, I rubbed my eyes and watched the lunch crowd. A group of several out-of-towners were sitting at tables on what used to be the stage. The men were clean-shaven and boisterous, the women pretty and wearing designer coats and scarves. Liz and another waitress brought out their lunch order, racks of ribs and burgers for the fellows, salads for the ladies.

After a minute, I went and asked Zak to throw a chicken breast on the fire for me. Then, I sat on a chair in the back of the kitchen and thought about what I'd learned from the recording. I had hoped taking a break from it might allow my subconscious to hit on some angle relevant to Valerie Horvachek's murder. Something between the lines, a hidden clue. Because at face value, the tape had revealed very little I didn't already know or suspect.

That Zayas was involved in cartel drug trafficking was neither surprising nor particularly illuminating. I was also not surprised he used his female employees, at least the ones from south of the border, as his personal sex slaves. More meaningful might be the escalating conflict between the Blood Bastards and the War Dogs. Roscoe, whose standing in his gang would now be marginalized, or worse, had tried to convince me the War Dogs may have killed Valerie for the drugs Roscoe had fronted her, or simply because they knew Roscoe liked her. Neither premise held water. Valerie had not been robbed, and no gangbanger would kill a rival's girlfriend just because the gangs were feuding. If the War Dogs killed Valerie, there would have to be something else involved. Maybe a personal vendetta or some other motivation.

There were a few more scraps, things that might provide direction. Zayas had spoken to a man named Virgil, who I assumed was Virgil Massie, Jake's estranged older brother. Virgil claimed he knew people in the Tahoe-Reno area, which could suggest a connection with Nick Galanis. Pretty thin, but something to keep in mind.

"Dan, what else you want?" Zak placed a piece of chicken in a Styrofoam container.

"Baked beans, coleslaw, and throw in some steamed broccoli."

"You got it, buddy."

I thanked him and walked outside with my to-go box and drove home, where I ate and then cued up the second recording, the one from Jake Massie's house. The first voice was time stamped at 8:30 P.M.

"Hey, man. We're at your house. You're not gonna believe this shit, but someone just shot at us. No, I'm not fuckin' kidding. There was a truck parked out front on the road. Gerhard and me went to check it out, and two shots were fired. Huh? No, we ain't hit. But they were close, like fuckin' close. It wasn't like anyone huntin' squirrels across the street, either, I'm talking sounded like a thirty ought six, or a nine mil. We weren't packin' you know, so we boogied like a motherfucker, came back about five minutes later, and the truck was gone. No, it was dark, never saw anyone. What, I can barely hear you, man. The truck? A big pickup, maybe one of those Jap rides, or a Ford, I don't fuckin' know. Hey look, the hell you expect us to do?

"The front door was locked. I'll check the others. Right. I'll go check out back too. Call you back in five minutes.

"Shit. Give the pipe a damn break, Gerhard. Grab that big flashlight in the drawer and come on."

The recording skipped forward seven minutes. Then, "The lab looks cool, Jake. No one's messed with it. No one's been in the house either, that I can tell. Right, we'll wait here."

For the next hour, I listened to a ceaseless stream of inane babble, clearly alcohol and drug induced. The conversation went in circles and was hard to follow, but the two men finally decided a couple of Mexicans from the Blood Bastards had likely fired the shots. Their blather then shifted to issues involving drug dealing turf, and their ideas on putting the hurt on the 'jungle bunnies and beaners.' They discussed the best methods for exterminating their enemies, debating over explosives, poison, and machine gun attacks. Then, the subject switched to torture, as in "You know what would really make my dick hard? Branding a spic with swastikas and then video him admitting that all Mexicans are good for is performing cheap labor for the white man. Then, tie him to a bumper and drag him until there ain't no brown skin left on him."

At 9:40, a door slammed, and a new voice spoke, one I recognized as Jake Massie's. "Tell me about the truck."

"Shit, we barely got to it before those shots. I was gonna slash the tires."

"And you didn't even see what make it was?"

"I think it was a Ford," the other man said.

"Yeah, looked like a Ford."

"You said it could have been a Jap truck," Massie said.

"Yeah, they make rip-off copies of Fords and Chevys."

"You fuckin' guys," Massie sighed.

"My opinion, it was probably the Bastards. It looks like your brother figured out we fucked his territory."

"Do yourself a favor, Strick. Don't think too hard. From now on, we don't leave this place empty. Someone needs to be here at all times."

"You got it, Jake."

Music came on, loud death metal, and it obscured any conversation for the remainder of the recording.

For a few minutes, I pondered what I'd heard. If any of it had the vaguest connection to Valerie's murder, it escaped me. The good news was Jake Massie might soon have his hands full with the trouble brewing between him and his brother. Whether Massie believed the truck belonged to the Blood Bastards, or if he was suspicious it was mine, I couldn't tell.

I exited the program and plugged in the external hard drive I'd connected to Massie's computer. The device whirred, and a file menu appeared on my screen. I clicked on the Word icon and found three documents. The first was titled "White Power Now," and it was thirty pages of racist propaganda, some of it well-written and trying for a scientific tone, but then, it dissolved into a slew of racial slurs that blamed nonwhites for all the world's problems. I scanned it for five minutes, then opened the next doc, one apparently written by Massie, titled 'War Dogs Manifest.' It read like a standard version of gang membership rules, all about loyalty to fellow members and secrecy and a pledge to never cooperate with the police. There was also a section specifying that since Jews, Hispanics, Blacks, and all nonwhites were inferior, crimes against them were part of the natural order and to be encouraged.

The third doc was a letter Massie had apparently begun writing to his brother:

Virgil,
We been thru a lot of shit together, you and me. I sometimes think about back in Tennessee. You riding that blue bike with the knobby tires. What happened to that bike? Was it stole or did the old man sell it for beer money? At least you had a bike. We had it rough then. Life's a bitch and then you die, huh? Except you never did hard time, that's why you don't understand things like I do. The old man always said you were the smart one and I was dumb as a rock. But he knew I was stronger than you. He always knew that. And he knew you were weak.

I never told you about my first week in the pen. You don't understand my ways because you ain't been thru what I have. You get jumped by the Mexican mafia or the black gorillas, you learn things. The light comes on, and the truth comes out. It ain't hard to see once you been thru it.

The letter stopped there, unfinished.

Next, I went to a file that linked to his e-mail account. Most of the activity was exchanges with four different women. After reading through dozens of messages, it became clear the women had contacted Massie through some sort of prison dating service. Much of the correspondence had pictures attached, mostly of the women posing nude in lurid detail.

It was almost happy hour when I finished up. Good thing, because I wasn't happy, and I needed a drink. Not a single thing in Massie's computer, or in any of the tapes I'd spent hours listening to, suggested either biker gang knew Nick Galanis or was involved in Valerie's murder. The only mention of Valerie was by a Suave employee talking to Zayas about Roscoe. Zayas's response did not indicate he was complicit or even interested.

I paced around my house, wondering whether the biker angle was a waste of time, or if the clues were there, but just hovering beyond my mental grasp. I sat and rubbed my jaw and tried to search through the jumble of information in my head. I'd learned a lot about the Blood Bastards, the War Dogs, and Mike Zayas. Unfortunately, none of it was getting me anywhere, and I'd just burned a complete workday reaching that conclusion.

At that moment, my phone rang, and I cringed when I saw it was the general calling.

"Investigations."

"It's Ray Horvachek, Reno. I was expecting to see another report yesterday."

"Sorry, I was working late last night."

"Spending the time productively?"

I paused. "I don't know yet."

"What's that supposed to mean?"

"I'm looking into Valerie's employment at the Suave Gentlemen's Club, and her relationship with a biker gang that frequents the establishment."

"Do you think these people are involved in her murder?"

"I have suspicions, but no evidence."

"What about your other leads?"

"I'm still working them. I'll let you know."

"Make sure you do. I want to make sure I'm not pouring money down a piss hole."

"I'll send you a report tonight."

"I'm looking forward to it."

We hung up, and I poured the last of the coffee from this morning's pot and heated it in the microwave. I went back to my desk and drank it halfway down, then assembled my notes on the case, both handwritten and typed. There were almost thirty names and numbers from Valerie's phone. There were also the names of four parties who had rented properties at Camp Richardson during New Year's Eve, potential witnesses to the dumping of Terry's body. In addition, I had the list of Blood Bastards and War Dogs members that Albert Bigelow had provided. Other miscellaneous things were scrawled in my notebook, like a reminder to reach Valerie's friend Christie Tedford, and also to interview Valerie's counselor in Sacramento. Also, a note about following up on snowmobile licenses. And a scribbled notion to interview Nick Galanis' partner, Greg McMann.

Smokey appeared at the doorway and started mewing. I picked him up and opened a packet of cat food. The kitten ate while I stood in the kitchen finishing my coffee. When he finished eating, he jumped onto my shin and began climbing my jeans. He made it to my knee before I pried him free and held him for a bit. Then, I called Marcus Grier's cell.

"Hello, Marcus. Got a minute?" It had just turned five o'clock.

"What's up?"

"Have there been any developments on Galanis and the two murders?"

"Not much. Galanis issued a formal statement saying he'll fully cooperate with all police agencies involved, and Douglas County resources will be focused a hundred percent on the case."

"He's trying to position it as if he has nothing to hide."

"Maybe he doesn't."

"I still think he may be taking dirty money from a biker gang."

"Have you found any evidence of this?"

"No," I admitted. "Just a theory."

"You come up with something better, let me know."

"I want to talk to Galanis."

Grier paused for a long moment, then he sighed. "At this point, I don't see why not," he said. "Doubt it'll do much good, though."

"We'll see. How about your detective, Worley? Is he getting anywhere?"

"He's working it. Listen, I'd love to pour over every detail of the case with you, but I gotta go."

"Talk to you later, then."

The squeak of the garage door told me Candi was home. I went to the garage and opened the door to her idling Subaru and took from her hand the large bag she carried to work.

"Thank you, Dan."

"Sure, babe. I'm gonna make us a homemade pizza tonight."

"Sounds great."

"Everything good at the college?"

She began telling a story about changes she was implementing to the art curriculum. I made a drink, she loaded her pipe, and we chatted while I spread tomato sauce on a premade crust and began shredding a ball of mozzarella. The oven heated the kitchen, and I looked over the counter at Candi and felt a surge of overwhelming affection. She had come into my life and brought brightness and warmth to my solitary existence. The sordid pall my work sometimes cast over me evaporated in her presence. The year before I met her now seemed like someone else's life, a long stretch of bar time broken by occasional one-nighters with women often more drunk and lonely than I was. I did not miss those awkward mornings after, fraught with furtive glances and sheepish regret.

It had been entirely different with Candi. We'd met out in Elko during a case. Our courtship had started tentatively, on my part anyway, but quickly evolved to the point where she was in my thoughts constantly. The second time we'd slept together, we began talking of her moving into my place. Though our careers were at opposite ends of the spectrum, we seemed to view life through the same lens. This I accounted to our similar backgrounds: we were both raised in families supported by men who worked in law enforcement.

While Candi was grounded, proper, and intelligent, she was also light-hearted, naughty, and quite willing to be silly. These contradictions were the basis of her personality, and though I tried to keep my emotions in check, I found her intoxicating and irresistible. I could no longer deny I wanted her to be a permanent part of my life.

Amid these feelings, or because of them, I had a growing trepidation over the danger she could be exposed to as the result of my work. Above all, I would not let her be at risk. Whatever I did, I would not let that happen.

The evening passed, and our conversation was light with casual familiarity. We ended up in the bedroom, made love, and dressed again for a continuation of happy hour. I was pleasantly buzzed when we came to bed to sleep, but the weight in my stomach was still lurking, like a roughly idling motor that begged for the throttles to be thrown wide open.

9

Clouds had moved in and there was no hint of blue when I checked the sky the next morning. I let Candi sleep in, took my coffee outside, and peered up at the distant ridgeline. The ski resort gondola heading up the mountain disappeared into a white mist.

By half past eight, we'd loaded our gear into my truck, and at nine sharp, we caught the day's first chair up the California side of the resort. Candi was wearing pink boarder pants and a lime green coat. On her snowboard, a yellow smiley face sticker winked at me.

"Looks icy," she said, looking down. The steep mogul run beneath us was shiny and hacked into sharp angles.

"It probably melted yesterday and froze overnight," I said. We both studied the snow and frowned.

"Don't worry, we'll make the best of it."

"Probably better at the top," she replied.

We reached the crest of the ridge and glided off into the flat light toward the chair that would take us to the summit. The lack of contrast between the sky and the snow was disorienting. If it was much worse up top, we might have to wait and hope for the clouds to lift.

Huddled against the cold in the summit chair, I put my arm around Candi and told myself to enjoy the day regardless of the conditions. Skiing was a sport where the weather could make or break any day. Blue sky powder days were every skier's dream, but today was the other side of the coin.

When the chair neared the summit, I told Candi to turn left, toward the Nevada side. There were runs there that didn't get much direct sun, so the snow would likely be in better shape. I skated along a flat trail, towing Candi with a pole. We dropped off the trail into the trees, and the visibility improved. The snow was chopped up but not hard, and we got in some good turns. Then, we came out onto a groomed run at speed, and I almost caught an edge and went down.

"Not bad," Candi breathed, as we headed back to the chair. More people were arriving, but the resort was still relatively empty.

"Be careful on the groomed. There're icy patches."

"I saw you almost eat it."

"What? I never wipe out."

"Super stud." She grinned, her teeth white against her flush skin.

We continued to find decent snow, until around 10:30, a lift line developed, and we moved on, deeper into Nevada. Traversing across the mountainside, we came around a wide bend and stopped to take in the view of the desert four thousand feet below. We were not far from the spot where I'd ducked the boundary ropes the morning I'd found Valerie Horvachek. But I'd promised myself I would not think about that today.

It was nearing lunchtime when we were on a broad groomed run, and I saw a man lose it on some icy bumps aside the piste. His tips crossed, and he got turned backward, tried desperately to save it, but a mogul caught him, and he somersaulted and lost his skis. After slamming off a bump, he slid to a stop, cursing and holding his leg. I gathered his skis and came up behind him.

"You okay?" I asked.

"Jesus, my knee. Oh shit." He was a middle-aged guy, his face twisted in pain.

I jammed his skis into the hard-pack, forming an X to signal he was injured.

"How bad?" I said.

He sat up and put both hands on his knee and tried to move it. "Bad," he said.

"We'll go get ski patrol," Candi said.

We skied down, and I told the lift operator a man was down and would probably need a toboggan. He spoke into a walkie-talkie, and we got on the chair and headed back to the summit.

Not ten minutes had passed, but three patrollers in red jackets had already reached the injured man when we came out of the trees above where he'd wiped out. Two of the patrollers knelt talking to the man while the third maneuvered a rescue gurney into place.

"Give me a second, Candi. I want to say hello to these fellows." I pushed off and made a wide turn and skidded to a stop near a patroller who had just stood. He had white sideburns and was in his fifties.

"I was the one who reported it down at the chair. He'll be all right?"

"Sure, thanks. We got it under control." The man smiled, his skin tan and sun-wrinkled. The other two patrollers glanced up at me. Both in their early twenties. One gave me a shrug while his partner secured the unfortunate skier to the gurney. His motions were sure, and he moved with the confidence of an experienced hand. Just as I realized I was staring, he looked over at me.

"Can I help you?" he said.

***

We had lunch outdoors on the large deck at the mid-mountain lodge. Rock and roll played from speakers mounted high, and people sat among their gloves and goggles and ate twelve-dollar burgers and drank beer. I ordered minestrone soup, part of my commitment to a healthier diet.

"What are you thinking?" Candi said.

I looked up from my food and realized I'd been ignoring her. "I think I promised myself I'd not think about my case, and I'm breaking that promise. I think I've got fixated on these bikers, and that's distracting me from where I should be focusing my effort."

"I thought you were convinced the bikers were involved."

"I'm not anymore."

"Do you have a new theory?"

I looked out beyond the railing at the skiers and boarders coming off the slope and merging into the roped aisles to the chair lift. Like a confused jumble funneled into an orderly sequence. "I'm starting to think Valerie and Terry were killed only because they slept with Nick Galanis," I said. "Not because of anything having to do with bikers or drugs."

She looked at me quizzically.

Afterward, we skied a couple more runs, but the visibility grew worse, and we called it day before two o'clock. When we got home, Candi left to go shopping, and I went to my office and pulled out the copy of the police report the general had given me. I reread the sections describing Douglas County's investigative work. They had done a seemingly thorough job interviewing potential witnesses. That was always the first tactic in an investigation. Find an eyewitness, and it was like knocking a hole in a dike. Soon the hole would expand, and information would start to gush.

Except no witnesses had been discovered, with the exception of Saint Alphonso, a homeless derelict who had claimed only to glimpse a dark pickup truck and a nondescript man wearing a beanie. And that was in connection with Terry's murder, not Valerie's.

I went back to the section where Galanis claimed to call Valerie a cab, which she left his residence to wait for. Although she had a heavy coat, it seemed odd she would not wait inside. Maybe she was anxious to leave Galanis' townhouse. Maybe she no longer felt welcome there, as in, *thanks for the piece of ass, honey, now show yourself out.*

I needed to contact Tahoe Taxi. Both Valerie and Terry had left Galanis' home to wait for a cab, which showed up and, finding no customer, left. Or did something else happen? Maybe the taxi driver was a predator, targeting sexy blonde women. Maybe the opportunity to kill Valerie and Terry, two women alone late at night, was too tempting to pass up. Was it the same cab driver that was supposed to pick up both Valerie and Terry? If so, did that cabbie own a dark pickup or a snowmobile? Or maybe he delivered the women to someone who did. Could be two killers involved.

Two killers. Possibly working together on both murders. Or could be two killers working independently, meaning Valerie and Terry were not killed by the same person, and there was no connection between their deaths. There was little commonality in where their bodies had been disposed—one in a remote, difficult to reach place, the other in a very conspicuous, public spot. But both had been strangled, and both of their purses had been recovered intact, save for their driver's licenses. And both had just had a sexual encounter at Nick Galanis' home.

Many possibilities, many maybes. Very little solid information. There was still the perplexing matter of how Valerie's body could have ended up in such inaccessible location. And there was also the elephant in the room, the obvious conclusion that somehow Nick Galanis must be linked to both murders.

I found the address for Tahoe Taxi on the Internet. Five minutes later, I was shaved and wearing the black coat I favored when trying to look official. I drove six miles west through town, past the timeshare resorts and hotels and tourist shopping complexes. When I reached the juncture of 50 and Highway 89 that locals referred to as the Y, I turned right and parked in front of a modest stand-alone building that had once been the business office for a used car dealership. A half-dozen silver vehicles were parked in the small, chain-link enclosed lot behind the building.

Inside the glass door, two desks sat in an office cluttered with newspapers and magazines. Behind one desk was a man with thick glasses popular in my parents' generation. His hair was black and definitely dyed, and he wore a plaid wool shirt. At the other desk sat a woman in a yellow dress, the bangs of her plastic blonde hair in a line midway up her forehead. A married couple in the latter part of middle age—transplants from some other state, not native Californians. They both looked at me with wary expressions. Maybe thought I was a salesman.

"Do you need a taxi?" the woman said.

"No. I'm looking into the deaths of two women who were supposed to be picked up by one of your cabs."

"Oh," said the man. "Yes, that. Terrible thing. We've spoke to the police twice already."

"I've been hired by one of the girl's parents. Can you answer a couple questions for me?"

They looked at each other, then the man said, "I didn't get your name."

I handed him a card. "Private investigator, huh?" he said. "Okay. Take a seat, mister." I lowered myself into a wooden chair in the corner.

"I doubt this will help you much, but this is the same as I told the police. It was my brother who went out to that condo on Christmas Eve and New Year's. He's our graveyard driver. Same thing both times. He showed up, no one was there, so he left."

"Did he call the number that called in for the cab?"

"I believe he did."

"Did he see anything unusual either night?"

"Not that he told me. You'd have to talk to him yourself."

"How can I reach him?"

He looked at his watch. "He'll be here in half an hour."

I left and drove down the street to a Mexican cantina and drank a soda while watching a sports talk show I couldn't hear. A group of young people with bright eyes sat at a nearby table drinking margaritas and shots. Their hair was mussed, their faces red from cold and wind. They bantered loudly, exaggerating tales of big air and wipeouts and injuries and epic moments. I sipped slowly, and when my glass was empty, I headed back to the Tahoe Taxi office.

The man and his wife were both at their desks talking on the phone. I sat and waited in the chair in the corner, and a minute later, the glass door opened. The fellow that hobbled in was around sixty, his face fleshy and mottled beneath his sparse hair. He had watery blue eyes and wore an elastic back brace around his thick midsection.

"Hello, sir. I'm Dan Reno, private investigations."

"Oh," he said. "You're here about those poor girls?"

I nodded and stood to offer him my chair.

"Thank you. I'm Art Crume."

"Hi, Art. I'd like to ask you about Christmas and New Year's Eve."

"Okay, young man," he said. He shifted his weight on the chair and winced.

"Can you describe what happened when you showed up at Nick Galanis' condo on December 23rd?"

"It was actually the 24th. I arrived at 2:15 in the morning."

"Right."

"I waited ten minutes in front of the driveway. The lights were out in the condo. When no one showed, I called the number we received the call from. A man answered, said he didn't know where the customer was. He apologized and hung up."

"Did you see anybody at all while you were waiting? Any people, or cars?"

"Nothing."

"How about when you arrived at the complex?"

"When I pulled in, I passed a car leaving."

"What kind of car?"

He shook his head. "I don't remember. It was dark, and its lights were in my eyes."

"Was it a pickup?"

He shook his big head again, folds of skin creasing at his neck. "Could have been, I suppose. The lights seemed high, so maybe it was."

"When you talked to the police, did they ask you about this?"

"Yes. And I told them the same as I just told you."

"All right. Let's talk about New Year's. What time did you get the call?

"1:55 A.M. Arrived there at 2:05. Same thing as Christmas Eve. I called the number after ten minutes, and the man said he didn't know what happened to the customer. Said she should be out there waiting."

"He didn't come out to talk to you, huh?"

"No, sir. The cop, Galanis, right? He was drunk, I believe. Sounded like I woke him."

"Hmm. Did you see anyone while you were there?"

"Not a soul. But I do remember a vehicle this time. It was parked on the side of the road when I turned into the condos. Wouldn't have noticed, except the headlights came on behind me. I saw it drive off in my mirror."

"What kind of vehicle?"

"A Ford Ranger," he said without hesitation. "I worked for years in the repair business. I know cars."

"Did you see the driver?"

"No."

"How about the color? Or any other detail?"

"Dark blue or maybe black. A 2000 model, I think.

"Any other detail you remember? Any dents?"

"Not that I could see. It was a regular cab model. Not a deluxe cab."

"Are you sure it was a 2000?"

"No, it could have been a '98 through 2002. The bodies are very similar."

I noticed the woman was no longer on the phone and was now listening to our conversation. I felt awkward standing over the cabbie and wished there was somewhere to sit so we could be at eye level.

"Do you mind if I ask you a couple personal questions, Art?"

He looked surprised, then smiled. "Why not? I doubt you'll offend me."

"I'll try not to. Are you married?"

"Not anymore. Wife passed on. Cancer got her."

"I'm sorry to hear that. How about kids?"

"Got two. Grown and raised. Son got his college degree and works for a company in Texas. My daughter is married back in Ohio."

"You're from Ohio?

"Spent most of my life in Akron. Moved here to be with my brother a few years back. Thought I might even try some skiing, funny as that sounds."

"Bad knee?"

"Knees are okay. Back and hip are the problems. Probably have to get the hip replaced here sometime, if it doesn't improve."

"You got a good chiropractor?"

"I've been seeing Gordy Chapman over on 50. He's got me in traction. Seems to help."

It was silent for a moment, then I handed him my card. "Please call me if you remember anything else," I said.

He handed me his card in return. "Call me if you ever need a cab."

***

You ran into all sorts in interviews. Criminals didn't usually cooperate much, regardless of their guilt or innocence, unless there's something in it for them. Then, there were those who didn't want to get involved because they feared being dragged into trouble. Conversely, I'd interviewed people who knew nothing but wanted to be my buddy and spewed forth all sorts of baseless conjectures. And occasionally, you got those wracked with guilt and anxiety, who would confess to anything.

Then, there were types like the cabbie Art Crume. Upfront and innocuous, apparently with nothing to hide. It was hard to imagine him being involved in the murders, hard to imagine him physically capable. Or maybe that was exactly what he wanted me to think.

I drove back up 50, and about a mile before Zeke's, I pulled into a parking lot serving a cluster of businesses. A neighborhood bar, a dry cleaner, a pizza joint, and tucked in the far end, a sign for Mountain Chiropractic.

I parked in one of the four vacant spots in front and went into the small lobby, where a too-skinny blonde with volleyball breasts sat behind a counter.

"Hi, I'm Crystal, welcome to Mountain Chiropractic, how may I be of assistance?" she chirped. She may have been legal drinking age, but I'd have bet a car payment against it.

"Gordy in?"

"Do you have an appointment, sir?"

"Nope."

"Oh. Please have a seat, and I'll be right back." She went through a curtain, top heavy and teetering on heels. A minute later she came back and said, "I'm sorry, Mr. Chapman is with a patient. Can I make an appointment for you?"

I ignored her and walked around the counter and through the curtain. Down a short hallway, I picked the first door to the right, where Gordy Chapin sat with his legs crossed reading a magazine titled *Hot Vacation Spots*.

"Keeping busy, Gordy?" I said.

He looked up, and his eyes jumped. "What the—"

"Is that your new squeeze out there?"

Gordy's face flushed red. He had curly blond hair and a fake suntan and wore a white puka-shell necklace. He unfolded his slender six-foot frame and rose from his chair, but froze when I took a step forward. Gordy had been arrested on a child molestation charge a while back for having sex with a thirteen-year-old girl. In his defense, he said she claimed she was eighteen. His attorney hired me to dig up the dirt on the girl, who I learned lost her virginity at eleven and had slept with a number of middle-aged men. But I'd also learned that Gordy Chapman had a penchant for school-aged girls and had narrowly avoided prosecution twice before. At the conclusion of the case, he tried to thank me, and I let him know where we stood. On the occasions I'd seen him around town afterward, he'd moved rapidly in the opposite direction.

"What do you want?" he stammered.

"You seeing a patient named Art Crume?"

"What if I am?"

"I want to see his file."

"There's a thing called doctor-patient confidentiality."

"That doesn't apply to you, Gordy. You ain't a real doctor." I stepped over to a file cabinet and pulled open the top drawer and grabbed a handful of files.

"You have no right to—"

The words became a gargle in his throat when I flung the folders at him and grabbed another bunch. "These aren't even in alphabetical order," I said.

Gordy came at me and tried to pry the folders from my grip, but I stopped him with a stiff hand to the throat. I tossed the files over my shoulder and pulled another batch from the drawer.

"They're in the bottom drawer, for crying out loud," Gordy said. I let him get to the cabinet. He poked around, muttering, then handed me the file for Art Crume.

"What's his condition?"

"He's got degenerative disc disease, a bulging disc, and moderate sciatica."

"What's the effect on his daily activities?"

"He needs to be careful with his posture, and extremely careful when lifting anything over ten pounds or so."

"How about fifty pounds or more?"

"He knows better. It could rupture his disc, meaning back surgery."

I looked through the file and stopped at a sheet showing MRI photos.

"You see there," Gordy said. "That disc is bulging against the nerve."

I slapped him in the chest with the file. "Have a nice day," I said, and walked back out to the lobby. The receptionist stared at me with big eyes as I opened the glass door. I paused for a second, but I had no advice for her.

***

While Candi got ready for dinner, I ran Art Crume's name through my people search program. There was a purpose behind the questions I'd asked him about his personal life: I wanted to see if I could catch him in a lie. But I verified he was in fact a widower from Ohio, with two children. Further, he had no police record. There was even a reference I found to his auto repair business, which was said to still be reputable after he sold it.

It began snowing when Candi and I left for a restaurant. Tiny flurries danced down from the darkness above and swirled in my headlights. As we headed toward the state line, the Friday night traffic slowed our progress, until we passed a rental sedan that had spun out and was blocking a lane. The rear tires were wedged in a snow bank and spun futilely, and the passengers sat staring and silent, as if mystified by their dilemma. I wondered if they regretted putting themselves in an avoidable situation, or if they were just oblivious. I shook the thought from my head and drove on.

10

The next morning, a few inches of fresh snow coated my deck. Wind swept in from the meadow, blowing white wisps from the huge pine out front. I drank coffee with Candi and watched Smoky bounce around the family room until 9:00 A.M. When she retreated to her room to paint, I left the house and drove into Nevada, to Nick Galanis' condo complex.

The development was carved out of a grove of evergreens where the land flattened at the end of a steep stretch of winding road. The condominiums were linked by cobblestone paths and little bridges that meandered through the acreage. There were a few small parking areas, but most of the units looked to have their own attached garages.

I found Galanis' address and parked down the road, then walked along the quiet street past his home. It was a two-story unit tucked between two others like it. The front door was natural wood and looked freshly lacquered. Above the door was a pair of large bay windows. On the nearby paths, the snow was neatly plowed, and a manmade stream meandered and gurgled quietly. Tall pines shaded the area and made for a private, secluded feel.

Across the street from the address was a swath of forested land. I walked over to the snow pack and saw I could hide behind any number of pines and view Galanis' place. From there, I hiked across the snow for about fifty yards until I reached the next street over. More condos and half a dozen parking spots lined the road.

I walked back the way I'd come, scanning the ground, but if there was any evidence, it had long been snowed over. I stood peering at the beige residence where two women had spent their last night alive. Was this the spot the killer waited out his victims?

Not likely—it would have been impossible to cross the street under the streetlamps without being noticed. More likely, he hid in a shadowy spot near the house where he could sneak up from behind. I moved to a thick trunk near the steps to Galanis' door. From here, the murderer could have attacked, striking from behind with a club. Then, with a single motion, he could have hefted the body over his shoulder and run into the dark trees, then fifty yards to his truck.

Back in the trees, I walked again to the next street. I knocked on ten doors and spoke with six people. None recalled seeing a dark Ford Ranger in the neighborhood. I came back to Galanis' condo and knocked on doors up and down the street with the same result.

Snowflakes began floating down from the white sky. I stared out beyond at Lake Tahoe. Five miles away, there was a clearing in the clouds, and the north section of the lake was glittery with sunshine. The view was unimpeded and almost as majestic as the vista from atop the ski resort. An expensive view, no doubt. For Galanis, likely one financed with dirty money. Whether that had any bearing on the murders, I didn't know.

I went back to Galanis' unit and considered ringing his doorbell. The temptation was almost overwhelming, but I knew it would be a bad move. If he had something to hide, he certainly wouldn't cooperate. And if he had nothing to conceal, he still wouldn't tell me much because he wouldn't want me interfering with his force's efforts—or worse, embarrassing him by solving the case before his detectives. The involvement of a private investigator meant nothing but trouble for Galanis. Best I lay low for the time being.

Before heading to my truck, I paced around in the adjacent trees for some minutes. My collar turned up against the light snowfall, I dug my hands deep in my coat pockets and walked down to the entrance of the complex and back again. I had almost entirely dismissed the potential the cab driver was involved, which meant someone must have invested quite a bit of energy in following Galanis. The killer probably was at the club where

Galanis met Valerie. He—I assumed the killer must be male—could also have been at Pistol Pete's when Galanis had hooked up with Terry. From those locations, the killer would have tailed Galanis to his home and waited in the shadows for the right moment to pounce.

I looked through the trees at the condos lining the street. There was another option I hadn't considered. A neighbor could have been staking out Galanis' place. It was possible the killer lived on this street. The thought was worth looking into.

Neighbor or otherwise, the killings required not only stealth and forethought, but also a certain bravado. To abduct two women in front of a police officer's home made a statement of sorts, perhaps a mocking affront to the police department. But strangling two women who had just been seduced by Douglas County's top cop sent a message beyond taunting. What that message was, I didn't know.

I drove home and ran Nick Galanis' name through my computer and learned he'd purchased his condo two years ago for $750,000. Unless he'd made a large down payment, the mortgage would be at least $3500, quite a stretch for his income level. I doubted he'd gotten an inheritance, because his parents were still alive.

By noon, I'd completed my online research on Galanis. Besides the data on his home and his parents, there wasn't much. I watched Candi finish a portion of the landscape she was painting, then she put away her brushes, and we drove out to Zeke's. When we arrived, Zak Pappas came out from the kitchen and greeted us effusively. We sat at the table next to the front window, and Zak brought us his new addition to the menu, spinach salad with hot bacon dressing and split barbecued prawns.

"What do you think?" he said. He wore a white chef's hat and a red apron stretched across his rotund torso.

"Damn decent, Zak."

"It's a wonderful dish," Candi added. Zak beamed and returned to the kitchen.

We ate while looking out the window. The snowfall had increased, the flakes heavier now, but still floating down at a languid pace. In the windless calm, the snow coated the parking lot and built gently on top of the cars. The huge pine out front stood immersed and unmoving, like a stoic guardian.

We didn't speak for a while. I sat touching Candi's fingers, lost in the serenity of the moment. Then, I heard a raised voice at the bar. It was only a man joking with his friend, but I found myself staring through him at the stool where Jake Massie had sat. My stomach tightened, and the muscles in my back and shoulders flexed. I felt my lips pulling back from my teeth, and I widened my eyes and exhaled.

"Dan?" Candi said.

"Yes?"

"What's up?"

"Nothing, babe."

"Maybe you should have a beer or two. It is the weekend."

"That's all right. I'll wait until tonight." I looked at her, and she was studying me, her face compassionate and concerned, and maybe a little angry. I reached out and gave her arm a squeeze. "No worries, doll. I have some work to do this afternoon."

She got up and went to the lady's room, her fingers drifting over my neck. I returned my eyes to the front window and watched an SUV back out of a parking spot, its tires slipping and spitting snow. Maybe the weather was thwarting Massie's plans to pay me another visit. Or maybe he was consumed with other priorities. I hoped that was the case, but hope is not much of a strategy, as my old man used to say.

Before heading home, we stopped to pick up groceries, and I bought Candi a new pair of gloves at a sporting goods store. When we got home, I tried to watch TV, then gave up and lifted some weights and cleaned the kitchen. At half past three, I went to my computer and searched for a phone number or address for Douglas County detective Greg McMann. Not finding a thing, I called the cell number I had for the recently transplanted cop from Texas, Bill Worley. He picked after three rings.

"Hi Bill, it's Dan Reno."

"Howdy, Dan. What can I do for you?"

"Thought I'd see if you'd like to compare notes on the murder cases."

"Well, that's neighborly of you, but there's not much I can share, being the cases are open and all."

"Yeah, I know. But we're both working toward the same goal, so I thought maybe we could help each other out. For the common good, you understand."

He chuckled. "For a PI, you're quite the diplomat."

"I try."

"Tell you what. You want to share what you know, I'll be happy to offer my opinion."

"All right. I found out the cocaine in Valerie's purse was fronted to her by a biker named Roscoe, rides with the Blood Bastards out of Sac."

"He did her wrong. That stuff was about eighty percent baby laxative."

"My guess is she cut it. Roscoe thinks a rival biker gang, the War Dogs, killed her for the drugs and to send a message to the Blood Bastards."

"Makes no sense. She still had the coke."

"Yeah, I know. You think bikers have anything to do with this?"

"They're not among our primary suspects."

"Who is?" I asked.

"We're profiling sex offenders who might carry a grudge against Nick Galanis."

"Sex offenders? Neither woman was raped, right?"

"True. But we think there's likely some underlying sexual deviance at play."

"Like, someone gets off on killing blondes seduced by cops?"

Worley cleared his throat. "By Galanis in particular."

"What does Galanis think of that theory?"

"He's been cooperative, but I don't think he has any more insight than we do."

"How do we know he didn't kill the girls?"

"We don't for sure. But other than the fact he was the last one to see them alive that we know of, there's no evidence he was involved in the murders. There's also no motivation we can come up with. And we don't think he could have taken that body up into the mountains. He claims he's only ridden a snowmobile a couple of times, and he ain't much of a skier."

"Maybe he had a partner."

"Sure, we thought of that. But who? And why?"

"Have you interviewed Galanis' neighbors?" I said.

"We talked to everyone in his complex. Didn't come up with a single suspect."

"All right. What's his partner, Greg McMann, have to say?"

"Not much, besides, *Uno mas cerveza, por favor.*"

"Huh?"

"McMann is a twelve-stepper. Just fell off the wagon hard, from what I hear."

"Do you have a number for him?"

"Not that I can give you. But you want to find him, try Hannigan's over in Zephyr Cove."

***

Five miles into Nevada, I stopped at Zephyr Cove's single traffic light. To my left, the rugged eastern shoreline of the lake was obscured in a white fog. I turned right into a shopping center that had recently been built out, and was now the town's predominant landmark. Realtor and doctor's offices shared the development with a large grocery store, art galleries, numerous restaurants, and an Irish pub I was fairly certain had been there longer than any of the other businesses.

I'd known plenty of bar owners, all drunks or reformed alcoholics. Some had done quite well with their bars, but I didn't think it was because they were exceptional business people. It didn't take much entrepreneurial flair or business acumen to run a successful bar. What it did take was a drinker's sense of what fellow drinkers wanted. A good bar was where you went to blot out the drudgery and demands of a harsh world, to feel the thrill of an early buzz among those there for the same reason, and to immerse yourself in dark, familiar confines, where responsibilities were forgotten, and the party was an ongoing event. Good bars never changed, because drunks didn't like change.

Hannigan's was similar to many I used to frequent. The décor was timeless, dark mahogany, red carpet, the pool table an island of green light. At first glance, the place seemed upscale; the stools were newly covered in burgundy leather and gold buttons, and the bar top looked freshly lacquered. But the carpet was worn and stained, and behind the odor of cigarette smoke, I caught a faint whiff of vomit.

At the bar sat a dozen people, mostly men. They wore winter boots and wool shirts, and their jackets hung on coat racks near the front door. I walked the length of the bar, used the men's room, and came back to where three men sat at the back corner of the bar near the pool table. They were cops. There was nothing overt in their outward appearance that made this obvious, other than an invisible barrier between them and the rest of the patrons, as if they were shunned or feared.

I recognized Greg McMann immediately. Sitting between the other two, he looked too short to be a cop. He had a squat physique, thick neck, stubby arms, barrel chest. His face was ruddy and his features small, and his short hair was almost the same color as his skin.

I hung back in the shadows for a moment. The trick would be getting McMann alone.

"Gentlemen," I said, stepping forward. "Can I buy you a round?"

The three men turned and regarded me. If I'd hoped for smiles, they didn't come.

"Who's buying?" said the youngest, an unshaven man with a nose like a hawk.

"Dan Reno." They stared back blankly. Some local cops recognized my name, but if these guys did, they weren't letting on.

"What's the occasion?" said the other fellow, lanky, grizzled, in his fifties.

"Wanted to introduce myself. I'm a private investigator out of South Lake."

They eyed me, their faces suspicious and unwelcoming. I waved at the bartender and tossed a couple twenties on the bar. "Gimme a Bud and a round here," I said. I stood behind the cops and waited for the drinks.

McMann drained the last of his highball and turned on his seat. "You're buddies with Gibbons, the guy that was with Terry Molina, right?"

"Yeah, that's right."

"Let me guess—you want to talk about the murders."

I watched the bartender make the drinks. "I've got a few opinions I'd like to run by you," I said. "You want to shoot a game of pool?"

McMann didn't answer, and I stood there awkwardly until the drinks arrived.

"Here's to you, men," I said, and tossed back my whiskey. They nodded and drank, then McMann climbed off his stool and picked a pool cue from the rack on the wall. I plugged quarters into the table's coin mechanism, and the balls clunked and rolled to a stop. McMann chalked a cue while I racked the balls.

A lit cigarette in his mouth, the stubby cop leaned over the table and lined up the break, then slammed the cue ball with such force that one of the balls bounced off the table. I caught it and set it back on the felt.

"Nice break," I said.

McMann nodded and proceeded to run the table until missing a difficult bank shot on the eight ball.

"Good thing we're not playing for money," I said. I took a shot and missed.

He deftly cut the eight ball into a side pocket. I plugged in more coins and re-racked. After a break that threatened to rattle the neon beer lights off the walls, he took a slug from his drink and said, "You've been looking into the murders?"

"I've been hired by Valerie Horvachek's father."

He grunted and finessed a ball into a corner pocket. "What have you found out?"

"The most solid thing is the killer may have been driving a Ford Ranger pickup."

McMann paused and stubbed out his cigarette. "Really. Where'd you hear that?"

"The cab driver."

He grunted again and starred at the table.

"I originally thought bikers and drugs were involved. I'm not so sure anymore," I offered.

"The Horvachek girl may have known some bikers, but we don't think Terry Molina did," he said. "Have you heard different?"

"No. How about Nick Galanis? Have you known him long?"

"A couple years." McMann missed a shot, and I walked around the table and sunk an easy ball.

"I have a theory," I said. "Whoever killed the girls is motivated by something involving Galanis. Like maybe a pissed off husband of a woman he seduced. Or even a jealous woman could be the killer."

"Doesn't make sense," McMann said. He took a long pull from his highball and finished it. I caught his eyes and, for the first time, noticed a drunken sheen. He took aim and banked in a tough shot.

"Ever play professionally?" I asked.

"Semi-pro, back in Chicago. Why would a pissed husband go after Galanis' floozies? They hold a grudge, they'd go after Galanis himself."

"Right."

"Besides, neither of the victims was married. Or even had a committed relationship. Right?"

"True," I said. McMann missed a shot, and I studied the table then looked up at him. "Galanis seems to be one hell of a lady's man."

"So?"

"Has he ever had problems with any of his women?"

McMann smiled, his teeth small in his mouth. "He gets more ass than a toilet seat. But I've never seen him have a problem. He could be bangin' three broads in the same week, and they're all callin' and beggin' for more and wantin' to be his girlfriend. It would drive any normal guy nuts. But to him it's nothin'. It's a skill he has."

"I can barely manage one woman at a time."

"Same here."

"How does he do it?"

He lit another cigarette, and I saw the bartender and pointed at McMann's empty glass.

"You think it would catch up with him eventually," I said.

McMann shook his head. "Let me tell you a story, maybe shed some light on this. I knew a guy back when I was in high school. Horniest guy I ever met, walked around with a hard-on so bad, he had to carry his books in front of his crotch. We had a lot of hot girls at school back then, and plenty of guys were getting laid, but not this guy. He tried, like hell, he tried. But the desperation was like a stink on him, and he flubbed his words, and no girls would have anything to do with him. And he even tried with the ugly girls and the fat chicks, and not even those would have him."

I went to the bar and got McMann his cocktail. "Thanks," he said. "So, the guy gets out of high school still a virgin, and by this time, he's probably set some kind of record for jackin' off. Then, I lose touch with him for a year or two, and when I see him again he's goin' to college, and he's like a new man. Changed his hair, dressin' stylish, and he's datin' a very attractive woman. Clearly, he's had a transformation of some sort. Good for him, right? So, we're havin' some drinks and he tells me, yeah, he ain't the same awkward doofus he used to be, and he's been humpin' the hell out many different pieces of tail."

"Okay."

"So, then, he tells me, the best thing about getting laid is every time it's like a big fuck you to the girls who had denied him when he was younger. More so, he's come to realize he has no sympathy for women, none whatsoever, because of all the misery they put him through. So now, it gives him great satisfaction to talk his way into a girl's pants and then dismiss her like she's nothing. He tells me he doesn't think he's a bad person, but there's a big dead spot in his heart for females."

"Interesting story," I said, as McMann chalked his cue and addressed his shot. "But what does it have to do with Galanis?"

"I don't know much about Galanis' past," McMann said from around his cigarette, his eyes glazed behind a swirl of smoke. "But the part about the dead spot in the heart for women—he's got that. It's what allows him to juggle so many. He doesn't care what they feel."

"So, he's hurt some women. How does that figure in the murders?"

McMann hit an impossible bank shot and sunk the eight ball, but there was no satisfaction on his face. "I don't know," he said.

***

After a dinner of chicken enchiladas and Spanish rice, Candi and I sat on the couch to watch a movie she'd rented. Smokey curled up and fell asleep in Candi's lap, and I tried to pay attention to the movie, but it didn't hold my interest. Finally, I admitted as much and went to my office and called Cody. Saturday night, nine o'clock, and given his bibulous tendencies, I doubted he'd be home, but when he answered, I didn't hear any music or voices in the background.

"Hey, buddy. Taking it easy tonight?" I said.

"Yeah, I'm beat. I spent all day chasing down Terry's family and friends."

"Find anything useful?"

He sighed. "Not really. I did learn some charming tidbits, like she got divorced after her husband caught her getting it on with two guys at once. I also heard she boned just about everyone on her high school football team, and one of her ex-flings showed me a copy of a porno mag with her in a lesbian romp with a black chick."

"Have you had yourself checked out at the STD clinic yet?"

"I also didn't find any evidence she was dealing blow or knew any bikers."

"I'm not surprised."

"Why?"

"I think this is all about Galanis, not drugs or bikers. I'd like to bug his house."

Cody gave a low whistle. "You could get yourself in a heap of trouble bugging a cop's pad, Dirt."

"Yeah, I know."

"You could put a tail on him instead."

"I'm thinking about it. In the meantime, I got a line on a vehicle. A dark color Ford Ranger, '98 through 2002, was seen near Galanis' condo complex around two A.M. New Year's Eve."

"Same truck as the homeless guy said?"

"That's what I'm thinking."

"What do you want to do with it?"

"Any chance you can talk to any of your old friends on the force, get a DMV listing for every Ford Ranger registered in Northern Cal and Nevada?"

He laughed. "You're joking."

"What about that lady detective you bedded down?"

"That was a few years ago. We're not really on speaking terms anymore."

"Maybe you could get reacquainted."

"Nope."

"Shit. I guess I'll have to ask Marcus Grier."

"Like you say, he's your good buddy."

***

Calling Marcus Grier on a Saturday night was not something I thought would be productive, so I slept on it. When I woke Sunday morning and remembered he'd be at church, calling him seemed even less promising. Problem was, Grier was a limited resource, and I had to play my cards carefully with him. But I didn't have the same reservations about Bill Worley. So far, the old Texan had been pretty cooperative.

"We're already working on the truck," he said, answering my call after a single ring. "Care to guess how many Ford Rangers are registered in California?"

"Thousands?"

"Many thousands. The '98 to 2002 models were a big seller."

"How about if you reduce it to Northern Cal and Reno?"

"Still thousands."

"How about just the Tahoe Reno area?"

"Hundreds."

I leaned forward, my elbows on my desk. "What are you doing with the list?"

"We're working it. But it's a lot of names."

"I know this is irregular, but I could help."

"I appreciate the offer, son, I really do. But you'll have to talk to the sheriff on that."

"Hell, Bill, it's Sunday. I doubt Marcus would take my call."

"You know him better than me. Maybe best you wait 'til tomorrow."

I thanked him, and after we hung up I sat for a minute. On my desk was the case file I'd compiled, containing the names and numbers from Valerie's phone, as well as a list of Blood Bastard and War Dog members. I looked over the names and considered devoting the afternoon to phone interviews. This was the proper thing to do, I told myself. It might well be a waste of time, but it still needed to be done. If I had a boss, I'd probably be ordered to do so. Cases could be solved by this type of due diligence. But my gut was pulling me in a different direction.

I closed the file, got into my truck, and backed down the icy driveway. Five minutes later, I crossed the state line and turned into Pistol Pete's. A stream of SUVs, skis and snowboards clamped on their roof racks, were exiting the parking lot as I arrived.

I went through the glass doors and hiked across the quiet casino floor to the roulette table where Terry Molina had met Nick Galanis. From there, I circled outward to a nearby bank of slots, then I walked over to the bar named the OK Corral. Except for a couple playing video poker at the bar, the area was deserted.

I sat at a cocktail table and imagined the casino swarming with gamblers and revelers. The tapes I'd viewed showed every seat taken at every table, around which the crowds jostled and maneuvered. If someone was following Galanis that night, the mass of people would make it easy to go unnoticed, but difficult to maintain surveillance unless in close proximity. Also, the person would have to be standing; sustaining visual contact from a seated position would be next to impossible.

I got up and walked to the security counter next to a cashier's cage. "Is Chris Davies here?" I asked a uniformed guard.

"I'll check," he said. "Your name?"

I gave him a card and waited while he spoke on the phone. It didn't take more than a minute for Chris Davies, the employee I'd met when I was here last, to open the door that led to the stairway to the casino video room.

"Hi, Chris. I didn't know if you'd be working today."

"I take off Mondays and Tuesdays. To avoid the crowds on the slopes."

"I never ski weekends myself."

He nodded. "You need to look at some more video?"

"I do." Pleased and a little surprised at his obliging attitude, I followed him up the stairs to his desk, atop which sat three monitors. He hit a couple keystrokes, and a screen showing an overhead diagram of the casino came up. It was marked with blinking red arrows showing camera locations.

"Which views do you want to see?" Davies said.

I studied the screen and selected three arrows pointing at areas from which a man might watch the gaming tables or the lounge area.

"These three. From 11:00 to 12:15 New Year's Eve."

"How's the investigation coming along?"

"Still lots of unanswered questions."

"I'll go get you some CDs."

"Thanks. Hey, Chris?"

"Yeah?"

"It looks like there are four exits from the casino."

"That's right."

"But the cameras would only show the faces of people entering, not leaving?"

"Correct. People leaving, you'd just see from their backside."

"Hmm. Can you also get me these four cameras, midnight to 12:30?"

He went to his desk and scrawled on a pad of paper. "I'll have our technician make the disks. Should be about twenty minutes."

***

Whoever had murdered Terry Molina and Valerie Horvachek had waited until right after Nick Galanis had seduced the victims. Clearly, this timing was part of the killer's agenda. I still had no solid idea as to the motivation, but I was beginning to suspect, as Bill Worley had suggested, that some dark sexual deviance was at play.

I'd always found Freud's interpretation of arson entertaining. He viewed it as a substitute for the sex act. The lighting of the fire represented foreplay, the inferno was intercourse, and the eventual extinguishing of the blaze was the climax. Maybe this killer needed to see Galanis hitting on a woman. That would be his foreplay. The strangling would substitute for intercourse. The dumping of the bodies, the climax.

The killer could have watched Galanis' pad, waiting for him to bring a woman home. Or he could have followed and staked out Galanis' car for the same reason. Both were somewhat passive approaches that might minimize risk. But the killings were not the work of a passive, risk-adverse personality. Instead, my hunch was the killer had tailed Galanis into both the Vex Dance Club and Pistol Pete's, in order to witness his seductive ploys. Once Galanis had hooked up with the unfortunate ladies, the killer then followed them to Galanis' place and waited for the right moment. As it happened, both women had decided to wait outside for their cab, creating the opportunity for the killer to strike.

Freudian theories aside, the good news was Pistol Pete's was under constant video surveillance, something the killer might not have anticipated until it was too late. My first viewing of the Pistol Pete's videos had focused on seeing if Terry had met anyone there. Today, I'd be looking for someone watching Terry, and then following her and Galanis out of the casino.

The young technician brought out two CDs and gave me a quick review of their computer program. After settling in front of a monitor along the wall, I called Candi and told her I'd be tied up until at least midafternoon.

For four hours, I stared at hundreds of faces. I saw two drunk young guys get in a scuffle before security guards took them away. I watched a man grab a woman's ass, and she turned around and slapped him so hard his glasses flew from his head. Many of the males stared in the direction of Terry, leers or smiles plastered on their mugs. People passed by the screen smoking and drinking and grinning, and they reappeared scratching their heads or wiping their mouths. Their lips moved in silent conversation, and many had eyes glazed in drunkenness, and those sitting dared not rise because New Year's Eve seats were a valued commodity.

I took note of ten different men. One was the ponytailed Blood Bastards member who'd tried hitting on Terry before Galanis made his move. The other nine were fellows of various ages. They all seemed to be alone, though some were only visible for a few minutes. None of them were obviously watching anyone. If the killer was one these men, he did nothing to distinguish himself.

From my previous notes, I knew Galanis and Terry had left the bar shortly after midnight. I scrutinized the videos from midnight to 12:15, looking to see if any of the suspects had left during that time frame. A few did, but that didn't mean they left the casino.

It was two o'clock, and I'd skipped lunch. I ignored my stomach and inserted the second CD, which covered the four exits from the casino. I spent an hour studying the doorways. Galanis and Terry had departed through a side exit at 12:10. Although it was difficult to tell since I couldn't see their faces, none of the men I'd noticed followed them out. More troubling, I didn't see any of the men leave from any of the other exits.

"Shit," I muttered. I rubbed my eyes and stood to stretch.

A side door opened, and Chris Davies came into the room. "You look like you could use some coffee," he said.

"No, thanks. I'm about done."

"Find anything helpful?"

"Hard to say. Are there any exits from the casino other than the four?"

"Besides the employees exit? Yeah, you can get to the parking lot from Puttanesca's, our Italian restaurant."

"Is it covered by a camera?"

"No."

***

I left with pictures I'd printed of each suspect, most of them face shots of fair to good resolution. The faces were totally anonymous, with one exception: the ponytailed biker. And I knew nothing about him, except that he was a member of the Blood Bastards. But what did that tell me? He didn't fit my Freudian profile, and he and Galanis didn't appear to recognize each other. His agenda seemed solely to charm Terry. He had looked unhappy when he had failed, but that hardly seemed motivation for murder.

My approach to the case at this point, I'd conceded, would be a process of searching for the intersection of data points. I was looking for a man who possessed the skills to navigate in the snowy wilderness at night, and who drove a Ford Ranger. I was looking for a man who harbored some bizarre grudge against Nick Galanis. Bizarre, because why would he target Galanis' women instead of Galanis himself? And, I was looking for a man who may have been at Pistol Pete's on New Year's Eve, and whose picture might be in the stack of papers I held.

When I got home, I began searching online for snowmobile clubs and extreme skiing groups. I found a few things, but not much. Most of the hits under snowmobile were for rentals, but there was one local club I put on my list to contact. My other searches came up empty. If I wanted to identify hardcore backcountry skiers, I'd have to do it the old-fashioned way: hit the streets and talk to people.

That's where this case was, I mused. Without a clear idea on motive, or an eyewitness, identifying suspects could require sifting through hundreds or maybe thousands of names. Cops hated this kind of work. It's not only laborious, but time intensive and potentially impractical from a resource point of view. The murders of Valerie Horvachek and Terry Molina, while a priority, were not the only cases the local police had on their plates.

As a dedicated private resource, I had no doubt I could be of value to the Lake Tahoe police agencies. Marcus Grier was a nine-to-five cop, and Bill Worley's prowess as an investigator was an unknown. On the Nevada side, Greg McMann had just tumbled off the wagon, and Nick Galanis, who, by all accounts, was a good if not excellent detective, had apparently removed himself from the investigation.

I spent an hour reviewing my notes and writing an update for the General. After a while, Candi peeked into my office and suggested we head out to for Chinese food.

"Sounds good," I said. Before I stood from my desk, I studied the pictures of the ten men. I stared into their faces, hoping for some subconscious revelation, some flash of light in the darkness. When none came, I stacked the pages neatly. The pictures might be valuable to the police, especially if they'd made progress on the list of Ford Rangers. I'd look into it first thing tomorrow.

11

Monday morning, and it took until eleven o'clock to get Marcus Grier on the phone. When he finally took my call, he sounded distracted and irritable.

"How about I buy you and Bill lunch over at Zeke's?" I said.

"What do you want to talk about?" A phone was ringing in the background.

"I've got some pictures of potential suspects."

"From where?"

"I want to see if we can link one to a Ford Ranger."

"We?"

"Consider me a resource, Marcus."

He snorted a laugh. "Bill's doing just fine without you, if you can imagine that."

"I'm sure he is. You want to see the pictures?"

His voice became muffled, his hand over the mouthpiece. Then, he said, "Bring them in."

"You got to eat, right? Tell Bill Zeke's has real Texas brisket."

His voice was muffled again, then, "All right, we'll be there at noon. This better not be a waste of time."

***

From my table near the saloon's front window, I watched Grier and Bill Worley climb from their squad car. Walking together, they looked like two different species. Grier was still puffy, despite his recent diet, his body thick and round beneath his chocolate-colored face. Worley's weathered mug looked cracked as a dry riverbed, and he ambled along in a bowlegged gait, all elbows and knees.

I waved at them as they came in. They nodded their hellos and sat across from me. Liz brought menus, and I told Grier the prawn salad was probably the lowest calorie option.

Worley raised his eyes from the menu, reading glasses on his nose. "Chicken good?"

"Yeah. Try the baked beans too."

"Awright, I'll do that."

"Let's get to it, Dan," Marcus said, clearly not interested in idle chitchat. "What about the pictures?"

"I'm thinking whoever murdered Terry Molina was at Pistol Pete's, watching Galanis hit on her." I opened the folder on the table in front of me. "These men were all at the casino on New Year's, near where Galanis met Terry." I slid the folder forward, and Grier and Worley began looking through the photos. A group of teenagers come in, followed by two harried adults. Liz steered them into the dining room.

"See anyone familiar?" I said.

Worley scratched his eyelid and flipped through the pages. He shook his head and said, "Nope. How about you, Sheriff?"

"This is Ben Pinkus," Grier said, holding a picture of a man wearing a lime green T-shirt. He's a hair stylist over at the salon next to the Rite-Aid. Lives with his boyfriend. I wouldn't consider him a suspect."

"Because he's gay?"

"That, and he's a longtime resident, never had a scrape with the law that I know of."

"Any idea what kind of car he drives?"

"I'll look into it," Worley said.

"This guy," I said, grabbing one of the pages. "He's a member of the Blood Bastards."

"So?" Grier said. "You still think the gang is involved with Galanis and the murders?"

"I think it's a lead. I think you should find this guy and question him. I'd do it myself, but without a badge, I doubt it would go anywhere."

"We'll take that under advisement." Worley took the page from me, but Grier shook his head and looked skeptical. I didn't blame him.

"Bill, I like your idea the killer is motivated by some sort of sexual deviance," I said. "I don't think the killer necessarily knew Valerie and Terry. But I definitely think he knew Galanis."

"I tend to agree." Worley's blue eyes met mine.

"Have you compiled a list of men Galanis has arrested since he's been a cop here?"

"It's one of the things we're looking at," Grier said.

"Maybe focus on those charged with a sex crime?"

"That too," Worley said.

"And if one of them drives a Ford Ranger, and also happens to be a backwoods adventure type, maybe you've found your man."

"Not bad, Dan." Worley showed a hint of a smile, his teeth a bit crooked but very white against his baked skin.

"Lots of information to sift through, I imagine."

"We're making pretty good progress." Worley shifted in his chair and crossed his legs. His silver hair was neatly trimmed except for the few errant strands that fell onto his forehead.

"You need some help, I'm offering my time." Neither responded to that, and after the silence grew awkward, I shifted the discussion to a previous case in which I'd supported Grier, hoping to remind him I was a friend of the police. But the conversation fizzled, and we didn't say much until Liz came from the kitchen with our orders.

After she left, Grier said, "Actually, Dan, Bill's already got most of the work done."

"Really? Any suspects?"

Worley cut a piece of chicken and dipped it into a cup of barbeque sauce on his plate. "We have a number of persons of interest."

"No one from the pictures, though, huh?"

"No. But we appreciate you letting us keep them." Grier took the pages scattered on the table and arranged them in the folder. He reached behind him and propped the file on the window ledge.

"Glad I could be of help, Sheriff," I said.

***

After Grier and Worley left Zeke's, I drove down the street to the Rite Aid on 50. The parking lot also served an adjoining strip mall. The neon signs in the window of the Starlight Salon advertised manicures, facials, and hair styling. I spent a minute driving down the rows of parking spots, looking without success for a Ford Ranger. Then, I parked and went into the place.

An Asian woman was bent over a middle-aged lady's toes, filing away. The only other person there was a man with a shaved head and earrings and a goatee on his chin. He sashayed toward me with a devilish pout on his face.

"Oh, lucky me, but aren't you a project. Well, you've come to the right place. I imagine you'd like a total makeover?"

"No, I—"

"Oh, look at those nails!" He grasped my hand. "How long since your last mani?"

"My last what?"

"Manicure, silly. Years?"

I took my hand from him. "Are you Ben Pinkus?"

"Why, yes."

"My name's Reno, private investigations. I'm looking into the murder of a woman named Terry Molina. Does the name mean anything to you?"

His hand fluttered to his chest. "No, no, it doesn't. Should it?"

"You were at Pistol Pete's New Year's Eve. Miss Molina was there. Knee-high boots, a white top split down the center, and a big head of frizzy blond hair. Do you recall seeing her?"

He put his finger to his chin. "That was so many, many brain cells ago. Was she the one with the giant gazoombas? Yes, I remember now, the ridiculous little twit. Loved her outfit, though. So *come fuck me.*"

"Did you notice anything unusual that night? Like somebody watching her?"

"She was really murdered?"

"That's right. Did you see anyone scoping her out?"

"Like every horny hetero there! I thought she was an escort, right?"

"What kind of car do you drive, Mr. Pinkus?"

"Baby blue Cadillac Escalade. See it?" He pointed out the window.

"Do you own a pickup?"

"Not for years."

"Know anybody who drives a dark Ford Ranger pickup?"

"No, I don't think so."

"How about your boyfriend?"

"Roger? He drives a Subaru Forrester."

I looked around the empty salon. "What time did you leave the casino?"

"Oh my. Must have been around three. Roger and I had a bite at the coffee shop, sobered up, then he drove us home."

"Would he confirm that?"

"Of course. You can call him now if you like."

"No, that's all right. Thanks for your time, Mr. Pinkus. Here's my card. Please call me if anything occurs to you about Terry Molina."

He held my card in his soft hand and mouthed the words to himself, then tried to take my hand again, but I was already moving toward the door.

"I could do wonderful things with your hair. You'd be amazed!"

"I'll pass."

"Good bye, Dan," he yelled after me.

***

When I got home, I sat at my desk and called General Horvachek. His wife answered, and I waited a minute for him to come on.

"Yes, Reno?"

"Have you read the report I sent last night?"

"I did."

"Have the police in Nevada given you an update recently?"

"I spoke with Greg McMann last week. He didn't provide any specifics, but said they're making progress. He asked me to be patient."

"I met with South Lake Tahoe PD today," I said. "They seem pretty optimistic."

"Is that right? But they're not investigating my daughter's death."

"No, but they are investigating Terry Molina's. And we're pretty sure the killer is the same person."

"What did they tell you? Have they found a motive?ave they Hhhhh"

"They think there may be a sexual predator with a grudge against Nick Galanis."

The line went silent, and I heard the General take a deep breath. "Meaning my daughter was just in the wrong place at the wrong time."

"It's possible."

"You have a friendly relationship with South Lake PD?"

"Somewhat. I share information with them."

"Do they return the favor?"

"As they see fit, I suppose."

"Do you consider them competent?"

I paused. "The lead investigator is a man I don't know well. He seems like he knows what he's doing."

"Send me his name and number."

"Okay. General, do you want me to continue my investigation?"

"Of course. Why would you ask that?"

"The police may solve the case before I do. And my hours are piling up. It's getting expensive."

"I don't give a good goddamn about the money. Stay at it."

"Yes, sir. In that case, I have a request for you."

"Yes?"

"I'd like to get a DMV report listing every 1998 to 2002 Ford Ranger registered in California, north of Bakersfield, and Northern Nevada too. If possible, I'd like to get the information digitally, so I can manage it on my PC."

"You think my daughter's killer was driving a Ford Ranger?"

"One was seen near the crime scene. I'd also like a list of every person arrested by Nick Galanis since he worked in the Lake Tahoe area."

"That's a pretty tall order."

"I believe you have the connections, General. But if not, I understand."

"You'll find I don't respond well to being patronized, Reno."

"No offense intended."

"I'll work on your requests. In the meantime, redouble your efforts. Find who murdered my daughter."

***

It was two o'clock, and the clear morning skies had given way to afternoon clouds that fell over the ridgelines like puffs of white steam. Carrying a second set of the pictures from Pistol Pete's, I gunned my truck up the grade on Ski Run Boulevard and pulled into South Lake Tahoe's ski resort. It was more crowded than I anticipated for a Monday, and I had to hike five minutes to the main lodge. I sidestepped skiers clumping around in unbuckled boots, their skis slung over their shoulders, and asked a woman at a coffee kiosk where the human resource office was.

"Down the hall, past the ski shop, turn left."

I followed her directions and knocked on a door beneath a sign that read *Business Offices*. A young guy with a foreign accent opened the door and led me to a small office where a woman sat behind a desk. Her blonde hair was up, and she wore a white turtleneck sweater.

"Hi, Miss…?"

"Adams. Haley Adams, Director of Personnel. What can I do for you?" Her brown eyes were quick and attentive.

I handed her a card. "I'm investigating the girl who was found Christmas Eve."

"Ahh," she said. After a long moment, she closed her mouth, and a vulnerable expression replaced the professional glean in her eyes. "We're all still kind of freaked out by that."

"I have some pictures. Can you tell me if any of these men work here?" I laid my folder on her desk.

"I'll try, but we employ over a hundred-fifty during the season, and at least half are new hires. But I'll do my best." She opened the folder and began studying the shots. Her brow furrowed, and she looked at some twice, but finally said, "No, I don't recognize any of them. But that doesn't necessarily mean none of them might work here."

"The man I'm looking for is likely an expert skier. Would it be possible to talk to whoever runs your ski patrol?"

"That would be Brent Corrigan. He's on the mountain right now. I can ask him to call you."

"I'd appreciate that."

"Something else to keep in mind," she said. "Many of our employees work here because we provide a free season pass. We employ lots of expert skiers and boarders, whether they're cooks, janitors, parking lot attendants, whatever."

"Thanks for the tip," I said with a sigh. I took my folder, and before leaving the lodge, I stopped at the retail store, the bar, and the rental shop. I showed the pictures to five employees. They all seemed happy to help, but none recognized any of the men who'd been at Pistol Pete's.

I hustled back to my truck. There were twelve ski resorts around Lake Tahoe. If I hurried, I could hit two more before five o'clock, when their hiring managers would likely call it quits. What were the chances the killer worked at a ski resort? Impossible to say, but at this point, I needed to be out there making my own luck.

Five miles and a dozen traffic lights through town, half of which I hit before I reached the Y and turned right onto 89. I sped past where Terry's body was found on the beach near Camp

Richardson and climbed the tight curves over Emerald Bay. The road around the lake was plowed and made narrow by walls of snow on either side. I checked my speed until I dropped down to lake level and the road straightened. Then, I drove hard for thirty minutes, skipping past Homewood, a small ski resort on the lake's west side. When I reached Tahoe City, I stopped at the red light at the junction, and ten minutes later turned onto the access road to Alpine Meadows, probably the third or fourth largest ski resort in the Tahoe region.

At ten past four, I was able to park a stone's throw from the ticket windows. Though considered a secondary destination for visiting skiers, Alpine Meadow's steep terrain made it a local's favorite. Besides the challenging runs, I was also fond of the resort for its tendency to remain open into May, and sometimes June. One year, I even skied Alpine on July 4th.

I found my way to an office marked *Employee Services*, where a young, bearded dude sat working on a computer.

"What's up?" he said.

I introduced myself and asked him to look through the pictures. "Is your boss in?" I asked.

"No, he split early."

"Do you know most of the people who work here?"

"Yeah, most. I've been here a couple years." He continued flipping through the pictures, then started chuckling.

"What's so funny?"

"This guy works here," he said, holding a picture of a man with a round head. "He's our CEO."

"Really?"

"Yeah. CEO, as in Chief Entertainment Officer. A major party animal."

"Is he here now?"

"Probably. He works in the rental shop. You want to talk to him, ask for Big Paul Castentino."

Down a flight of stairs, the rental shop looked to be winding down operations for the day. I spotted the man named Paul

Castentino immediately. He was about five feet ten and easily 250, maybe closer to 300 pounds. His voice was loud, and he was laughing and bantering with two other employees.

"Hey, Paul," I said, standing at the counter.

"What can I do you for, my friend?" he said, jolly as Santa Claus.

I handed him a card. "I'm investigating the murders of two women, one who was at Pistol Pete's New Year's Eve."

"Shit, I heard about that. You catch the bastard yet?"

"If I had, I'd be skiing today, not working."

He laughed and reached out and patted my shoulder. "I hear you, bro."

"The woman had frizzy blonde hair, big knockers ready to fall out of a white top. Do you remember seeing her?"

"Oh, hell, yeah. Shit, she got murdered?"

"Did you notice anybody paying maybe a little too much attention to her?"

"Yeah, me," he laughed. "She was something else. But there were plenty of other guys checking her out too."

"Do you remember anybody in particular?"

"Jeez, I'd have to think about that. You mean like someone suspicious?"

"I think the killer might have been there at the casino."

"Whoa."

The other two employees were busying themselves, but they were moving closer and obviously curious. I opened the folder on the counter. "Do you recognize any of these guys?"

He took his time with the pictures, and I waved at the two men to join us. After a minute, Paul said, "I know a lot of people who live here, but I don't recognize any of these guys. My guess is they're from out of town."

The other two nodded in agreement.

"What time did you leave the casino, Paul?"

"Oh, about one. Had some folks come over to my place."

"Anyone here that can verify that?"

"I can," said one of the employees. "We partied there until past three."

"All right. Thanks, fellas." I gave cards to each of them and wandered out toward the cafeteria. I spent the next thirty minutes showing the pictures to a variety of employees, until I spotted a ski patroller, an Asian man with a serious face and square shoulders.

"Excuse me," I said. "Dan Reno, private investigations. Do you have a minute?"

"What for?"

"I'm investigating the murder of a young lady. Her body was found the day before Christmas in the backcountry outside of the ski resort in South Lake."

"I heard about that."

"I'd like to talk to whoever runs ski patrol here."

"That's me. Ken Sato."

We shook hands and sat at on a bench near a bank of lockers. He looked at the pictures closely, but said none of the faces, except for Paul Castentino, looked familiar.

"Here's a question for you," I said. "How many guys do you know who could transport a dead body deep into the mountains in the dead of night?"

He thought about it for a second. "Transport how?"

"Either a gurney or a snowmobile, unless you know of any other way."

He shook his head. "In the dark? Unless they were on a well-marked trail, someone would have to be pretty gonzo."

"How about any of the ski patrollers who work here?"

He took a moment to recognize the implication of my question, then raised his eyebrows. "All my team is proficient with a gurney or on a snowmobile. Does that make them suspects?"

"No, but they might be able to provide clues. Could you help me arrange a time to meet with them?"

"You could show up here at seven tomorrow morning, if you want. Our first shift starts then. We also have a shift that starts at ten."

"Thanks. I appreciate it."

"Sure thing."

"You ever hear of anybody skiing or snowmobiling at night?" I asked.

"For the sport of it? People do a lot of dumb things in the snow, throw themselves off jumps, ski off cliffs, you know? But you have to be able to see."

"Snowmobiles have lights," I said.

"True, but people rarely ride at night, especially off-trail. Too dangerous."

"You'd have to be nuts, or ballsy, or both, huh?"

"Or maybe a member of the Carberumdum Kegger Council."

"Who?"

"They're a group of some of the most extreme skiers and boarders in the world. Local guys, all professionals with sponsorships. You can see them on TV in the winter X-games. Skier-cross, snowmobile racing, first descents in the Himalayas, that's yesterday's news to these guys. They're into stuff mere mortals wouldn't even think about."

"Like what?"

"Wingsuit base jumping. Speed flying. Thousand-foot cliff jumps."

"Do you know them?"

"Not personally. But they shouldn't be too hard to find. Their home resort is right up the road, at Squaw Valley."

***

In the last few years, the resort developers had sunk their fangs into Squaw Valley big time. I wandered through the cobblestoned base village, past bistros, wine bars, a Starbucks, and a blur of retail stores. Once inside the main lodge, I was told by an employee the ski patrollers had just gone into a meeting on avalanche safety. I went back out to the village and eventually landed at Le Chamois, an indoor-outdoor pub. A boisterous group sat drinking around a fire pit on the patio out front. The dozen or so surrounding tables were full, and it was getting dark. I went inside and dodged waitresses in the crowded restaurant until I made my way upstairs to the loft bar.

A group of young fellows in beanies sat at the bar drinking cans of Pabst beer. I took a seat at the end, and after a minute, the lady bartender brought me a Pabst and a shot of CC. I drank the whiskey, and when the cold beer hit my throat, it tasted so good, I finished it. One long pull and the can was empty, the crushed aluminum clattering on the bar top.

The fellows next to me were discussing something that happened at a party, a friend who had snowboarded off a roof. They sat on their jackets, season passes dangling from metal rings. I eavesdropped for a minute, and when one of them signaled the bartender for another beer, I said, "Let me buy you boys a round."

Unshaved faces with studded ears and surprised expressions turned toward me. I gave the man next to me a card.

"I'm investigating a murder in South Lake. The man I'm looking for is probably an expert snowmobiler, or skier."

"Wow."

"Dude, we're not two-plankers. We're boarders," said a guy with pale blue eyes and a mole on his lip.

"Are you guys pretty good?"

Nods and shrugs. "Austin's fuckin' rad," one said, and nodded toward a small dark-haired kid at the other end.

I cracked my fresh beer. "I'm just talking to locals, trying to get a line on a guy that would have the ability to haul a dead body deep into the backwoods at night. You guys mind taking a look at some pictures?"

They all stared at me and nodded. I handed the file to the man on my right, and the pages made their way up and down the bar. Besides Paul Castentino, whom they referred to as a drunk, they didn't recognize any of the faces.

A freckled youngster with curly blond locks said, "Dude, anybody decent on a snowmobile could haul a body, if they're motivated enough."

"Do you know any guys really into snowmobiling?"

"Not really," the kid with the mole on his lip said. "You mean, like racing them?"

"Yeah. Do you know any snowmobile racers?"

"There's no snowmobile racing going on in Tahoe," the dark-haired kid said.

"How about the Carberumdum Kegger Council? Do you know them?"

They all turned toward the dark-haired kid.

"I did some runs in the park with Doug Copeland earlier this year."

"Who's he?"

"He's aiming to set the world record for longest gap jump on a board. He boards with Shaun White sometimes."

"You know who Shaun White is, right?" Curly Locks said.

"Yeah, the Olympic gold medalist. Do you know the names of the other Carberumdum members?" They all began talking at once, and I started to jot the names down, until one said, "Hell, just Google it. They're all on the internet."

"Are these guys around here?"

"Not now," the dark-haired kid said. "They're doing some filming in the Chugach up in Alaska."

"I heard they were heading to Chamonix and then the Swiss Alps," Curly Locks said.

***

After I left the bar, I looked for ski patrollers in the main lodge again, but they were nowhere to be found. I walked to my truck and assembled my notes on the passenger seat, then drove off into the dusk. The Truckee River flowed alongside Highway 89, the white caps breaking around snow-covered boulders, the water gray and churning under the darkening skies. In Tahoe City, I almost pulled into a liquor store off the highway, but kept both hands on the wheel and steered past it, then past a corner bar that used to be one of my favorites. If Candi wasn't waiting at home, I'd probably have picked up road beers or, better yet, parked my ass in a bar and tried to cleanse my mind in a frothy haze of booze. Get drunk and wait for my scattered thoughts to blur and hope they'd reassemble in a singular construct, one clear and purposeful. And if that wasn't forthcoming, then wait for the hangover, a numb fog in which the brain slowed and details were forgotten and sometimes complicated things became simple.

"Bullshit," I muttered. Ask anyone who'd had booze problems if they were fully recovered and it was easy to spot the liars—or those still in denial. My problem drinking was maybe five years past, but I still sometimes suddenly longed to take happy hour into extra innings. Or maybe pull a double header, close a bar, stagger out and weave home at 2:00 A.M., and drink an ice-cold six-pack for breakfast. Then, out to a bar again, with a bindle of Colombian flake tucked in the foil of a pack of hacks, and really work on those demons. Kill some brain cells and stop giving a shit. Drink until the angst was gone and replaced with dry heaves and the shakes.

Those were my old days, the memories not so distant, but I was nowhere near the class of some I'd known over the years. Like my old party buddy Gardner, who loved booze so much that whenever he got a break from his wife and kids, he'd rush to the liquor store and pack his pickup truck with booze and start pounding double-fisted. To him, a case of beer and a fifth of hard liquor in a day was nothing. It made him happy as a pig in shit to be drunk, but when the family was around, he sobered up in a hurry. His wife had grown up around violent alcoholics, and she did not tolerate drinking. I could never figure out why she'd married him.

Of course, for many, turning the habit on and off was not an option. I once knew a man named Joe Lane who was a wonderful talent on the guitar. Wrote some of the saddest and most haunting love songs I'd ever heard. The songs were about the one woman he loved, who left him because he was a drunk. After she left, he turned his drinking up a notch, and his friends staged interventions, he went to rehab centers, he did stints in the county jail. He always returned to drink as soon as he possibly could. He drank every day before his liver gave out, and he died penniless and wracked in pain. Never drank the hard stuff, just beer. But he drank lots of it. Said he liked the way it tasted.

No doubt I didn't have it as bad as some, and I seemed to drink less as I got older. For the most part, my thirst was no longer prone to run amuck. But my confusion and frustration over the case was eating at my resolve to stay sober.

"Bullshit," I said again. Instead of fogging my brain with alcohol, I needed to organize my head, check my thought process, stick to the fundamentals, get creative. I wanted to think about the case in a linear way, like moving in a straight line from point A to point B. But the lack of clues kept forcing me to restart, to pursue different lines of inquiry. As a result, I felt I was in a maze, one that might lead nowhere. In the meantime, the murderer of two women was running free, and I was being paid good money by a grieving parent for not doing much more than floundering about like a fish out of water.

I blew out my breath and wished I had a cigarette. There was nothing on the radio but static and commercials, and by the time I had passed the little communities on the west side of the lake, it was full dark. The fundamentals. One, the killer had to know Galanis. Likely, Galanis knew him too. Why the hell else would the victims be the two women Galanis had just slept with?

It was time to stop fucking around and go talk to Galanis. If he weren't a high-ranking cop, I would have grilled his balls first thing in the investigation. And if the right answers weren't forthcoming, turn the screws until he talked. But since he was a cop, hard-assing him would probably do nothing but land me in jail. I'd have to play it different.

As for the angle on the backwoods expert, it seemed half the population of the Lake Tahoe area might be capable of taking a body into the woods at night. But capable was one thing, and actually choosing to do so was another. I still thought the killer had to be a proficient backcountry man, but I needed to narrow the field. Chasing down extreme winter athletes was one approach. But celebrity daredevils who may or may not be in the country? A better bet might be focusing on ski patrollers. As a group, they were all trained on gurneys and snowmobiles. Given that Valerie's body was found not far outside a ski resort, the idea made sense. I'd start at Alpine Meadows and Squaw Valley, and then hit the South Lake resort. How many certified ski patrollers worked in Tahoe's dozen ski resorts? A hundred? Two hundred?

When I got home, Candi had stoked the stove, and a smorgasbord of food from Zeke's was on the table. I had one small drink, and we ate, and then, I took her into the bedroom and undressed her. I went at her body like a man starved, and we had raucous sex, switching positions, panting, her climaxes loud and long. When we finally slowed, she hovered above me, her dark hair lying just above her pink nipples, her hips still gyrating slowly.

"What got into you, cowboy?"

"I don't know." Then, before I could consider my words, I said, "I think I love you."

"Of course you do, silly."

12

At six thirty, the morning was pitch black and ten degrees above zero. I huddled in my jacket and drove out of my neighborhood and through the silent town. There was no wind, but the weight of the air made me certain a storm was coming.

I stopped at the traffic light at the Y and turned right, banging over a pothole. Then, it was miles of darkness through the tall trees, broken only by the white pierce of my high beams. I sipped from a steaming cup, and there was no sound except for my tires humming on the road. It wasn't until I'd driven all the way around the lake and into Tahoe City that the first pale hint of dawn appeared. The dark gave way reluctantly, but when I parked at Alpine Meadows, it was light enough to see the clouds coming in from the west, thick and roiling and battleship gray.

The lodge doors were locked so I hiked around to the back, where the chairlift to the top of the mountain was already running. A pair of large snow tractors were grooming a run midway up the face, the lights atop their cabs burning into the cold. I checked my watch and it had just turned seven-thirty, but the back doors were locked. I was ready to return to the front of the building when the door opened and the head of Alpine's Ski Patrol, the man named Ken Sato, stuck his head out.

"Good morning. Come in and get some coffee, if you like."

"All right."

"I wasn't sure you'd come."

"Me neither, when my alarm went off at five-thirty."

Five patrollers were milling about inside. Two held drills with three-foot auger bits attached. Between them, a bundle of metal poles and orange plastic fencing rested against a wall. Another man lugged a toboggan across the floor. The other two studied a computer screen on the ski rental counter.

"Listen up, guys," Sato said. "This is Dan Reno, private eye from South Lake. He's investigating the girl who was found dead over there. He wants to ask a few questions. So, stop what you're doing for ten minutes."

The men laid down their gear and assembled near the computer. They were all guys in their twenties. Ten minutes. Have to make it a group interview.

"What happened, guys," I said, "is someone strangled a girl and dumped her body overnight about eight thousand feet up in the backwoods outside the ski resort in South Lake. Over on the Nevada side. This happened very early the day before Christmas."

"Near Got Balls?" one said.

"Yeah. You're familiar with the area?"

"Sure, I've skied it."

"Has anybody else?" I said, looking from face to face. Two said yes, two said no.

"You're all trained on snowmobiles and know how to maneuver a gurney in the snow, right? How hard would it be to transport a body out there at night?"

"A bitch."

"And dangerous."

"Stupid," a third said. "No one would do it unless they were desperate."

"My theory is a ski patroller did it," I said. I tried to catch each of their reactions. A smirk, a shrug, some blank stares.

"Have you heard of anybody into backwoods snowmobiling, or skiing, at night?"

"Nope," one said, and the rest shook their heads.

"Okay," I said, and tried to smile. "I don't want to be a headache, but could you all write your names and phone numbers, and where you were on the evening of December 23rd, and the early morning of December 24th?"

They could have said no. Or write fake names and numbers. But Ken Sato said, "Let's help him out, men," and one found a piece of paper and began writing.

***

I spent the remainder of the morning bouncing between Alpine and Squaw Valley, where, at 8:00 A.M., I found the ski patrol manager. He was a helpful sort, and though I only spoke to three patrollers, the manager provided a list of the names and numbers of all twelve of his team. Then, I returned to Alpine and spoke with another four patrollers when the late shift started at ten, and then caught three more at Squaw a little before noon. I also drove through the employee parking lots at each resort, looking futilely for a Ford Ranger.

Still, not bad for a half-day's work, though none of the patrollers or the other employees I'd spoken to recognized any of the men who'd been at Pistol Pete's. I looked over the list of the twenty-one patrollers I'd compiled, and drove fifteen minutes north to Truckee and found a bar and grill on the main drag, one popular with tourists, but not on a wintery Tuesday; I was the lone customer at the bar. I ordered a turkey burger and watched a football program, and just as the food arrived, my cell rang.

"Yeah, this is Brent Corrigan, returning your call." The ski patrol manager from South Lake.

"Right, thanks. I'm Dan Reno, looking into the Valerie Horvachek murder. Could we schedule a time to talk?"

"Be happy to. You want to come by the resort about four?"

"That works."

I tapped my fingers on the bar. My plan to put together a list of every ski patroller in the region was making good progress. And if any of them owned a Ford Ranger, I'd have a real suspect. Next on my list would be Mount Rose ski resort, up on the top of Route 431 outside of Reno, about an hour-and-a-half drive from here. I ate fast, and while I waited for the check, a man came to the bar and joined a couple that had sat shortly after I did.

The couple struck me as locals. The woman had rosy cheeks and a little ski-jump nose, and her hair was tossed and wild in a way that made me think she'd just got out of bed and hadn't necessarily been sleeping. Her companion was a short fellow with a crooked smile and a round chin. Their voices had been a murmur, but the volume picked up when a second man arrived. He was six feet, his blue eyes framed with a sunglass tan. He smiled while he spoke, and the woman laughed and stared up at him, while the other fellow fidgeted and tried to inject himself into the conversation.

The bill came, and I left cash on the bar and walked outside, listening as the woman's laughter trailed me out of the building. I stopped at my truck. A man's laugh, deep and carefree, had replaced the woman's. The snowbank surrounding the parking lot was shoulder high and streaked with dirt inside the spiral patterns left by the blades of a snow removal machine. I stared over the bank at a boulevard lined with old bars, hotels, and shops selling T-shirts and retail artwork. The sky was heavy with rolls of gray, and the sounds from the street seemed muted. I started to get in my truck. Then, I stopped and punched a number into my cell phone.

"Good afternoon, Dan," answered my friend at University of Reno, ex-biker Albert Bigelow.

"Hello, Albert. Is that European professor still at the college, the psychologist?"

"You must be talking about the Count Unger von Zenz."

"Count?"

"Yeah. A descendent of Austrian nobility. Lives in a mansion in North Reno. I drove by it once. Looks kind of creepy from the outside, but they say he has Rembrandts hanging on the walls."

"I'd like to ask a shrink some things about the case I'm working on. You think he'd be a good guy to talk to?"

"Could be. His specialty is dark stuff. Darker the better. He spent years working at a state hospital for the criminally insane in Colorado. You want to talk the psychology of a murderer, he's your man."

"How can I reach him?"

"Hold on, I'll check his class schedule." A pause, then, "Looks like he's lecturing right now. Class ends in an hour."

"What room?"

"A-100. Our big auditorium. If you're facing my building, go two buildings to your left."

I thanked Albert and roasted the tires out of the parking lot and onto Interstate 80. The road was clear, but the wind had kicked up, and the clouds overhead were ominous. I drove east at eighty-five, my speedometer bouncing off a hundred on the long, straight down-hills. The same down-hills where I got pulled over when I was a teenager for going one-ten. If I recall, I'd ripped up the ticket and tossed it out the window to impress the girl I was with.

Just as I crossed the border into Nevada, the first snowflakes danced silently across my windshield. My foot stayed heavy on the gas until I reached Reno and turned off on 395 and ran into snowplows and traffic. Swearing, I weaved through the slow-moving cars until I came to the exit for the college.

The count's lecture was scheduled to end as I jerked to a stop in the university parking lot. I jogged through the campus and found the lecture hall. The door was open, and a swarm of students filed out. I went in and saw a middle-aged man standing at a podium facing the hundreds of now empty seats rising to where I stood. Even from the back of the hall, I could see the man's posture had an aristocratic bearing. A group of students surrounded him, and he seemed to be answering questions, but when I got closer, I saw he was referring most of the questions to a younger man next to him, perhaps a teacher's aide.

The count wore slacks, a brown sports coat, and a white button-down shirt. He was of average height and neither fat nor thin. The skin on his face was tanned, but so uniformly it appeared unnatural. His cheek bones and jaw line were all right angles, and his blond eyebrows slanted downward over his greenish eyes, creating a tragic effect, as if years of dealing with sordid circumstances had left him in permanent despair.

"Excuse me, Professor Unger von Zenz?" I said, after the last student left. He had not acknowledged my presence while I had been waiting, and he had his briefcase in his hand and was eyeing the exit.

"Yes." Brusque, impatient. An important man. Used to dealing with underlings and naive questions.

"Dan Reno, private investigations. I'd like your help in profiling a murderer, one who committed a double homicide I'm investigating."

He stopped, and his eyes panned me, his expression sharp. "Thank you, Robert," he said to his aide, who quickly gathered his things and climbed the stairs to the doorway.

"A local case?" the count asked.

"Yeah. Two women murdered. One on Christmas Eve, the other on New Year's Eve. Both hit over the head, then strangled."

"Raped?"

"No."

"Mutilated?"

"No."

He rested his briefcase on one of the foldout desktops attached to all the chairs in the auditorium.

"Tell me more details, please." He had an accent, but not one I could clearly identify. A cross between German and Russian, perhaps.

"Both of the woman had just been seduced—or rather, had consensual sex—with a police captain who has a reputation as a prolific ladies' man. They seem to have been abducted upon leaving his residence."

"Did the women know each other?"

"No."

He stood with his hands at his side, and his lips were bloodless against his skin. "Have you eliminated the police captain as suspect?"

"Not entirely. But let's say so, for the sake of argument."

"As you like." He paused for a brief moment. "Have you considered the killer may be a woman?"

"A woman? Why?"

"A jealous lover, spurred by the policeman."

"The bodies were transported post-murder. I think it would take a strong individual to do that. Unless it was an unusually strong woman, I don't think so."

"A gay lover, then. Outraged at not being chosen over the opposite sex."

I repressed a smile. "There's no indication the police captain has any gay tendencies. He seems entirely focused on women. Blondes, in particular."

The count regarded me silently. He did not blink or take a breath. "Does the policeman have a son?" he asked.

"I...I don't know."

"Has he been married?"

"I don't know," I said, and felt a rush of blood crawling up my neck. These were simple questions, obvious questions. They were questions I should have been able to answer.

"He may have a son who resents that his father invests all his time in womanizing," he said, his voice dispassionate. "Or one who's jealous his father enjoys many women, while he does not."

"That's an interesting angle."

"Sexual desire is a vast component of deviant psychology. The need for sex, especially among the younger, is second only to the need for food and shelter. When sexual gratification is unavailable, for whatever reason, serious emotional turmoil may ensue."

"As in, if I don't get laid, I'm gonna go crazy?" I said, but immediately regretted my flippant tone.

The count's expression didn't change. "That's a simplification," he said, and if his intention was to make me feel like a simpleton, it worked.

"Sorry," I said.

"I've seen murders motivated by sexual jealousy or resentment. It's something you may consider. The fact the women weren't raped or tortured suggests the motive is not based on hatred of women, which is quite common, but instead on something else.

"Like what?"

He checked his watch. "Hatred," he said, "of the policeman."

"I see."

"I do beg your pardon, but my time is tight. If you'll excuse me."

"Of course."

"Best of luck to you," he said. He nodded curtly and strode up the stairs toward the exit.

I followed him out of the building into the cold white of the afternoon. He stepped briskly away, and I jogged to where I'd parked. I wheeled out of the parking lot and back to the freeway, thankful it was only snowing in light flurries. In perfect driving conditions, I could make it down 395 through Carson City and over Spooner Pass to South Lake Tahoe in less than an hour. Factor in today's weather, it might take more like ninety minutes. It was already almost two-thirty. I wouldn't be able to visit Mount Rose Ski Resort today. It was more important to make my four o'clock appointment with Brent Corrigan at the South Lake Resort.

But I was already mentally leapfrogging the angle on the ski patrollers. Yes, it was plausible a ski patroller was the murderer. Yes, it was worth following up on. But the fact that I'd not yet spoken with Galanis was a problem. And the blame for it rested squarely on my shoulders. I needed to question Galanis, and I needed to do so without delay.

A few minutes outside Reno, the landscape turned stark. The straight highway split empty flatlands glazed with snow, and to the east, the pastures stretched for miles until a hillside rose and merged with the iron sky. Beyond the hills lay five hundred miles of high desert terrain and the labyrinth of peaks and ranges that made Nevada the most mountainous state in the U.S. The land between here and the Great Salt Lake was sparsely populated, and some of the rural towns looked much like they had in the 1950s. Some were ghost towns, gray and decaying, abandoned after the silver mines went bust. Places where if you listened closely late at night, you might hear the tinny rattle of an old time piano, the clink of whiskey glasses, and the lost voices of bearded men whose luck had run out.

Spooner Pass was slick with ice and slush, and it took half an hour to make the twelve miles over the barren hills to Lake Tahoe. Then, I got on the gas again and made time around the lake until I hit the light at Stateline right before the casinos. The snow was falling in heavy, wet flakes, and the neon casino lights flashed and beckoned through the haze.

At four o'clock, I parked at the ski resort, snow melting off my hood, and hiked into the lodge. I ran my hand through my wet hair and went down a flight of stairs to an area where rubber mats lined the floors. I asked the first person I saw with a nametag to direct me to Brent Corrigan. A minute later, I stood in his small office.

I immediately recognized Corrigan as the patroller I'd seen on the slopes when I skied Friday. He had a head thick with white hair and full cheeks and friendly eyes. About fifty-five years old. His body thickening with middle age, but still powerful. A man used to working with his hands, not a desk jockey.

"Mr. Corrigan, Dan Reno."

"Yes, have a seat." He grimaced at some paperwork and pushed it aside. "You wanted to talk about the poor girl found out there."

"Right."

"Well, how can I help you?"

"I have a theory, Mr. Corrigan. I think a ski patroller may have killed Valerie Horvachek and dumped her body."

He raised his eyebrows in surprise. "Why would you think that?"

"Her body was moved into the woods either by snowmobile or gurney. Ski patrollers are trained on both."

"Yes, that's true, but…is that your only theory? I mean, do you have any other clues?" Doubt and a hint of sympathy etched his face.

"Yes, I do. I think the killer might have been driving an older model Ford Ranger. Do any of your patrollers drive one?"

"I can't say for sure, but I can definitely get you an answer to that."

"Thank you, I'd appreciate it. How many patrollers work here?"

"We have eighteen total, including me."

"Can you get me their names and addresses?"

"Ahh. For that, you'd probably have to go through HR."

"You have the information, don't you?"

"Yeah," he nodded. "But we're owned by a big resort conglomerate. Employee information is confidential, and I'd probably lose my job for sharing it. The person you should talk to is Haley Adams in Personnel."

"I see. I'll do that. Mr. Corrigan, have the police spoken to you yet?"

"No, no one's contacted me but you."

"Hmm." I sat and stared at Brent Corrigan. He had a caring, fatherly aura about him and vaguely reminded me of some character I'd seen on a TV sitcom years ago.

"Here's a question for you," I said. "Are all your rescue gurneys accounted for?"

"Well, yes. None are missing, that I know of."

"If one was missing, would you know?"

He paused. "Our patrollers sign an equipment sheet after every shift, accounting for all our valuable gear, including sleds, drills, communications gear, etcetera."

"Is it possible a gurney's missing?"

"I suppose it is. I'd have to double-check."

"That would be very helpful."

His lip turned downward, and I imagined he was thinking that not only was the chore a pain in the ass, but if a sled was missing, it might bode poorly for him.

"I wouldn't ask if it wasn't important," I said. "We think the murderer has killed two women, and might kill again."

He met my eyes. "I have a twenty-one-year-old daughter myself. I'll cooperate in any way I can."

"Thanks." I laid a manila folder on his desk and opened it. "Can you tell me if you recognize any of these men?"

He studied the pictures of the men at Pistol Pete's carefully. After a minute, he shook his head and passed the file back to me.

"None of these guys work for you, huh?"

"No, sir."

"Just hoping I'd get lucky."

"I'll call you tomorrow after I check on our gurneys."

"Good deal." I stood to leave, then stopped. "One more question, Mr. Corrigan. Can you tell me where you were Christmas Eve?"

The white-haired patroller looked perplexed for a second, then he smiled. "Of course. My family from Minnesota came to visit. Twelve all told. We had dinner, then went to midnight mass at Our Lady of the Lake."

"Okay. Thanks again for your time."

"You're very welcome."

We shook hands, and I left his office and went up the stairs and down a hallway to the office of Haley Adams, the woman I'd met previously. But her office was locked, and when I asked someone, they said she had just left.

I yawned and pressed my palms to my eyes, which felt bloodshot. I spotted a wood bench and was tempted to sit and close my eyes, just for a minute. Instead, I went to the bar and asked for a cup of coffee.

"I'll have to brew a new pot," the bartender said.

"Shit. Don't you have any old stuff?"

He walked over to a percolator tucked in a corner and held up the pot. "Been here since morning. Probably taste like tar."

"Perfect. Pour it."

The coffee was thick and acidy. I sat hunched over the cup, and the stale brew coated my throat like a bitter syrup. Outside the floor-to-ceiling windows, the snow was falling, and the slopes were deserted. The only other people in the bar—a group sitting near the windows—gathered their coats and gloves and walked out, their ski boots clunking against the wooden floorboards.

The bartender departed on some errand and left me alone in the cavernous room. I looked up at a huge stuffed California golden bear standing on a platform built over the bar. Its mouth was set in a roar, the yellowed fangs exposed. It was hard to say whether the bear was roaring its approval or unhappiness at being displayed at the bar. It was probably pissed, I decided. It certainly didn't look cooperative, unlike most of the folks I'd interviewed in the last two days. For the most part, they'd all been friendly and willing to answer my questions. In my experience, that's not always a good thing. People cooperate when they had nothing to hide, but that also meant they likely didn't know much of value. Better to find those who evaded questions, or who were outright antagonistic. Then you knew you were getting somewhere.

The ski resort employees, the snowboarders, the taxi driver, they all seemed perfectly willing to cooperate. I didn't see any sign they were withholding information, and that was something I was pretty good at recognizing. Tells, they called it in poker—the rubbing of the face, an involuntary wince, a glance askew, the conversational hesitations while a story was concocted. It wasn't hard to spot after a while.

I looked up at the bear again. Hell, maybe it wasn't pissed, but instead, happy to overlook the daily revelry. Maybe in death, animals or people can take on a meaning altogether different from that of their lives. Just like the two women who died after sleeping with Nick Galanis.

I tipped the mug back and swallowed a mouthful of grounds. Then, I went out to my truck and drove back over the state border and up the winding road to the upscale condominium complex where Galanis lived.

13

It was twilight when I pulled up to Galanis' house. A pair of pickups with snowplows attached were working the area, and the streets were more wet than icy. Yellow street lanterns were lit in front of every residence, creating a quaint, welcoming effect. The half-dozen guest parking spots down the street were taken, so I parked right in front of Galanis' address, near a no-parking sign.

I rang the bell and waited on the step. After a minute, I rang again. It was possible he was still at work, and I considered leaving and coming back later in the evening. But then, the door opened.

Galanis wore running shoes and black sweat pants with stripes down the sides. His tank top showed arms and shoulders more muscular than I'd imagined. He blinked when he saw me, then smiled. His curly black hair was flawless.

"Hey, Dan Reno. What's happening?"

"It's *Reno*, Captain. I'd like to share with you some things I've learned, some ideas I have on the murder cases."

"You do, huh?" His smile was casual, but maybe a little forced. He was freshly shaven, and there was an amused glint in his eye that looked practiced. "I heard you were hired by Valerie's father."

"That's right."

"You didn't catch me at the best time. I usually work out before dinner. But I've got a few minutes, I guess. Come on in."

I stepped out of the wet light into a tiled foyer. "You'll have to forgive me, I have company," he said, as I followed him down a short hall to a room with a fire crackling in a marble fireplace. The flames reflected off a large picture window stretching to the top of the peaked ceiling. Outside the window was a view of a forested valley that dipped then rose into a distant ridgeline.

A band of mist hovered low in the valley, the vaporous tendrils threaded through the pines like ghostly fingers.

But that wasn't the only scenery offered in Galanis' home. On a furry white rug in the center of the room was an easy chair, and sitting in it was a woman in a crème-colored robe. Her hair was platinum blonde and silky straight, and the bangs were cut in a line low over her eyebrows. One of her legs was hiked up on the chair's arm, revealing a bare foot with silver nails, a shapely calf, and the smooth flesh of her inner thigh. The skin was bronze and glowed with an inviting sheen.

She turned her head from the television. With the motion, the satin material opened from her neck and slid aside, revealing the curve of her bare breast just shy of the nipple.

"Hello," she said. She had large green eyes and amazingly full lips. She took me in for a second then lazily returned to the television and continued surfing the channels, gold bracelets dangling from her wrist as she pointed the remote control.

"Marla, I've got some business," Galanis said. She nodded briefly, her profile almost cartoon-like in its perfection. I followed him away, past a kitchen and to a room with a desk, a stationary bike, and a row of dumbbells on a rubber mat. There was only one chair, so we both stood.

"Well?" he said.

I squelched an urge to ask him about the young lady in his living room. Instead, I said, "Have you ever been married?"

He nodded. "About twenty years ago. Lasted a little over two years. She went on to date an NFL running back. Can you believe that? Guy played for the Saints, I think."

"Did you have any children?"

"No," he chortled. "We avoided that, thankfully. Why does it matter?" His voice was easygoing and conversational, but the affable expression on his face receded some.

"I don't know that it does. I talked to a headshrink who asked the question. He theorized the murders might be part of some inner-family jealously."

Galanis tilted his head, and one eyebrow dipped. "Really, a headshrink?"

"That's right."

"Let me ask *you* a question or two, Dan. Take a seat." He moved aside and turned the swivel-back chair to face me.

"Okay," I said. I stepped past him and sat, my hands resting on my knees.

"Have you identified any suspects?" Galanis stood over me. His shirt clung to his torso, his midsection convex and his chest cut at a sharp angle.

"Not specifically, no."

"Have you identified any specific motive?"

"No, nothing definite."

"Where are you in your investigation, then?"

I looked up at Galanis. If he was trying to intimidate me, it was pointless. I had every intention of playing it straight with him. I had nothing to lose in doing so, and if I was lucky, he might share something of value in return.

"I burned a bunch of calories looking at two biker gangs," I said. "The Blood Bastards and the War Dogs. Also, a Mexican businessman named Mike Zayas. Runs a strip club in Sacramento, and has cartel connections. He supplies drugs to the Blood Bastards."

Galanis' face betrayed nothing. If he was involved with either gang, or even knew they existed, nothing in his manner let on. But I believed Galanis to be a cold-hearted son of a bitch, and I didn't expect him to react, even if he was up to his eyeballs in dirty money from the Blood Bastards.

"But the biker angle fizzled out," I continued. "I don't think either gang was involved in the murders. I also don't think drugs had anything to do with it."

"What else?"

"The cab driver that showed up here on New Year's claims to have seen a Ford Ranger nearby. It's possible it was the killer's vehicle."

"Go on."

"Whoever dumped Valerie's body had to be skilled enough to transport her body out to that location at night. I'm working on putting together a list of every ski patroller in the Tahoe area. Then, see if one drives a Ford Ranger."

"Is that it?"

"I also compiled pictures of a dozen men who were at Pistol Pete's, near where you met Terry Molina New Year's Eve. My theory is one of the men might have been tailing you."

"How did you get the pictures?"

"I asked politely."

An impatient flicker crossed Galanis' face. "Have you got anywhere with the pictures?"

"Nope. But I brought you a set." I handed him the folder I'd been holding.

Galanis gave the pages a cursory glance, then set them on his desk.

"Recognize anyone?" I asked.

"No." He looked at his watch.

"Captain, I think the murderer is someone you know. Either a man you've arrested, or maybe someone you've injured in your past."

"Injured?"

"Yeah. As in grievously offended."

"Grievously offended." Galanis spoke slowly, as if deeply contemplating the meaning of the words. "What do you think a cop's life is, a popularity contest?"

"I'm not talking about a cop's life."

"What you talking about, then?" A bubble of white spittle appeared at the corner of his mouth.

"Your personal life. I bet you've bedded down hundreds of women, right? Maybe even had kids you don't know about."

"Jesus Christ. So what if I have?"

"Maybe there's someone out there, someone closer to you than you think, someone with a lot of resentment."

Galanis rolled his eyes, but it was calculated, and I didn't buy it. "I bet you could make a list of ten people, and one would be the killer," I said, standing. "I think you know who murdered those girls, Detective. Whoever it is definitely knows you."

Galanis' body tensed, and he looked away, his eyes shrunken and gleaming darkly, his cavalier aura gone and replaced by something hard and callous and self-serving. In that instant, I sensed I was glimpsing the real man beneath the movie star looks, an inner being that was ugly and cold and kept tucked away behind a glossy exterior. For a moment, I thought he might take a swing at me. Then, his stance relaxed, and he smiled again.

"Those are interesting ideas you have, Reno. I'll definitely do some, uh, soul searching. Now, like I said, I have things to do." He opened the door and held it for me.

"Have your detectives identified any suspects?" I asked.

"We expect an arrest soon. So, I wouldn't go get yourself too wrapped around the axle with your theories."

"I'll try not to." I walked out of the room, and he led me to the front door, taking a different route than when I'd arrived.

"The girl in your living room," I said, as we stood in his foyer. "I'd say she's beautiful, but that doesn't quite do it."

"Maybe stunning is the word you're looking for."

"You using her as bait?"

"Not her." His expression was one of mock pain.

"Anyone else?"

"Nope. That's not a tactic we're using."

"Does she know the last two blondes you seduced were murdered?"

"She does."

"Despite that, she just can't resist you, huh?"

Galanis winked knowingly, as if I'd just professed my admiration for his sexual prowess. "You said it, not me."

***

I drove away from Galanis' condo and out to Pioneer Trail. After a minute, my jaw started aching, and I realized my teeth were clenched. I opened my eyes wide and tried to relax my facial muscles, but my head felt like it was in a vice, and I couldn't relieve the tension that had taken hold behind my eyes. Maybe two stout belts of whiskey would help. But what I really wanted to do was turn around and ram my fist into Galanis' face.

The fact that Galanis was unwilling to put his womanizing on the shelf for even a brief time was beyond irresponsible; it was reprehensible. The piece of eye candy in his living room could well have a target on her back. And if she was murdered next, Galanis' attitude seemed to be not much more than a big, "Whoops."

It was inconceivable to me that anyone, much less an officer of the law, could behave in such a manner. But who was there to stop him? Who could tell him to cease his social life, his sex life? Only Galanis could make that decision. And apparently, he'd decided he would change nothing, make no compromises.

Compounding things, I did not believe the Douglas County PD was close to finding the killer. For that matter, I also didn't believe the South Lake Tahoe police was nearing an arrest. Despite what both Galanis and Marcus Grier had claimed, I didn't think either side was close to solving the case. Maybe part of my thinking was ego-driven, but it was beyond that. The reality was, I simply saw no indication either police agency was willing to delve deep enough to uncover what motivated the killings.

There wasn't much snow on the road, but when I steered into a gentle corner, my truck swerved, and I had to fight the wheel. Then, I felt a rhythmic bump and realized I had a flat tire.

I pulled onto a dark side street and rolled to a stop on the shoulder. My left rear tire was hissing and rapidly settling onto the rim. I swore and kicked the tire. Then, I got the flashlight from the glove box and knelt down behind the tailgate and started removing the bolt that held the spare.

The tire had just come free when I felt an electric sting in the thick muscle beneath my shoulder. I jumped up and tried to reach the pain with my fingers, but it was beyond my grasp. It felt like I'd been bitten by a wasp, but I wore a heavy coat.

"What the..." I tried vainly to shake free of the pain, but I couldn't reach it, and it was getting worse. Then, a wave of vertigo made me reel. I clutched at my truck, but my head was spinning madly, and my stomach was in my throat. I fell backward, my breaths labored, and rolled off an incline onto a patch of broken snow and pine needles. "Move, move," I told myself, and I tried to claw into the forest where I might hide. But I was clammy and sick, and the light was fading at the edges of my consciousness. I pushed with my boots and crawled forward. The last thing I remember was curling around the base of a pine, my cheek pressed against the rough bark.

***

My first thought when I woke was there was sand in my mouth. My tongue was thick, and I was massively thirsty. When I was able to raise my head, there was a sharp light on my eyelids. I dropped my head again, but a blast of icy water in my face stunned me. I blinked and licked my lips, grateful for the few drops that trickled down my throat.

"Wake up, toadstool," a voice said.

I opened my eyes to fuzzy shapes. I tried to rub the cobwebs from my eyes, but my hands wouldn't move. I shook my head and blinked rapidly and became aware I was tied to a chair.

"Come on. You need to be awake for this. You wouldn't want to miss it, I promise." Through the fog, I felt a surge of alarm. The voice was Jake Massie's. I stared upward, into florescent tube lights hanging from cross-beams in the ceiling. When I lowered my head, I was looking at Massie's face. His flesh was pale and coarse, and the thin scar above his lip was gleaming in the artificial light. In his pale eyes was a glow of anticipation, as if he was a hungry man ready to begin a meal.

I flexed my arms. My wrists were bound by rough twine to a wooden chair, as were my ankles. The floor was concrete, and the room was cold, except for a ray of heat coming from behind me. We were in a garage of some sort.

"What did you shoot me with?" I rasped.

"Oh." Massie turned and reached to a bench that lined one side of the garage. "Horse tranquilizer." He held a syringe in his fingers. "At first, I thought we might have OD'd you, but it looks we used the right amount."

"We?"

"Yeah. Hey, Tipper. Come say hello to our friend."

The man who stepped into view was bone skinny and had the yellowed pallor of a meth addict. He wore black leather pants and was shirtless beneath an unbuttoned black vest. His emaciated torso was snakelike, hairless and almost translucent to the ribs. Around his neck was a tattooed collar broken by a Nazi cross etched on his throat. He tilted his shaved head at me, as if I was a specimen in a cage. His face looked deformed, his nose horribly crooked, his skull cratered around a half-shut eye. He opened his mouth, and it was like a dirt hole in the nest of his scraggly goatee.

"Howdy hi," he said. "We're jist about ready." His breath was rancid.

Massie nodded, and the reptilian man went behind me and returned holding a branding iron. On the red-hot end was a swastika, about two inches in diameter.

"Get that fucking thing away from me," I said. He cackled, and I jerked in the chair. The legs shook and scraped against the concrete.

"Yeah, that's right, fight it," Massie said. "It's always best when they fight. Right, Tip? Give me the iron."

The man cackled again, and then, Massie had the metal rod in his hand. He held it under my nose, the heat nearly singing my skin. I pulled my head back, and he followed my motion.

"First, I'm gonna brand your forehead, you weasel cocksucker," Massie said. "Then, I'll take some pictures to capture the moment for our enjoyment. Maybe send them to your friends and family, too, just so they understand how pathetic you are. Then, I might let you live for a bit, watch you suffer, before I snuff you out. But I haven't got to the best part yet. After I kill you, Tip and me, we'll pay a visit to your bitch. I'm getting a big hard on just thinkin' about it. We've been checking her out, and I got to hand it to you, she is one fine piece of bitch meat. We're gonna take her and fuck her right, we do this double penetration thing, and Tip's got a dick about ten inches, I shit you not. It will be a real tube steak boogie."

I felt my eyes bulging. "No," I said.

Massie laughed. "Oh, yes."

"No," I said again, panic creeping into my voice. "Don't do this. My buddy Cody Gibbons will hunt you down, and he'll never stop until you're dead."

The man named Tip raised his hand and moved his fingers open and shut in a mocking pantomime. "Bwa, bwa, bwa," he said.

"Here, Tip. You do the honors." Massie handed him the branding iron.

My heart pounded in my ears and every muscle in my body flexed as I pushed back from the man who looked like he climbed from a grave. Then, my ears popped, and a burst of images flooded my head, snapshots of my father and of Cody's wisecracking face, of Candi's smile and my sister in San Jose, and of my mother playing with me as a child. I felt myself coming apart, bright shards of light raining like breaking glass around me, and all the pain and sorrow and joy in my life merged in a singular moment. And then, like lava reaching the point of critical mass in a volcano, a blast of adrenaline surged through my heart, and something inside me exploded.

I bucked, and my body went straight, the veins in my arms engorged as if I'd just finished a set of hundred-pound curls. I saw the hot iron moving closer, then the chair broke apart in a burst of loud cracks. I hit the ground and jumped up, my face screwed in a mask of rage. Splintered wood hung from my limbs, and in my right hand, I held the arm of the chair where the wood had split diagonally. The man named Tip jabbed the branding iron at my face, but I grabbed the shaft with my left hand and pounced with my right, swinging down in a vicious arc with my fist.

It was a lucky shot. The jagged point of the chair's arm found his eye, and he barely had time to scream before I drove it home and felt the point hit the back wall of his skull. Blood spurted from his eye socket, and he gurgled and shuddered, and as he fell, I wrenched the hot iron from his hand. The thick splinter, still bound to my right wrist, came free of his face when he dropped. It was coated with blood and bits of brain matter.

"You die, fuck!" Massie shouted, his hand reaching inside his jacket.

I leapt at him and swung the iron, but my legs were tangled in a mess of rope and wood, and I stumbled and missed. His hand came out of his coat holding an automatic, but before he could point it, I lurched forward again and slashed the red-hot swastika down on his wrist. He howled, and the wound smoked, and the gun clattered to the floor. I swung the iron in a backhanded arc, and when Massie dodged back, I rolled and came up with his gun in my hand. He scrambled toward the large, hinged doors behind him. I rose to a knee and had him dead in the sights, but when I pulled the trigger, the gun didn't fire.

I checked the safety, and Massie yanked up the long bolt securing the doors to the floor. My finger squeezed the trigger again, and once more, the gun dry-fired. Cursing, I jerked the chamber and ejected a jammed round. Massie pushed the door open and disappeared from my line of sight just as I pulled the trigger one more time. This time, the gun boomed, and I started after him, but the ropes around my ankles slowed me to a hobble. The garage door swung shut, and I heard a metallic clunk.

When I reached the doors, I pushed, and they didn't budge. I rammed my shoulder into the wood planks, but they held firm. From outside, I heard a motor start, and then, the sound of tires spitting snow. I stepped back and fired three times into a square of rusted nuts and washers imbedded in the wood. Splinters flew, and I heaved my weight against the doors again, and this time, they gave way. I fell outside to see a pickup truck fishtailing through a clear-cut area.

I rapid-fired three rounds. One bullet hit the tailgate, and I aimed lower with the next shot, hoping to puncture the gas tank, but the shot was too low. The third round, aimed at the driver, struck the roof of the pickup with a spark that flashed brilliant in the darkness. Then, the truck turned where the trail led into the trees, and I fired once more, but in a second, the vehicle was obscured by a dense shroud of pine boughs.

Three more times I fired and heard each bullet thunk into a tree. I heard the sound of the truck's motor grow distant. "My shooting sucks," I mumbled, and stumbled back into the garage. My coat lay in a corner, and my cell was still in the pocket. I called 911 and told them to get a squad car to my house right away. Then, I called Candi and, my voice thick with emotion, I told her to lock the house, get her gun, and wait for the police. I gave her a brief explanation and promised more detail later. She asked if I was safe, then asked no more.

After we hung up, I took a knife from the belt of the corpse lying on the cement. I cut the ropes from my limbs and tossed aside the debris from the chair. Bile rose in my throat, and I coughed and spit a wad of bitter phlegm in the face of the sadist who almost branded me.

"Burn in hell, motherfucker," I said. Then, I threw up.

***

When I was done retching, I called Cody.

"Wait a minute," he said, after I told him what happened. "You're still there?"

"Yeah. I don't know where, though." The adrenaline rush had subsided, and I was light-headed. I walked around the dead biker, carefully stepping over the pool of blood in which his head lay. It had stopped snowing outside, and it was dark, but the white clouds provided some visibility. I stood looking out from the doors, and through the silhouettes of the pines, I could make out the casino lights. A road led from the garage down a slight grade and past a clear-cut area, off into the forest. To my left, I could just make out lift cables over the trees.

"I'm in an old garage where they park snowplows during the off-season, I think. About a half-mile from the lake, in the woods near where the gondola runs."

"Where's Massie?"

"I don't know. He drove off."

"Did you tell the cops it was Massie?"

"Not yet. I only spoke to the 911 operator. I got to call back and get someone to pick me up." A wave of dizziness made me drop to my knees. "I feel like shit."

"It's probably residual from the tranquilizer," Cody said. My face was clammy, and I lay down, then crawled out to a clean patch of snow and started shoveling handfuls into my mouth.

"Dirt?"

"Yeah?"

"Hang up and call 911 again. But don't tell the cops it was Massie."

"Huh?"

"Don't tell the cops it was Massie." Cody's voice sounded like it was in a tunnel.

I rolled on my back and felt the snow on my neck, and I stared up at the trees. Sweat rolled off my face, and I thought I would vomit once more. Cody was still talking, but I hung up, and I think I dialed 911. But I don't remember doing so.

***

"Hey," a soft voice said. I opened my eyes and saw Candi's face. She squeezed my hand. "The doctor gave you a shot in case there's an infection. He says you'll be fine."

I pushed myself to a sitting position. I was on a hospital bed. "Are you okay?" I said.

"Of course. Are you?"

"Yeah." I looked around the room. There were empty beds to either side of me, and a uniformed officer stood in the hallway. "What time is it?"

"Eleven-thirty."

"I've been out for hours."

"The doctor said you were shot with a strong animal sedative. The police found a syringe."

"I want to get out of here."

"The cop out there brought me here. He's been waiting for you to wake up."

The uniform in the hallway peered in at us.

"All right." I flipped back the sheet and swung my legs over the bed. I was happy to see I was still fully clothed and not wearing a ridiculous hospital gown. My shoes were in the corner of the room.

"Dan, I overheard the police say they found a dead body when they found you."

"It was either him or me, babe."

She drew me closer and put her head on my shoulder. "No one's gonna take my man away from me."

"Not if I have anything to say about it." I felt her eyes wet on my face, and I pulled back and wiped a tear from her cheek. "There, now, doll. Can you grab my boots?" Once the cop saw Candi walk away, he came into the room.

"Excuse me," he said, his eyes round and close-set. "Kent Walters." He was bald, and his ears stuck out like small flaps. The file cards in my mind flipped, trying to recall his face. He reminded me of an old school comedian. Rodney Dangerfield, maybe. Despite his comical appearance, he had a serious demeanor about him.

"I need to take your statement," he said. He held a pad of paper and a portable tape recorder.

Candi came back to the bed, and I began tying my bootlaces. She stood at my side, glaring defiantly at the cop.

"Candi, you should wait outside for this," I said. "It won't be long."

"It was self-defense," she said to the uniform. "You need to find these lowlifes and put them in a cage."

"I know, ma'am."

"Good." She stood with her hands on her hips for a long moment before walking out of the room.

"Is she trained to use a firearm?" Walters said.

"Yeah. Why?"

"When I went to your house, she answered the door with a .38 in her hand."

"I told her to arm herself. The men who kidnapped me intended to rape and kill her. And one is still out there."

"Did you recognize them?"

"Not the one I killed."

"You told the 911 dispatcher there were two men."

"That's right. The one who got away is leader of a neo-Nazi biker gang out of Stockton. His name is Jake Massie."

"We'll put out an APB on him."

***

The interview was over in five minutes. Before I left, Walters told me Marcus Grier instructed I be released following my statement. Grier also left order that I be at his office at nine sharp the next morning.

There was almost a foot of snow in the parking lot where Candi had parked, and it was coming down hard. I took her keys and drove through the drifts out to Highway 50. She sat in a rigid posture, her eyes shifting from me to the windows.

"You shouldn't worry," I said. "Massie's long gone by now." I hoped to sound soothing and confident, but I felt naked without my gun.

"I hope you're right," she said. "But we both know guys like him are capable of anything." When I looked at her, I saw an expression on her face I'd never seen. And then, in a faltering voice, she said, "There's something in my past I never talk about. It's something I wish I could forget forever. I hope you'll forgive me for not telling this before."

"Telling me what?"

She stared out the windshield. "When I was a sophomore in high school, it was in the hundreds every day that summer in Austin. We'd turn the on sprinklers in the front yard, and the kids from the neighborhood, boys and girls, would come over and run through the water. Then, we'd sit in the shade and drink lemonade and flirt.

"My older sister Felicia had gone off to her first year in college, and she came home that summer. She was tall and beautiful and talented, and she could have had anything she wanted. I worshipped her. One day, she joined us, running through the sprinklers in her bikini, and the boys couldn't take their eyes off her.

"I came home from a friend's the next day. When I went inside my house, a man was raping Felicia on the kitchen floor. I was still a virgin, but I damn well knew what rape was. I ran into my father's room for a gun. But I knew he kept them locked up. Instead, I grabbed a baseball bat he kept near his bed. When I came out, the man was getting off Felicia, and there was blood on his crotch, and she moaned and cried, and I swung the bat.

"I would have hit him in the face, but he ducked, and it was just a glancing blow. Then, he got up and hit me hard enough to give me a concussion.

"My father arrested him that night. He lived in the neighborhood, and people said he was mentally disabled, his mother took drugs, he didn't know what he was doing. He spent two years in jail, that's it. Before he got out, Felicia hanged herself. She just couldn't live with what had happened."

"I'm sorry," I stammered, a lump in my throat. I wished I knew how to say something more. Candi continued staring out the windshield, as if unwilling, or maybe afraid, to look at me. But she was not crying, nor was pain etched on her face. I imagined her trauma was so personal, she loathed sharing it, hated imposing it on anyone. Instead, she internalized it, tried to relegate it to a deep, seldom visited chasm in her mind. I knew of such wounds. They bled, they scabbed over, they faded and retreated into the past, and over time, they were replaced with brighter memories. The human psyche heals itself. But the scar resides permanently on the soul. I reached over and took her hand, and she finally turned toward me.

"The world's a beautiful place, but there's danger out there. You don't have to try and hide it from me. Don't try to tell me otherwise."

"I'm sorry," I said again, and when I looked in her eyes, I felt an odd kinship, one born of grief and suffering, and the horrible realization that our fellow man had the capacity to commit acts so heinous that the agony never stopped, but lived on eternally in those who survived. You were never the same after a loved one had been victimized. You lost a basic faith in humanity, in the belief we all shared a common decency. And that changed a person.

"Now, tell me how you killed the man who tried to hurt you," Candi said.

***

I drove to where my truck was parked and dug the spare tire out of the snow and replaced the flat. Despite being unlocked, the interior of the cab appeared undisturbed. I unlocked the steel box in the bed and saw that my gear was intact. My Beretta automatic lay atop my body armor. I picked up the gun, feeling its weight, the grips caressing my palm. Then, I followed Candi home.

It was past midnight, but Candi claimed she couldn't sleep. We sat on the couch, her .38 resting on the coffee table. It wasn't long before she lay down, her head in my lap. As for me, the dope Massie shot me with must have run its course, because I was wide awake. Once I felt her steady breathing, I covered her with a blanket and went to my office and called Cody.

"Hey," I said, "Did I wake you?"

"Do I sound like I just woke up?"

"No. What are you doing?"

"Driving."

"Oh. Listen, I just got home from the hospital. I was there for five hours or so, recovering."

"You're fine, then?"

"Yeah. Hey, man, did you say something to me before about not telling the cops it was Massie?"

"Are you telling me you forgot about that?"

"I was nearly passed out when we talked. I just remembered it."

"So, you told the cops?"

"Yeah."

Cody laughed.

"What?" I said.

"Nothing. It doesn't matter now, anyway."

"Why not?"

"Did I tell you about that case in San Francisco where the Mafia kid was trying to impress the big bosses?"

"What does that have to do with anything?"

"Humor me, Dirt. I've got a long drive in front of me."

"Where are you?"

"Bungfucked Egypt. Now, listen up. The young son of a Mafioso takes it upon himself to wage a one-man war against his family's enemies. He sees this as a shortcut to being a made guy. But his method ain't guns or knives. He somehow got ahold of a stock of military-grade C4 cartridges. The same stuff the Navy SEALs and the black ops commandos use. A cartridge the size of a wallet can blow a car to smithereens, I mean, doors flying off, the frame a twisted mess, the whole thing burnt to shit. So, the kid starts with cars. Plants a cartridge on a greaseball's car, underneath near the gas tank where no one can see it. Then he waits until the right moment to dial a cell number that triggers a fuse, and, *blabloowie*! The car launches into the air and parts go flying, and there ain't nothing left of the unfortunate goombah."

I heard the gurgle of a bottle, followed by Cody's sigh.

"The kid's having so much fun, he decides to take it to the next level. He creeps the home of his pop's arch-enemy, a mobster who lives in a big mansion across the bridge, there in Sausalito. He plants enough C4 on the place to not only reduce it to rubble, but to likely take down the whole freaking block."

"You worked this case?"

"Yeah, I was hired by an interested party, so to speak. Anyway, me being the concerned citizen I am, I intervened and stopped the imminent slaughter of not only the mob boss, but also many innocent civilians. In a sane world, I'd be granted a medal, but I'm still waiting on that."

"What are you trying to tell me?"

"A story, what does it sound like?"

"There's an APB out on Massie, Cody."

"And I bet they'll find him soon. In the meantime, I wouldn't worry."

"Why the hell not?"

"Hey, I got to get off the freeway. There's this country western bar up here that's supposed to be packed with babes."

"Goddammit, Cody. I'm sitting here with my gun, wondering if Massie's still in town."

"Hang loose, Dirt. He's probably at home, throwing a barbeque."

"What the fuck is that supposed to mean? You're drunk."

"You ought to have yourself a drink too. I'm serious. I'll catch you later."

"Cody?" I said. But he'd hung up.

I found a pack of cigarettes, stood in my kitchen, and stared at nothing for a long time. I didn't know what to make of Cody's drunken babble. Or maybe it wasn't drunken babble; maybe he was really, finally losing his mind. Regardless, I decided to take his advice. I poured a jolt of whiskey in a water glass and put on my heavy coat and went outside to the deck. The snowfall had lessoned, and I could see the moon in a black clearing in the sky. With my arm, I swiped the snow off a section of railing and set down my drink. The blanket of snow covering my yard was unblemished. Out on the street, my neighbors' homes were dark, save for a few scattered lights that broke the darkness like random campfires in a desert. I lit a smoke and drank from my glass in one long, continuous pull.

After a minute, I walked the perimeter of my property, the white fluff coating my shins. I saw no tracks, except those of a small animal, and heard nothing but my footfalls. The whiskey had settled pleasantly in my gut, but my fingertips were going numb, and the cold was penetrating my coat. I double-checked the hidden wiring for my home alarm system, then kicked the snow off my boots and went back inside.

Her lips parted as she slept, Candi looked angelic. I lifted her from the couch as gently as I could and brought her to the bedroom. She murmured in protest, and after I pulled the blankets around her, I returned to the couch and surfed the channels, hoping to find a movie to keep me occupied. When that failed, I sat in darkness, wandered the house, and sat some more. The hours passed slowly.

14

Candi woke me the next morning. I'd fallen asleep shortly before dawn, and slept fully clothed on the couch.

"Here," she said, handing me a coffee cup. "Did you get much sleep?"

"Enough."

"Dan, is it safe for me to go to work?" It was Wednesday, and her first class was at eight-thirty.

I rose and stretched and sipped at the coffee. "Even if Massie is foolish enough to hang around town, he won't try anything in broad daylight, with witnesses. Just stay away from any secluded area."

"I'm taking my gun in my purse."

I knew that was coming, and though I wasn't entirely comfortable with the idea, I wasn't about to stop her. Not that I could if I tried. "I don't think you'll need it, but just be careful," I said. "Why don't I drive you this morning? Grier wants me in his office at nine anyway."

"You better go take a shower."

"All right. I'll come get you at noon, take you out to lunch."

She smiled. "Okay, my guy."

We left the house half an hour later, and I saw no sign we were being watched or followed. Stalking a target in daylight was difficult if the target was on the alert. And I didn't suspect Massie was trained in the art. He'd taken me down at night when my guard was down, but he'd blown his chance, and I would not grant him another.

I dropped off Candi at the campus and made it to Grier's office fifteen minutes early. He came through the glass doors five minutes after nine. I was reclined in a plastic chair, my legs stretched out straight, and my hands clasped on my stomach.

"Morning, Sheriff."

"My favorite PI, alive and well," Grier said. He wore a police-issue winter coat and a hat with earmuffs. "Let's go," he said, and walked back toward the doors.

"Where?"

"I want you to take me to where they took you."

"What for?"

"Would you quit asking questions? Come on."

I followed Grier out to his Ford Explorer sheriff's vehicle. "I doubt this rig will make it," I said.

"It's got four-wheel drive. We'll chain up, if we need to."

We drove away from the lake to Pioneer Trail and followed it toward the state line. The landscape was buried under last night's storm, the main road plowed, but everything else covered in white. Clumps of snow fell continuously from the pines as we drove, landing on the road and hitting our windshield with dull thumps.

Once I saw the gondola cables rising up the mountainside, I said to Grier, "Hang a right."

We turned into a residential area, the road slick with packed snow, and weaved our way through a series of turns before reaching a wire fence bordering the forest. We drove parallel to the fence and past a hillside meadow, until there was an open gate and a faint trail leading up the grade. The trail was covered in fresh snow, but I could still make out tire tracks.

"Stop," I said.

Grier looked up the trail, and his face creased in doubt. "This is it?"

"Yeah, I think, so."

"Chains?" he said.

"Chains."

Grier pulled a heavy box from the rear of the SUV, and after a minute, it became clear he was not particularly adept at chain installation. I told him to stand aside and completed the job. Then, he drove up onto the trail and nearly ran into a tree.

"Where'd you get your license, Cracker Jacks?"

"There must be a sheet of ice under all this snow." Grier inched forward at a speed that did not register on the speedometer.

"I do have other things to do today, Marcus."

"You want to drive?"

He stopped, and I took the wheel. Five minutes later, we came into the clearing leading to the wood plank A-frame garage.

"It was two patrolmen who found you passed out last night," Grier said. "Bill Worley and another detective came afterward and secured the crime scene."

I pulled up to the garage doors. Yellow tape in a giant X stretched from one side to the other. We got out and tromped through the snow to where a padlock hung from a metal slide bolt that had been mangled by the shots I'd fired. The padlock had been clipped with bolt cutters.

We went inside and he hit the light switch. A chalked outline of the man I killed was the only sign anything had taken place. That, and the congealed puddle of blood where his head had come to rest. Everything else was gone; the branding iron, the remnants of the chair, the small propane stove. We stood in the middle of the room, looking around and blowing steam. It seemed surreal, as if my abduction had occurred in a dream.

"They're looking at some prints they took from the door," Grier said.

"They might be able to lift something off Massie's gun. Did they find it?"

"Yeah, it was outside. Next to where you were lying in the snow, Worley said."

"Have the police in Stockton raided Massie's house yet?"

"Raided? An APB is out on him. But he could be in Mexico by now, for all I know."

"He tried to kill me and said Candi would be next."

"I know that. What else can you tell me about what happened last night?"

"Like I told your man at the hospital, Massie shot me with horse tranquilizer, kidnapped me, and tried to brand a swastika on my face."

"I read the report," Grier said. He hooked his thumbs in his belt loops and walked around the garage, peering in the corners and up into the rafters, as if searching for some hidden artifact. Then, he walked out the garage doors.

"You stood here and fired at Massie as he drove away?" Grier pointed down the trail we'd driven up.

"That's right. I hit his truck twice, once on the tailgate, and also on the roof."

Grier took a handkerchief from his pocket and blew his nose. "We need physical evidence to prove he was here."

"Find his truck and maybe you can find a slug, run ballistics."

"That's pretty weak. Maybe the prints will pan out."

"Are you saying you don't have enough to arrest him?"

"Arresting him is one thing. Trying and convicting is another."

I opened my mouth to speak, but Grier's cell rang. He turned his back and walked a few paces away and had a brief conversation consisting mostly of "okay" and "got it." Then, he turned toward me.

"What?" I said.

"Douglas PD made an arrest in the murders of the two girls."

***

We didn't talk much as I drove Grier's rig back to the police station. The sun had burned through a smear of purple-tinged clouds, and the sky was tiger-striped in blue and white. Crystals glittered in snowfields along the road where streaks of sunlight fell with blinding intensity. On another day, I might have paused to marvel at the setting, at the reminder of why I chose to live here. But today, the moment escaped me, because I was consumed with Grier's remarks about the potential difficulty in prosecuting

Massie. I could not tolerate Massie remaining free, not after what he said he'd do to Candi. But if he was really tied to the AB, even jail did not eliminate him as a threat.

I parked and followed Grier through the lobby to Bill Worley's office. The detective from El Paso wore a bolo tie, and in the corner of the room a beige cowboy hat banded with silver squares hung from a rack.

Worley looked at me and hesitated. Grier nodded at him and said, "Just tell us what you got, Bill."

"Awright, then. Greg McMann called and said they made the arrest this morning. The suspect is named Tim Elkind. Lives out in Fallon. He's got a rap sheet chock full of small time stuff. Busted for drugs, DWI, domestic abuse, shop lifting, and, get this, he was also jailed once for having sexual congress with a sheep." Worley handed Grier a stack of papers.

"What kind of evidence do they have?" I said.

"McMann wasn't specific, Dan," Worley drawled. "Reckon they had enough to make an arrest."

"Does it say what kind of car he owns?" I asked Grier, who was flipping through the pages. He grunted ineligibly.

"He was one of the men whose picture you had from Pistol Pete's," Worley said. "White trash hillbilly type, straggly beard. Remember him?"

"Yeah."

"Galanis busted him years ago on the bestiality charge. Elkind got probation, but apparently, the rap ruined his marriage and forced him to move."

"And that's the basis of his grudge against Galanis?"

"It was no small thing for him, according to McMann. He worked at his father's ranch near Carson City, but after the bust, he became known as Ol' Sheep Dip, both behind his back, and some called him that to his face. After his wife left him, he moved out of state for a while. Then, he moved back to Nevada, out to Fallon."

"Says here he owns a black 1999 Ford Ranger," Grier said.

"McMann said we're free to interrogate him this afternoon, after they're done." Worley looked at Grier, who still was studying the pages.

After a moment, Grier's eyes rose. He looked at neither of us, his expression glazed and tentative, as if he was deciding how to deal with a problem not of his making.

"Well, I guess that's what we'll do," he replied.

***

Before I drove from the sheriff's complex, I unlocked the steel box in my truck bed and shrugged into my Kevlar body armor. The vest had stopped lethal rounds on four occasions—more than that, if I counted a couple shots that probably wouldn't have killed me. It was heavy and not particularly comfortable, but it was my favorite goddamned piece of clothing. I looped my shoulder holster over it and snapped my Berretta automatic into place. I'd cleaned and oiled the weapon around three in the morning.

Did I think it likely Massie was lurking around town, waiting for the right moment to finish the task at which he had failed? The police were looking for him, and he was someone who would stand out in a crowd. The logical thing for him to do was head for a different state, or even a different country. But hardcore felons often didn't subscribe to logic that prioritized staying out of prison. That's why recidivism rates were so high. Career criminals didn't know how to behave otherwise. It's the same concept as trying to force-feed democracy to third world countries that had known no political system other than dictatorship.

I drove to the community college where Candi was teaching and spent half an hour scouting the surrounding area. Then, I parked and walked the campus. After that, I spent another fifteen minutes watching with binoculars from different vantage points.

Satisfied the campus was secure, I drove over the state line and past the casinos, to the Douglas County police complex. I parked under a huge fir on the edge of the lot and sat for a minute, wondering if Galanis and Greg McMann were still with their suspect. If they weren't, maybe I could have a word with them. Perhaps they'd share how they figured a man with a history of mostly petty crimes, a man caught screwing a freaking sheep for crying out loud, was the brazen yet elusive killer of two young women.

I looked at the white stucco façade of the two-story police building. Even if I could get an audience with Galanis, he'd probably just tell me to get lost. After my visit to his condo, my status with him was somewhere between barely tolerable and complete asshole. Like he said, sometimes life ain't a popularity contest. Regardless, Douglas PD would not formally release details on the arrest until they were good and ready. But McMann, he might be a different story. Our meeting over a couple games of pool and a few drinks had been reasonably amicable. And he didn't seem to be a big fan of Galanis. If I caught McMann at the right moment, he might talk.

Before I got out of my truck, I called Cody Gibbons. It went straight to voicemail. He was probably shacked up with a woman somewhere, sleeping off a hangover after a long night in a bar. Obviously, he was drunk when we spoke last night, but that didn't excuse his irreverent attitude about Massie. That was something we needed to get straightened out.

I sidestepped patches of ice and boilerplate snow and followed a plowed section of asphalt to the main entrance. Just inside the door, they'd installed a metal detecting machine similar to the contraptions used in airports. I removed my vest, my shoes, my belt, and handed my holstered piece to a uniformed officer along with my license to carry a concealed weapon. Another uniform eyeballed the situation and came over to give me a thorough pat-down, legs spread, hands against the wall. When he was done, I sat on a metal bench to put my boots on. Then, I had a quick moment of regret when I heard a familiar voice.

"Hey, what do ya know, it's 'No Problemo' Reno." I looked up and saw Galanis and McMann walk from a doorway into the lobby. They were both dressed in slacks and button-down shirts.

Galanis' dark clothes were freshly pressed and tailored to match his physique. McMann wore a wrinkled brown shirt that looked unwashed and fit like a burlap bag yanked over a fire hydrant. Only his belt lent some organization to his appearance and kept him from looking completely disheveled.

"Morning, Detectives."

"Here to see anyone in particular?" Galanis said. He smiled with half his mouth, but his expression was sharp as a razor.

"I heard you made an arrest in the murder case."

His smile faded. "Word travels fast in this town."

"Yeah, sometimes. You sure you got the right guy?"

"I wouldn't have arrested him if I wasn't."

"Has he confessed?" I finished tying my laces and stood.

"Just a matter of time."

"I guess that means no."

Galanis' eyes receded in his face. "Do you have any purpose here, Reno, other than making asinine comments?" He was no longer handsome, but instead looked like an angry rodent. He stepped closer to me, and behind him, I saw McMann's cheeks go round as he blew out his breath.

"Not really. I'm just continuing my investigation into the murder of Valerie Horvachek."

"Knock yourself out, then, waste all the time you want. Just don't interfere with my department's business."

"The worst thing your suspect ever did was bugger a sheep, and you think he's a killer?"

Galanis' nostrils flared and his lips curled as if a noxious odor had invaded his sinuses. "Here's my advice for you, Reno. Call General Horvachek and thank him for paying you for mucking about. You can also tell him it was money wasted." Then, his facial muscles relaxed, and his smile returned. "You know, something just occurred to me," he said. "You probably contacted him after you found his daughter's body and convinced him to hire you. Is that what you did, take advantage of a grieving parent?"

"No, Detective," I said. "There're a lot of corrupt and self-serving people running around these parts, but I'm not one of them."

"That's a relief," Galanis said with a smirk. "Now, unless you'd like to spend the night in a cell, get your ass out of here."

I bit my lip and resisted a reply. I was already mad at myself for stupidly walking into an avoidable situation. The result was, I'd learned nothing, plus I'd ruined any likelihood McMann would talk to me later. My own goddamned impatience was to blame. It would have been easy to bide my time and catch McMann alone, maybe tonight. But since I couldn't wait, I'd blown the chance.

I collected my firearm from the uniform, who stared at me as if I'd tracked dog shit onto the carpet. When I went out the door, my ears felt hot, despite the cold. I hurried toward my truck, fighting a childish but very strong impulse to head back to the building to continue the conversation. Preoccupied with the thought and not paying attention, I was almost at my truck when I stepped onto a strip of black ice, and my feet went out from under me. My arms wind-milled, and I fell hard on my back. Laughter erupted from the front of the building, and I turned and saw Galanis, McMann, and a uniformed cop standing at the curb watching me, grins splitting their faces.

***

By the time I got home, I'd rationalized the situation the best I could. I'd been imprudent and made a mistake. My motivation may have been noble, but my execution was flawed. As a private investigator, I often had to deal with the police, or dodge them, as the circumstances dictated. Usually, I did a pretty good job of it. Today was an exception. Then again, I'd never had a case where I suspected a police officer was somehow complicit in two murders.

I sat at my desk and stared at my blank computer screen. My anger over being treated as a punch line by Galanis and his lackeys was still boiling in my gut. If Galanis was a civilian, we would have come to blows, and he'd probably end up hospitalized.

The thought provided little solace. Galanis was a cop, and I couldn't touch him.

After a minute, I got up and went to where I kept a bottle of bourbon on my kitchen counter. I filled a shot glass and contemplated the amber liquid. Eighty-proof, straight. Just what I needed to take the edge off my recriminations. I rolled the glass between my thumb and forefinger. In no time at all, I could be drunk, and my concerns about the Valerie Horvachek case would become scattered and forgotten. And then, I might load my shotgun and pick up a half-rack of road beers and head west over Echo Pass and off the mountain down into San Joaquin Valley. In less than three hours, I'd be in a little-known farm town where a decrepit house flanked by an aluminum-sided shack sat a quarter-mile off the road. After that, it was anyone's guess.

The scene played itself out in my mind. My truck power-sliding to a stop in front of Massie's dilapidated shit hole. The door to the house flying open, the doorjamb splintered where my boot heel slammed into it like a battering ram. Bodies moving in a blur, yells and screams, the roar of my shotgun, breaking glass, blood on the walls, men running, more shots fired, then Massie wounded and pleading before I ended his life in a spray of gristle, bone, and red splatter.

I carefully poured the whiskey back into the bottle. The scene was from a different time in my life. I would not revisit it. Not in a drunken rage, and not today.

Instead, I went back to my computer and ran a search on Tim Elkind, the man Galanis had arrested. Among other things, his public record listed numerous misdemeanors, a personal bankruptcy, addresses past and present, and the name of his ex-wife. I ran a search on her and found a phone number in Carson City. Her name was Dolly. I punched the number into my cell.

"Who is it, and what do you want?" The voice was female, but had a hoarse, deep tenor that could have mistaken for a man's.

"Dan Reno, investigations. May I speak with Dolly, please?"

"You got her."

"I'd like to ask you a couple questions about your ex-husband."

"We're divorced."

"Yes, I know."

"Is he in some kind of trouble?"

"Looks like it."

"I'm not surprised. He's a dumbshit and a pervert. What did he do this time? Rip off a candy bar?" She brayed loudly, greatly amused by her remark.

"Actually, he's been accused of murder."

She laughed even harder. "That chickenshit? He's scared of his own shadow."

"They say he strangled two women."

She brayed again. "If you said he'd been busted for sticking his pecker in a pig, I'd believe you," she said between hoots and trying to catch her breath. "But Timmy ain't no killer."

"Did he ever do much skiing?"

"Skiing? Hell, no. He cain't hardly walk and chew gum at the same time." She launched a laugh so loud, I held the phone away from my ear. "Harvey!" she yelled. "Bring that bottle over here, goddamn you!"

"How about snowmobiling?"

"He's drove plenty a' tractors, but he ain't ever rid a snowmobile I know of."

"I see. Well, thanks for your time."

"You got it." She started yelling for the bottle again and hung up.

I spent the next hour updating the case report for General Horvachek. When it was finished, I looked it over from beginning to end. It was ten single-spaced pages packed with names, dates, times, interviews, and my own opinions. The report concluded with the arrest of Tim Elkind and a recounting of the conversation I'd just had with his ex-wife. I was ready to e-mail it to the General, but instead, I called him.

"Good morning, Reno." His voice sounded old and resigned. It didn't sound like he was having a good morning.

"An arrest was made a few hours ago by Douglas County PD, General. They think they've found the man who murdered your daughter and the other woman."

"What? No one from Douglas County called me."

"I'm calling you. I can't speak for them."

"Was Nick Galanis involved in this?"

"My understanding is he was the arresting officer."

The general paused, then said, "Who is the suspect?"

"His name is Tim Elkind."

"Was he one of your suspects?"

"Yes and no. He was at Pistol Pete's the night Terry Molina was murdered. Other than that, I don't think he fits the profile. I think he was arrested based on circumstantial evidence."

"That's what you think, huh?"

"Yes, sir."

"Well, since they didn't call me with this news, it looks like I'll have to call them."

"I'm sure they'll be happy to hear from you. General, I would typically conclude an investigation after an arrest is made. But I'd like to continue looking into this. I'm willing to do it on my own time."

He grunted. "Please continue until I say otherwise. I'll pay you."

"As you see fit. I have a status report I'm ready to e-mail. You should probably read it before you contact either Douglas County or South Lake PD."

"I'll do that. Send it now."

***

At noon, I drove over to the community college and spent a few minutes casing the area before walking to Candi's classroom. Hoping I wasn't interrupting a class in session, I opened the door and peaked inside. There were no students, only Candi at her desk.

"Hey there," I said.

She held a pair of sketches in each hand, seemingly absorbed in comparing the two. "Oh, hi. I've got a few pretty talented students in this class. Check these out."

I walked over and saw the drawings were of a naked woman on horseback, galloping through a meadow. The artist had captured a certain grace and wanton desire.

"They're very good," I said. I looked around the classroom, where clay sculptures sat on tabletops, and easels held paintings in progress.

"Art is a funny thing. What an artist creates exposes their heart. What kind of person do you think made these sketches?"

"Uh, a girl?"

"Yes, but you might be surprised if you met her. She's the most tiny, timid thing, a little stick figure. What do you see in these sketches?"

"Something sensuous and carefree."

"Exactly," Candi said, her green eyes staring into mine. "That's what's in her heart. The drawings are a form of release."

I turned to a nearby lump of clay that vaguely resembled a dog. "What's this one mean?"

Candi made a face. "Not everyone has the knack is what it means. Where are you taking me for lunch?"

"Wherever you like," I said, and when I turned, I saw a painting of a mountain landscape. A snowy glade and a distant granite ridge were depicted on a canvas about two feet square. The quality of the artwork was fair at best, certainly far from professional grade. But the perspective and depth of the scene were well done.

Candi took off her smock and grabbed her purse. "Let's go," she said.

"Wait a sec." I stared at the painting.

"What's so interesting?"

I tilted my head to one side and the other. Then, I walked closer and reached out with my finger and traced the border of the glade.

"I'll be goddamned."

"Why?"

"This is a painting of the snow field where I found Valerie's body."

"Are you sure?"

"I swear, it was right here." I pointed at the bottom of the canvas. "And I tied my bandana to this tree here."

We both stood staring at the painting. "And this is where her body lay," I said.

"Well, Marty probably skied there, just like you."

"Yeah, maybe." And then, I saw a tube of pink oil paint resting on a pallet, along with green and white tubes. Pink, just like Valerie's purse, hanging from the tree.

"Marty who?"

"Marty Nilsson. A quiet student, for the most part."

"What's he look like?"

"About six feet. Big arms, like a body builder. He's also got something weird with his lip. Almost like a deformity, but maybe it's just a scar."

"What color skin and hair?"

"Olive complexion, some acne, and curly black hair."

"Nilsson is a Scandinavian name."

"He doesn't look it."

***

We went to a small café with a view of the lake. We ordered soup and sandwiches and chatted about small things. I forced myself to push away all thoughts of the murder case and Jake Massie. I wanted to enjoy the normalcy of the moment. Just a quiet lunch in an inconspicuous place. I looked at Candi, and an unexpected and powerful sense of calm came over me. She was my lover and friend, our relationship unencumbered with accusations and resentment, because we understood each other, and understood the world together. I relaxed for the first time in what seemed like weeks and simply enjoyed the company of the woman I loved.

The lunch hour ended too quickly. I drove her back to the college, and we walked to her classroom together.

"Can you pull up Marty Nilsson's home address?" I asked.

I saw her hesitate, and I knew I had asked her to bend the rules. "Of course," she replied. She wrote it on a piece of paper just as a pair of students came through the door. I took one last look at the painting, then told Candi I'd be back to pick her up at five.

***

I drove home and ran a trace on Marty Nilsson. Very little information came up. No surprise there. Like most twenty-one-year-olds, he'd not yet amassed much of a public footprint. Never married, no record of owning real estate, no listed arrests, liens or bankruptcies. No siblings listed, either. His mother was listed, however: Anne Nilsson, last known address in Ogden, Utah. I ran a trace on her and found she'd been at the address for less than a year.

The address Candi had provided for Marty was for a street near where Highway 50 and 89 split. It took ten minutes to get through the lights on 50, then I turned onto a steep road next to the 7-Eleven on 89. I climbed the grade and made a sharp right into a residential area. The homes were modest. Like most Tahoe neighborhoods, the properties were either owned by locals or by real estate speculators who rented them out while waiting for the right time to sell.

Marty Nilsson's house was a white, wood-sided place with peeling blue trim and gutters overflowing with pine needles. An orange Chevy SUV sat in the driveway, the paint faded and the oversized off-road tires cracked with age and nearly bald. The gate to the side yard was an ancient-looking chain link unit that hung crookedly on rusty hinges.

I walked past the SUV to the concrete porch and knocked on the front door. Heavy footfalls sounded before the door opened. An unshaven man about thirty stared out at me. He wore hiking boots and work jeans and a padded vest over a blue sweatshirt.

"Is Marty here?"

"He ain't around." The man was about my size. The bristles on his face were thick and coarse, and the heavier growth circling his mouth made me think of a toilet brush. His head was covered with brown hair that grew in clumps and looked like grease-smeared paper napkins kneaded in a sweaty palm.

"Do you know when he'll be back?" I said. I tried to keep my tone friendly.

"I ain't his babysitter. Who are you?"

"Private investigations."

"A rent-a-cop, huh? What's this about?" He leaned forward, and there was dried mucus in the corners of his eyes.

"The murder of two women. I want to ask Marty a few questions. You know where he is?"

"Murder, my ass," he scoffed, and he made a backhanded gesture, his fingers square, the nails caked with dirt. "Like I said, pal, I don't keep track of him."

"Look, man, I'm not trying to be a pain in the ass. I just—"

"You are being a pain in my ass. And I got shit to do. So, take a hike." The door began closing.

Just before the latch clicked shut, I reared my leg back and shot my heel into the knob. The door flew open and slammed into the man. I jumped through the doorway and saw him staggering pack, blood streaming from his nose. "What the fuck?" His voice was guttural, caught somewhere between rage and confusion.

"Take a swing, champ," I said.

He looked at me for a second, struggling to decide if my intrusion on his day would become something worse than it already was, or if perhaps this was an opportunity to reclaim the pride and machismo he may have enjoyed in his younger years, but had been systematically stripped from him by an unfair world.

Or maybe I was reading too much into it. Maybe he was just deciding how to go about kicking my ass.

He feinted with a left jab, light on his feet, then threw a big roundhouse with his right. If he landed the punch, it probably would have probably knocked me out cold. But I ducked under his fist and caught him with an uppercut just below his ribcage. His breath left in a whoosh, and he doubled over. A nasal wheeze escaped from his throat as he tried to catch his wind. I kicked his legs out, and he fell face down, then I dropped a knee on his back. In ten seconds, I had him hog-tied, plastic bands binding his wrists and ankles behind him, one band looped between the two. He lay writhing until his breath returned with a gasp.

"You lousy cocksucker," he panted. "You let me go, or I swear you'll pay."

"I can leave you like this, maybe duct tape your mouth so no one can hear you yell," I said pleasantly. "Or you can stop acting like you got something to prove and answer my questions. I know it's a tough choice. I'll leave it up to you."

He lay on his side and looked up at me. He had a cut on his lip and his teeth were red with blood. "What the fuck you want to know?"

"Where's Marty Nilsson?"

"He said he was driving to Utah to visit his mom."

"When did he leave?"

"Two days ago. Three days ago. I don't fuckin' remember."

"When's he coming back?"

"I don't know. By Friday night, cause he's working."

"Where?"

"The Rusty Scupper. He's a cook, like me."

"How well do you know him?"

"Barely. Met him about three months ago. We work the same place but never together. So, I don't see him a lot."

"Where's his room?"

"Down the hall, door on the left. But it's locked."

"You got a key?"

"No."

"Too bad."

I went down the hall and tried without success to jimmy the door with a credit card. I saw no reason to damage the property unnecessarily, especially given that I didn't want to alert Marty Nilsson he was a suspect. But the roommate would tell him anyway, so there was no point. With a sigh, I hit the door with my shoulder and splintered the frame.

The room was too neat for a twenty-one-year-old male. Hell, it was too neat for me, and I could barely remember twenty-one. The bed was made military crisp, and the bookcase and small desk were free of clutter. A blank pad of paper and a pen rested on the desk beside a keyboard and a monitor. There was no PC. He probably owned a laptop—probably took it with him.

I went through the desk drawers, the dresser, and his closet. In the closet, a snowboard leaned against the wall next to a ski coat on a hanger. Beneath the coat was a pair of boarding boots and a plastic crate stacked with mountaineering gear. Crampons, an ice pick, a collapsible shovel, an avalanche beacon, and underneath it all, a coiled rope. I ran my hand along the coils until I found one of the ends. It was cut cleanly and not sealed with black, as new ropes are.

I checked under the bed, then spent a few minutes fanning the pages of his books and a half-dozen Snowboarder magazines, hoping Valerie and Terry's driver's licenses might fall out. No such luck.

"Hey fuck-face, you done yet?" came the voice from the hall.

I went back out to where the man lay on his side. His eyes were bulging, and the tendons in his neck stood out.

"What kind of vehicle does he drive?"

"You gonna let me go?"

"Answer the question."

"A gray Ford Ranger."

"What year?"

"How would I know? Older, like ten years old. This is getting pretty uncomfortable, man."

I looked down at him. "It's supposed to be uncomfortable. You brought it on yourself, my friend."

"Guys like me never learn. My old man used to say that."

I unfolded my pocketknife and slit two of the plastic ties, but left his ankles bound. He sat up and rubbed at the dried blood on his lips and jaw.

"You keep proving him right, huh?"

"Go fuck yourself."

"You want to do something smart? Repair the busted door, and don't say a word about this to Marty when you see him."

He pushed himself to his feet, working to keep his balance, and snorted a laugh. "You're dreamin', pal."

"My free advice might keep you out of jail."

"For what?"

"Aiding and abetting a murder suspect."

His lips moved silently, and one eye shrunk in his skull while the other protruded. "Bullshit," he spat.

"You want to risk doing time for a roommate you barely know? That could be quite a learning experience."

"Get out of my goddamn house," he said.

***

I called the number for South Lake Tahoe PD as I drove off, and the receptionist told me Marcus Grier was out on patrol. Grier had told me not to call his cell during working hours unless it was an emergency, or at least urgent. Whether he would view my new information as such, I wasn't quite sure.

"What is it, Dan?" Grier said, after about ten rings.

"I just identified a strong suspect for the murder of Valerie Horvachek."

"A strong suspect?"

"He drives a Ford Ranger. He's into mountaineering."

"Hooray."

"I'm not done, Marcus. He's a student in Candi's art class. He's working on a painting of the exact scene where Valerie's body was dumped. Plus, in his room, there's a climbing rope, cut at one end. I think the piece he cut off is the murder weapon."

Grier made a huffing sound, then said, "I'll call Bill Worley. We'll call you back. Keep your phone with you."

I drove back through town, cursing at each light. The highway was busy with tourists pulling in and out of shopping areas and restaurants. Over the lake, the sky had settled into a shifting porridge of gray and white globules, as if in some kind of meteorological purgatory.

When I got home, I went to my PC and checked flights from Reno to Salt Lake City. If I could get in and out of Utah quickly, I'd visit Marty Nilsson's mother. If I was lucky, he'd be there. But there were very few direct flights, and most of the connecting flights involved layovers that were impractical. There was a 6:00 P.M. flight today that would get me there at midnight, through Las Vegas. The next option was an 8:15 direct departure tomorrow morning, arriving at 10:15, with a return flight at four in the afternoon. That might work.

I looked again at the flight leaving tonight and briefly considered driving to Reno to get on the plane. I'd have to leave right away. But that would mean leaving Candi alone overnight, and that was not something I was willing to do.

As I weighed my options, my cell rang. "Dan, I've got Bill Worley on the line," Grier said. "Repeat what you told me."

I told Worley the details surrounding Marty Nilsson. When I finished, I said, "Can you get a warrant to search his house tonight?"

"Possibly," Grier said.

"Might be awkward, being that Douglas County's already arrested a man," Worley added.

"That arrest is bogus, and Galanis and his dream team know it," I said.

"I know this is a lot to ask, Dan, but I'd really appreciate it if you could keep your sarcasm to yourself."

"I'll work on it. In the meantime, I'm planning to fly to Salt Lake tomorrow morning and drive out to Ogden to speak with Nilsson's mother."

"What if he's there?" Worley said.

"I'll make a citizen's arrest, secure him, and call you so you can arrange for the local police to hold him."

"Save yourself the trip," Grier said. "If we decide it's the right thing to do, we'll call the police in Ogden."

"Forgive me, Marcus, but there's too many ifs in that equation. If you get a search warrant tonight and find enough to issue a warrant for his arrest, I'll back off. Otherwise, I'm going. Nilsson murdered those girls. It all adds up."

"I could order you not to go."

"I'm going, Sheriff."

Grier sighed. "Whatever you do, you better not break the law."

"Call me if you get the warrants."

***

When I left my house at dawn the next day, there was no moon and no hint of light on the horizon. The neighborhood was quiet and shrouded in an eerie darkness, as if a black hood had been pulled over the valley. I drove around the block twice, then headed out to the deserted highway, out toward Spooner Pass.

Last night, I'd set up Candi's smartphone with an emergency alert. If she pressed the designated button, my cell would ring, and the GPS function would show me her location. That, and the fact that she was still carrying her loaded pistol, provided a certain comfort.

An hour later, I parked at the Reno airport and went through the rigmarole required to check the case containing my pistol and stun gun. After that, I killed a few minutes playing slots until the flight boarded.

It was not a crowded plane, and I had a row to myself in the back. We climbed over Reno, and I watched the city fall away, then we were over the high desert, the sun low and white on the horizon. Brown flatlands spread from the shadow of the Sierras, the land scarred with sinkholes and buttes and fissures. Thin roads led off until they faded from sight or terminated partway up snow-covered ridges. Then new mountains rose, white-capped and foreboding, the terrain uninhabited for a hundred miles in any direction. As the jet continued eastward, the ridges receded and were replaced by the salt flats.

I filed out of the plane and left the Salt Lake City terminal in a compact class rental car. It was as cold in Salt Lake as it was in Tahoe, but evergreens did not grow here, and the surroundings were void of color. Skeleton trees lined the roads, and the grass looked dead. Every building was brown or gray, as if mandated by some misguided legislation.

I got onto the freeway and headed upstate on 15, Utah's main north-south artery. To the south were Zion and Bryce National Parks, home to some of the most spectacular natural scenery in the world. But there wasn't much to look at heading north, except for the formidable granite faces of the Wasatch Range, which ran parallel to the freeway off to the east. There were eight or nine world-class ski resorts tucked back in those canyons. I suspected Marty Nilsson was intimately familiar with them.

Thirty miles later, I exited the interstate and found the neighborhood where Anne Nilsson lived. The streets consisted of small, pastel-colored homes on small lots, each home well-kept and consistent with the next, the architectural style from the post-depression 1940s housing boom. I drove up her street and back again. There were patches of snow here and there, and little piles of leaves in the gutters. If it wasn't for the cars parked in the driveways, I imagined the neighborhood would have looked almost identical sixty years ago.

On the curb in front of Anne Nilsson's address was a late model Ford Mustang with black racing stripes on the hood. Parked in the driveway was a silver Chevy sedan. The house was a faded pink, and Christmas lights were strung along the eaves and shutters.

I followed an old brick walkway to the door and knocked. When no one answered, I rang the doorbell, then knocked again. "Shit," I mumbled. Two cars in front, somebody had to be home. Maybe she worked a late shift and was asleep. Maybe she'd taken her dog on a walk. Or maybe she thought I was a solicitor.

I knocked one more time, banging my knuckles hard against the wood. Then, I tried the doorknob. A click, and the door eased open. I stuck my head in.

"Hello? Police business. Hello?" No one was in the front room. I stepped inside and looked at the modest kitchen visible from the doorway. To the left was a hall. "Police! Is anyone home?"

There were three doors in the hall, and all were closed. I felt the hair on the back of my neck tingle, and I reached into my coat and pulled out my Berretta.

The first door was to a bathroom. Empty.

The second door opened to what looked like a guest bedroom. Also empty.

I crept toward the door at the end. My heart thudded in my chest, and I felt a trickle of sweat begin down my side.

I knocked on the door. "Police business. Open up!"

Nothing.

I turned the knob and pushed the door open, panning the room with my pistol.

"Oh my god," I said.

A naked woman lay face up on the bed. Her legs were straight before her, her bare feet splayed, her hands rested at her sides. The sheets were streaked with blood. She had long blonde hair and her eyes were sky blue, and her pubic hair was as blonde as the hair on her head. When I reached to check her pulse, her wrist was ice cold. She'd been dead for hours.

Beside the bed, a man was curled in the fetal position. He was covered in blood and the carpet surrounding his torso was crimson. I could see two puncture wounds in his neck, and one clearly had found the jugular vein. He was naked as well, short dark hair and an athlete's body, brown eyes wide and staring. About twenty-five years old.

I looked at the woman again. Her toned curves were those of someone who spent considerable time at a gym. Her nipples pointed at the ceiling, the breast implants oblivious to her death. Purplish ligature marks circled her neck, and her mouth was open, as if in protest. Estimated age, forty. A box of condoms sat on the nightstand, next to an opened wrapper.

I backed out of the room and called 911, then went outside to wait. A gust of wind sent a scattering of leaves across the street, and the cold cut through my jacket. A cat sauntering across the shingled roof eyed me with distrust, and down the street, two children rode their bikes in circles, their distant voices tiny. I walked to either side of the house and peered into the side yards. There was no sign of forced entry, no broken windows, no damaged doors. The house looked calm and peaceful, and no more remarkable than when I'd first seen it, as if the dead bodies inside were snapshots out of a nightmare fabricated solely by my mind.

In less than two minutes, a pair of squad cars pulled up, followed by an ambulance and an unmarked sedan. I gave my ID to an older uniformed cop with a meaty face and a nose crisscrossed with threadlike veins. Two plainclothesmen went into the house, and I leaned against my rental car and answered questions I knew I'd be asked again when the detectives were ready to talk to me.

It took twenty minutes for the plainclothesmen to come back outside and tell the medics to remove the bodies. The uniformed cop passed my driver's license to one of the detectives. I handed him my PI license.

"You're a long way from home," the man said. He wore slacks, a tweed jacket, and a long black overcoat. The garments did little to hide his powerful build. His dark hair was neatly combed and probably hair-sprayed, and he had a five o'clock shadow, even though it wasn't yet noon.

"I came here looking for a man named Marty Nilsson. He's suspected of two murders in Lake Tahoe. I heard he was visiting his mother." I pointed to the house with my thumb. "But it looks like I missed him."

"She doesn't look like anyone's mother," the other detective said, a taller man with a round head and a complexion as pale and cratered as a full moon.

"Marty Nilsson's twenty-one. My guess is she's forty."

"You don't think he killed his mother?" the swarthy cop said, and I couldn't tell whether he was skeptical or just perplexed.

"Yeah, that's exactly what I think," I said.

"Why?" Moon-Face said.

"I think he came home to pay her a visit and found her in bed with a younger man."

"You're losing me here," the swarthy cop said. "You think he killed his mom, just because she was getting it on with some young buck?"

"The marks on her neck were identical to the two women strangled in Tahoe."

"You have any evidence on him for the Tahoe murders?"

"Sheriff Marcus Grier in South Lake Tahoe is working on getting a search warrant for Nilsson's house. Grier knows I'm here. You should call him."

I gave Moon-Face Grier's cell number, then said to the other cop, "Was the man wearing a condom?"

"Yeah," he sighed. "Jesus, what a way to go."

Moon-Face began speaking, and after a minute, he hung up. "They searched Marty Nilsson's house and found a rope. They're testing to see if it's a match for the ligature marks on the victims."

"Did Grier issue an arrest warrant, or at least put out an APB for Nilsson?" I said.

"No, they're waiting for the test results on the rope."

I put my palm to my forehead. "You got to be fucking kidding me."

"Watch your language, please," Moon-Face said.

"Listen, this guy is like a nuclear plant in meltdown mode," I said. "He needs to be contained, and fast. What do you guys think? You want him roaming free in your town?"

"Back up for a second," the swarthy cop said. "Why the heck would he kill his mom?"

We stood there facing each other. The medics came out the front door, wheeling a corpse on a gurney. They struggled as they maneuvered through the doorway, and from the profile of the black plastic bag, I could tell it was Anne Nilsson's body.

"Find him, and maybe he'll tell you," I said.

***

On the way back to the airport, I called Grier. "You need to go tell the judge that Marty Nilsson's mother was killed last night," I said. "Strangled, probably with the same rope used to kill Valerie and Terry."

"So I've been told. As soon as we confirm the rope in Marty's room is a match for the one used on those girl's, we'll issue an arrest warrant."

"He could be anywhere in Utah by now, Marcus. Hell, he could be in Colorado or Idaho. Or heading back to Tahoe."

"Would you let us do our job, for Christ's sake?"

I dodged a three-trailer rig that swerved into my lane and stomped the gas pedal until the truck was behind me. "All right. Has there been any sign of Jake Massie?"

"Not a thing."

We hung up, and I called Candi and told her I'd be home on time. She said everything was fine, and she'd have dinner ready when I arrived. Then, I called Cody, but like the last few times I'd called, he didn't answer. It was past noon, but I wasn't hungry, and I wondered if there was any chance of getting on an earlier flight. I knew there wasn't, but I drove hard anyway, straight through the pallid landscape to the airport. I was a couple hours early, but I wanted to make damn sure I made my flight home.

15

When I woke the next morning, the angst that had taken hold in my chest over the past week seemed to have relaxed its grip. I felt satisfied that I'd identified the murderer, and now, it was up to the police to bring him to justice. My investigation was coming to a close. How the rest played out was up to the authorities. Like Grier said, I needed to let them do their job.

As for Jake Massie, he was one of many enemies I'd made in my career. He wasn't the first to try to take me out. Maybe we'd meet again, or maybe he'd find easier targets for the sadistic turmoil raging in his heart. Predators were drawn to the weak, those who couldn't or wouldn't fight back. When confronted by capable adversaries, the Massies of the world became cowards. It was a survival instinct, pathetic but predictable.

Whether my assessment was a false hope or not, time would tell. Regardless, I would not live my life in fear. By the same token, if I ever laid eyes on Massie again, I'd kill him without hesitation. The certainty of that fact made me feel quiet and content.

I drove Candi to the college and came back home. The sun had come out, and the sky was a deep shade of blue, and the only clouds were thin bands low over the mountains. I was in my garage lifting weights when my cell rang.

"Sorry I've been off the air, Dirt," Cody said, clearing his throat. "I've been on a bit of a roll."

"Where?"

"Here, there. I actually ended up down in Bakersfield."

"The armpit of California."

"Tell me about it. You wake up there with a hangover, there's only one thing to do."

"Keep drinking," I said.

"Exactly."

"You make it back home yet?"

"Yeah. Nothing but good, clean living for me now. Everything copacetic in your neck of the woods?"

"Pretty much. No sign of Massie in town."

"Listen, Dirt, about the War Dogs—"

He stopped when my cell blared. I felt my heart skip. It was the ring tone I'd programmed for Candi's emergency alert. "Call you back," I said, and jumped into my truck bed and unlocked my gearbox while checking the phone GPS. The alert had been sent from the college.

I yanked on my body armor and holster and hopped behind the wheel. I hoped she'd hit the emergency button by mistake, but Candi knew her phone well and was not prone to error. All four tires spinning madly, I roared down the street and took the corner in a power slide. I turned onto 50 amid blaring horns and jammed the accelerator to the floor. A bus turned in front of me, and I swerved into oncoming traffic to get around it and narrowly avoided a head-on.

A minute later, I skidded into the campus parking lot. When I got out of my truck, I heard sirens. Whether they were after me for my lunatic driving, or someone else, I didn't know. I ran from the parking lot to Candi's classroom. People stared at me like I was a madman. Other than that, nothing looked out of the ordinary. But when I looked in the small, rectangular window in the door, I saw a man in the room, standing next to Candi.

The sirens were loud as I opened the door. Candi was standing at a long table in the front of the room, and the man had moved behind her. He had curly dark hair and a face bumpy with acne. His upper lip was pitched on one side, showing a bit of tooth.

"Freeze right there," he said, pointing a revolver at me. On the table, Candi's phone lay next to her open purse. I looked at the pistol and realized it was Candi's.

"Take it easy, now," I said, stepping into the room. The door closed behind me.

"Marty had me call 911. The police are coming," Candi said.

The man nodded. His arms were massive, his acne likely caused by steroid abuse. "So, don't try to be a hero," he said.

I watched him from the far side of the room, my hands half-raised. "You called 911 on yourself?"

"That's right."

"Why don't you put the gun down, then?"

"On one condition."

"What?"

Before he could answer the door opened, and Marcus Grier stuck his head in. When he saw me, he blinked in surprise.

"Show your hands, real slow," the man named Marty said, the gun at Candi's temple. Grier moved through the door, hands out from his sides. Bill Worley followed behind him, and then two more uniformed cops.

Marty crouched low behind Candi. "Take those seats back there," he said. "You too." Candi stared at me, pale and speechless.

"What's this all about?" I said.

"Where's Nick Galanis?" Marty said, his eyes wide with a crazed intensity. "Sit down, or I'll kill her, I swear."

Grier lowered himself into a student desk. "He's on his way."

"Keep your hands on the desk tops," Marty said. "Don't make me tell you again."

I sat next to the cops, five of us, all armed and watching the man with the revolver. He had put his left arm around Candi's waist from behind, shielding his body with hers. His jeans and shirt looked like he'd slept in them, and the oily sheen of his face glowed in the artificial light. He must have driven all night across the Nevada desert after killing his mother and her lover. I felt the weight of the Berretta on my chest, and it took a very conscious effort to keep my hands still.

Marty Nilsson looked consumed with hatred, his deformed lip set in a snarl. Then, as he peered out from behind Candi's head, I saw an odd transformation in his countenance. His anger seemed to recede, and his visage became that of a vulnerable child's.

There was an awkward silence, until Bill Worley said, "Son, what's your interest in Nick Galanis?"

"None of your business. I'll surrender after I speak with him."

"You'll need to lay down your weapon first." Grier said.

"Once we're face to face."

We waited a minute, and then another. Candi stood in the clutch of Marty's oversized arm, and I considered a quick draw but immediately rejected the notion. If I sensed she was in imminent danger, I would have gone for my gun. But Marty seemed to have another agenda in mind.

Footfalls sounded from outside, and the door slowly opened. Marty trained the revolver at the Douglas County policeman who peered in.

"Just Nick Galanis. No more cops," Marty said. A brief hubbub, then Galanis stepped into the classroom. He wore pants with a sharp crease and a black suit coat over a lime-green button-down shirt. A tiny smile began on his lips, but ended when his eyes met Marty's.

"Come here," Marty said.

Galanis pointed with his finger. "You put that gun down."

"If I wanted to shoot you, I'd do it now. Come here."

Galanis looked over to where the four South Lake cops sat, and when his eyes passed over me, his lips curled in a brief scowl. Then, Grier nodded, and Galanis walked to the front of the room, to the side of the table opposite where Marty held Candi.

"Come around here, and I'll let her go," Marty said.

As Galanis stepped slowly around the long table, the officer next to me dropped his hand and released the snap on his holster. But Marty didn't notice. His eyes were following Galanis, who came to within three feet of Marty, then stopped.

"Now put the gun down," Galanis said.

Marty removed his arm from Candi's waist and said, "Go."

Candi ran to the side of the room to where I sat. "Get behind me," I whispered.

"Hello, Father," Marty said. His voice took on a childlike tone, as if he'd regressed to a prepubescent period. "How come you never answered any of the letters I sent you?"

Galanis winced and his head jerked as if Marty has spat full in his face. "Letters? I never received any. Your gun?"

Marty still held the revolver, pointed at the floor. "You shouldn't lie to me, Father. I'm your son. You wouldn't lie to your son, would you?"

"You're not...why do you think we're related?"

"My mother told on you, Father. She admitted you fucked her and wanted nothing to do with either of us."

"I have no idea who your mother is. You're crazy. Now, put that gun down. Do you think you can get away with this?"

"Do you think you can get away with what you've done? Every birthday and holiday that went by, me alone while you were sticking your cock in any skank you could find. And you know how my slutty mother celebrated Christmas this year? She fucked some guy about my age."

"You're nuts. Put the gun down, and we'll get you some help."

"Maybe you're right. That might be the best thing."

"Put the gun down now."

"Yes, Father," Marty said, and set the revolver on the table.

Galanis glanced toward the back of the room, a smug expression beginning on his face, as if he'd not only absolved himself of guilt or responsibility, but also showcased his talent at managing dangerous situations. And then, he reached forward to pick up the gun.

What happened next occurred in no more than a second. Later, I would think about the moment as similar to the frozen pause an eyewitness experiences before the impact of a high-speed traffic accident.

When Galanis moved within reach, Marty's left arm shot out and grabbed him by the wrist. Then, a silver blade flashed in Marty's right hand, and he thrust it into Galanis' neck. A fountain of blood spewed from the wound, and Marty jabbed three more times, blood shooting everywhere. Galanis' arms flailed, and his features contorted in terror. Then, Marty released his grip, and Galanis spun and dropped to the floor.

We all jumped up, and I pulled my piece quicker than the others. Marty dropped the knife and began to raise his hands. The cop next to me was a fraction slower, but he did not hesitate. "No!" I yelled, but it was too late. His first shot hit Marty in the chest, and then, the uniform nearest the door fired, the slug tearing a bloody smear in Marty's shoulder.

Marty fell, and we ran to the front of the room. The two men lay in a spreading pool of blood. Galanis blinked once, and a tiny cry escaped his parted lips. Then, his eyes froze, fixed and staring. Marty lay next to his father, their heads nearly touching. Marty turned his head just enough for his nose to graze Galanis' curled hair.

"Now, I'll never have to wonder where you are on Christmas, Dad," Marty said. His head lolled back, and he stared up at us and smiled. Then, he died.

16

The paramedics tried without success to revive the two bleeding men. Meanwhile, police from both sides of the border flooded the campus. Then, the press vans arrived. Reporters with shoulder-mounted cameras and microphones ran around making jackasses of themselves, and when they tried to film the paramedics removing the bodies, Marcus Grier exploded and arrested a pair who ignored his commands to stand back. An hour of chaos ensued as the cops cleared the campus. Finally, the reporters, students, and most of the cops were gone, and things quieted down. Candi and I sat with Bill Worley in an empty classroom and completed our statements.

"I found Marty Nilsson's truck parked out there," Worley said.

"You go through it yet?"

"Yes, sir. Found a three-foot length of rope."

"That settles that."

"I reckon so."

***

I walked with Candi to where I'd parked. In the vacated parking lot, a tow truck finished hooking up Marty's gray Ford Ranger and began pulling away. I watched the vehicle disappear down the road. Then, I drove us home through crisp, sunny weather that seemed incongruous with the day's events.

"I could use a drink," I said.

Candi sat with her arms wrapped around each other. "When he came into the classroom, I went for my gun. But I screwed up, and he took it from me."

"And then, he used your phone to call 911?"

"He had me call the police. But first, I pushed the emergency button."

"You didn't screw up, babe. You did great."

"Really? It sure doesn't feel like it."

"Are you okay?"

She looked at me and made a face. "As okay as anyone can be after watching two people die."

I pulled into my garage, and we went inside. Candi asked for a drink, and I made her a weak vodka and fruit juice and poured myself a whiskey-seven. Then, we sat on the couch, and she loaded her pipe.

"In a way, I feel sorry for Marty," she said. "My god, that stuff he said."

"Most psychopaths come from horrific childhoods. But I don't think that applied to him."

"He felt abandoned by his father, and maybe his mother too. I think it drove him over the edge. I always thought there was something a little off with him."

"No doubt he was tormented. But that's not an excuse to kill people."

She walked to the window and exhaled a puff. "What is?"

"Self-defense."

"How do the laws define that?"

I looked at her and took a healthy slug off my drink. "State laws differ. Some states say it's permissible to kill an intruder in your house."

"How about proactive self-defense? Like someone threatens to kill you, so you kill them first?"

"You'd have to prove the threat is imminent and deadly."

She made a scoffing sound with her mouth. "By that time, you'd probably already be dead."

"The proper legal recourse would be a restraining order."

"You think that would work on Jake Massie?"

I set my drink down, unfinished. "Nope."

***

Later that afternoon, I called Bill Worley.

"Howdy, Dan."

"Hey, Bill. Have you learned anything more about Marty Nilsson?"

"A few things. He was a ski patroller for a couple years out in Utah. He's moved here only a few months before the murders."

"You think he moved here because of Galanis?"

"Maybe. We'll never know for sure."

"Anything on how he moved Valerie's body to the backcountry?"

"Probably never know that, either."

"How about Tim Elkind, the sheep lover? He still locked up?"

"They'll kick him free shortly, I understand."

"At least they're doing something right in Nevada."

Worley laughed dryly. "I also heard a couple Douglas County officers are calling for an examination of Galanis' bank records. They think he was being paid off by various parties."

"Galanis was suspected of being on the take since day one," I said. "And they wait until he's dead to open an investigation?"

"Looks that way. Maybe you ought to go talk to them about a job."

"I'll pass."

"Awright, then."

***

I spent the remainder of the day concluding my report for General Horvachek. He had said he wanted closure, and now, he would have it. I doubted it would provide him and his wife much solace or satisfaction. Their rebellious daughter was still dead, and there was no changing that. She'd done nothing terribly stupid or irresponsible. She hadn't even been specifically targeted. Her promiscuous behavior had simply landed her in the wrong place at the wrong time. I stopped for a minute and imagined the general and his wife sitting on their living room sofa, hunched and teary-eyed, looking through a family album, the pictures capturing Valerie as a cute little girl, smiling and happy with her family.

When I'd finished typing, I read over the report. There were a slew of details I'd never followed up on. Names from Valerie's cell phone, names of Blood Bastards and War Dogs that Albert Bigelow had provided, and also the names of the ski patrollers that I'd compiled. Hell, I'd never even interviewed Valerie's best friend, Christie Tedford, who'd been in Tahoe when Valerie was murdered. In retrospect, though, none of it would have mattered.

I shook my head and rubbed at the stubble on my chin. If not for seeing Marty Nilsson's painting in Candi's classroom, I might have never identified him as a suspect. In that light, much of the investigative work I'd done prior to that had been meaningless.

I attached the report to an e-mail and sent it. Almost immediately, my cell rang. Could the general have gotten my e-mail that quickly? No, it was Marcus Grier.

"What's happening, Sheriff?"

"Paperwork, that's what's happening, if you're really interested. I just got a phone call you should know about."

"You did?"

"The sheriff in Stockton called to tell me that Jake Massie's house burned to the ground last Tuesday night. They just completed their forensic work and have a positive ID on Massie's body."

"A fire?" I sputtered. "You're just telling now?"

"I just found out about it. Massie and five other bodies were found."

"Tuesday night? That was when Massie kidnapped me."

"He must have drove home after that," Grier said, his keyboard clattering.

"That was a stupid thing to do. He should have figured the cops would be waiting for him."

"Well, he didn't, and they weren't."

"Six people dead? Did anyone get out alive?"

"No survivors."

"They probably were sleeping."

"Not necessarily. The sheriff said there was evidence of a massive explosion. They found lumber scattered in a hundred-foot radius. Are you still there?"

"Yeah," I said slowly. "Massie was cooking meth. His lab must have exploded."

"Most of the bodies were dismembered and burnt beyond recognition. They had to ID Massie by dental records."

"They're positive it was Massie?"

"The ID was a hundred percent. Dental records don't lie."

"He will be missed."

Grier chuckled. "I'm glad you haven't lost your sense of humor."

"Me too."

***

It wasn't until late that night I called Cody.

"How's your sobriety coming along?" I asked. I'd taken Candi to dinner and poured a couple margaritas on top of the whiskey I'd drank earlier in the day.

"It's a relative thing," he said.

"Marcus Grier called me and said Jake Massie's house was leveled by an explosion last Tuesday night. The body pieces were unrecognizable."

"Oh my."

"His meth lab must have blown up."

"What a shame."

"Six people dead, one of them Massie."

"It's a sad day for the community."

"I was thinking about that story you told me, Cody. About the Mafia guy and the C4."

"I told you about that? Shit, the court told me to not talk about that case. Me and my big mouth."

"You didn't happen to plant some of those plastic explosives at Massie's house when we were there, did you?"

"Dirt, you're slurring your words. I think you've had too much to drink."

"I remember your hand was coated in mud."

"Christ, I'm getting a contact high just talking to you. But I'd be celebrating, too, if I was you. Six shit-bag racists X'd off the list. All probably planning to torture and kill you and your girl. The only pity is, they likely didn't suffer much."

"Did you plant the explosives?"

"You need to concentrate on what matters. No one puts a hit on my buddy Dan and gets away with it."

"Can you just give me a straight answer?"

"Yeah. The world's a better place with those assholes dead. I can't think of anything straighter than that."

"That's it, huh?"

"I got to boogie, man. I'll catch you on the flip side."

"Hold on," I said, but for the moment, I was out of words. I sighed. How could I be mad at Cody Gibbons, a man who had my back at any cost? Cody's lifestyle and lawless ethics made him who he was, and whatever faults he possessed were superseded by his friendship and loyalty. His tactics sometimes seemed a little excessive, but who was I to judge him?

"I think I need another drink," I said.

"Pour yourself a stiff one, Dirt, and raise your glass. It's a happy day."

I hung up and took his advice.

***

A few days after Marty Nilsson's demise, an Alaskan storm blew into the Tahoe valley. The morning after the storm passed, I put a bouquet of flowers and a wooden cross in my pack and rode the gondola to the summit of South Lake's ski resort. When no one was looking, I ducked the boundary ropes and skied through the backcountry until I reached the cornice over Got Balls Bowl. The snow twenty feet below looked as soft as a bed of pillows.

I backed up and pushed off toward the launch and landed in a blinding blast of powder, then came out of the fluff and made effortless turns until I reached the tree line. From there, it took ten minutes to reach the glade where I'd found the body of Valerie Horvachek.

The glade was as pristine as when I'd first skied it. The snow sparkled in the morning sun, and the gentle swell of the surface was smooth as cream. I made a few turns, powder whisking away beneath my skis, then I stopped at the tree where I'd tied my bandana to mark Valerie's body.

I never knew Valerie Horvachek. What I'd learned about her during my investigation was not endearing. But her parents loved her, and perhaps there was goodness in her heart. She may have turned out to be a good person, had she lived. Sometimes, you cut people a break, especially those too young to have found themselves. And sometimes, you did things because it filled an emptiness inside you.

On the cross, I'd written Valerie's name and the dates marking her short twenty-one years. I nailed the cross to the tree and propped the flowers beneath it. A cold gust blew through the pines, and as I skied away, my bandana fluttered on the branch where I'd left it tied.

***

The weeks went by, and it was a good winter, cold and snowy and better powder conditions than I'd ever seen in Tahoe. I worked a few minor cases and put in a fair amount of time bartending at Zeke's. Things returned to normal at the college, and Candi continued teaching and working on her art projects. In early April, she finished her oil painting, a surrealistic rendition of the view from the big window in my living room.

We had the painting framed and hung it above the fireplace. We were drinking our morning coffee and admiring it when Cody called.

"Hey, Dirt. What are you and your old lady doing tonight?"

"No plans that I know of. Why?"

"San Jose is getting to be a drag, and I was thinking of driving up."

"Alone?"

"No, I've got someone I'd like you to meet."

"Oh, god."

"Now, why would you say that? I think you're going to really like this girl. I think Candi will too. Her name's Heidi Ho. I call her my Swiss Miss. She used to be a gymnast."

"She ever done any stripping?"

"No. Absolutely not. Give me a break, would you? Now, I want to make up for that New Year's Eve fiasco. I made reservations for the top of Pistol Pete's."

"Hold on," I said, and muted the phone. "Candi, Cody wants to introduce us to his new girlfriend over dinner tonight at the Gold Lantern. What do you say?"

She looked surprised, then burst out in laughter. "This is like déjà vu. Sure, why not? Wait—don't answer that."

I joined her in laughter, then said to Cody, "Okay, we're in. What time?"

"What's so funny?"

"Life's good. Why not enjoy a few laughs?"

"That sounds like one of my lines," he said.

"Maybe it is. You're beautiful, man. Don't ever change."

"I couldn't if I tried."

ABOUT THE AUTHOR

Born in Detroit, Michigan, in 1960, Dave Stanton moved to Northern California in 1961. He attended San Jose State University and received a BA in journalism in 1983. Over the years, he worked as a bartender, newspaper advertising salesman, furniture mover, pizza cook, debt collector, and technology salesman. He has two children, Austin and Haley. He and his wife, Heidi, live in San Jose, California.

Stanton is the author of five novels, all featuring private investigator Dan Reno and his ex-cop buddy, Cody Gibbons.

CPSIA information can be obtained
at www.ICGtesting.com
Printed in the USA
LVHW112337311022
732062LV00005B/479

9 781912 604173